The cavalcade of horsemen reappeared suddenly. It swung for the house, the men of it spreading fanwise. Bill Maude turned sharply, arm dropping, and the girl saw how incredibly fast the lazy, serene humor of his face gave way to a tight and mask-like expression of watchfulness. The horses came on and a part of Maude's rigid attitude vanished, though not all; for as the flanks of the party spread around him, he slowly backed his pony as far as the porch and squared himself to command them. The party halted and one man came forward.

"Want you, Bill," said he, solemn as a sphinx. "Hand over the gun."

Maude drawled dryly: "Lickshaw, you get some of the nuttiest ideas a man ever heard of. Yesterday you wanted me to be deputy. This mornin' you want my gun. Settle down and explain."

"You know why, Bill."

"Yeah? Well, let's hear your version of it."

Lickshaw replied: "For the murder of Tom DeLong . . ."

—From "Ride Out!", one of a 'Trigger Trio' of gripping Westerns by Ernest Haycox, all of which appear in this single exciting volume.

Trigger Trio
by
Ernest Haycox

ACE BOOKS

A Division of Charter Communications Inc.
1120 Avenue of the Americas
New York, N.Y. 10036

CONTENTS

THE OCTOPUS OF PILGRIM VALLEY

I

THE LONE BUCKAROO

"Politeness is shorely a shield that stops many a bullot. Still an' all, if a feller has got to insinuate hisself into another party's quarrel, it's plumb best to omit apologies until the shootin' is over. . . . I nev' yit did see a red-headed gent that wa'n't burnin' to right the wrongs of thisyere unjust world."—Parting advice of Joe Breedlove to Tom Lilly.

THE BLAZING, blood-red sun dropped over the western rim and left the valley to a twilight peace. Tom Lilly, riding his weary buckskin toward the distant huddle of buildings that formed the isolated town of Powder, felt the first of the evening's breeze. It had all the effect of a cold shower on man and beast; Lilly wiped the crusted sweat from his face and washed his parched throat with a drink.

"Another day, another dollar. Buck, you got a restless, homeless no-account for a rider."

The pony raised its ears and quickened the pace. Dust rose behind in swirling eddies. Night threw successive darkening cobalt shadows across the land, through which twinkled here and there the light of a

7

homesteader's shack; eastward the high mesa became nothing but a stark outline against the sky.

It was new country to Tom Lilly. For that reason and no other was he here. The lure of the unknown, the unseen drew him like a magnet. Beyond the hill was always the promise of fairer fields, the hint of great adventure. And as tired as he was, a small excitement burned in his blue eyes and compressed the muscles of his lean, sun-blackened face as he drew upon Powder and beheld the lights shining out of the windows into the rutty, dusty street. This was the whole story of Tom Lilly and explained the wistfulness of his features, the temper that slumbered fitfully beneath the sorrel-red thatch of hair. He was a wanderer, a seeker of something that could never come to pass; Joe Breedlove, his partner back on the H-H, had said this in plain blunt language—though rather sorrowfully—when Tom was on the point of moving.

"Yuh ain't foolin' me, old-trapper, with that poker face o' yourn. I reads you mos' clearly. Yore a red-haired gent with misbegotten idears o' romance. All red-heads is the same, which is a fact. Yuh have traveled a hell of a lot o' trails before yuh camped here, without findin' anything to please yuh. Better stick to these diggin's, amigo. Yuh won't locate any better. All you'll do is grow gray an' mis'ble. Ain't I seen how these roamers end up? Usually over a bar'l o' spuds in some town restaurant. Yeah, a broken-down old codger washin' dishes fer a livin'. Ain't that a fine end fer an A-1 top hand?"

But Tom Lilly tightened his cinches and tied down his blanket roll, smiling in a faint sheepish way. "Lots of country I ain't seen, Joe. If I don't like it I'll mosey back."

Joe Breedlove shook his head. "Yore kind don't back track." Then the man's big paw gripped his friend's arm. "Well, yuh know best. If yuh ever git in a jam, drop a line or send up a smoke signal. I'll come-a-runnin'."

"Sho'," muttered Tom, losing his grin. He had ridden off with a very brief farewell. Now, as he entered this straggling town street, he was recalling those words. "The hardest part about movin'," he said to himself "is leavin' a good Joe like that behind." He had said good-bye often, yet never with quite the same depression of spirit. "He was shore a square gent. Well, here we are, and where are we?"

Powder was just another desert town. Tom Lilly had seen a hundred built in the same loose-jointed shackling fashion, with a dozen or more false-fronted frame buildings abutting a dirt street. There would be two or three saloons with their kerosene lights beckoning through the swinging doors, a general store, a restaurant, a jail and, somewhere near the edge of town, a livery stable. Lilly rode slowly, looking for this latter establishment. Men moved in the shadows, their cigarette tips gleaming. Dishes rattled in the restaurant and from the nearest saloon came the flat, unmelodious notes of a piano. Powder was tuning up for the night, given a new lease on life by the evening breeze. Lilly, turning his horse into the stable, felt depressed. It was the same old story over again; Joe Breedlove was right—he would travel the long trail until he could no longer sit in the saddle, looking for something not to be found. How could he find it when he didn't know what he looked for? Just another stray critter never thrown and branded. He slipped off the buckskin, seeing the stable roustabout amble through the door.

"This pony," said he, "gets oats. Where's yore brush and currycomb?"

He led the animal to a stall, slipped off the gear and set to work with the implements the roustabout produced. The latter, displaying the indirect curiosity of his kind, spoke casually.

"Hope it ain't this hot where you come from."

"We had rain there in 1903," opined Tom gravely. "Where's a good place to eat?"

"They's only one place, which is the Star. You won't mind it too much if yore hungry, I might add they's usually a gentleman's game o' poker in progress at Jake Miner's place. Mos' stranger like to know, so I'm a-tellin' you. Mama Ringo runs the hotel if it's your desire to sleep on a real four-bit bed. The sher'ff an' marshal are both tol'rant to'rds ord'nary misdemeanors o' the peace. I might add the likker here abouts is thirty proof an' the cards entirely without marks. Which constitutes the whole story o' this hole in the ground. It's a nice leetle place—if you don't stay long."

"You shore are a compendium of useful knowledge," averred Lilly, strolling out. "Civic pride is a jewel of great renown."

The roustabout's retort was a short and emphatic word that exploded in the darkness. Tom Lilly, smiling slightly, crossed to the Star and had his supper in solitary state. Powder had unanimously eaten and departed to its pleasures, leaving the latest arrival to finish his steak and onions among a débris of dishes. It was a meal, nothing more than that and Tom paid his bill and walked out, hungry; not for food, but for the palaver of his own kind, for the rough joke and the twang of a familiar voice. It was always thus when restlessness drove him onward and away from friends. He was forever an alien in a strange land, left to his own sober, wistful thoughts. Under the impulse of this loneliness, he built himself a cigarette and headed for Jake Miner's.

But before he reached the door the jingling of the

piano, the rattling of chips and the hum of voices suddenly ceased. A silence, uneasy and expectant, pervaded the place and when he pushed through the swinging portals he became a witness to a scene that jerked at his nerves and sent a warning down his right arm. There was something going on here out of the ordinary, something that made him brush the butt of his gun with careful fingers and move quickly to a rear wall. It was such a little drama as he had often seen before and within thirty seconds his quick-acting, partisan temper was thoroughly engaged on the side of a man who appeared to be the under dog. And of a man not of his own kind or profession.

He was a nester, this fellow. That was obvious from a glance at the shabby overalls and the sallow, be-whiskered face. He had a gaunt, weather-beaten frame and a pair of hands warped out of shape by hard labor. A very homely man, who leaned uneasily against the mahogany bar and gripped a glass of whisky that had not been touched. He was perhaps forty, but he looked older, and from beneath bushy sun-bleached brows a pair of faded blue eyes stared out in mixed defiance and fear. Lilly leaned against the wall, hearing a faint whisper float across a near table. "Trono'll shore kill 'im. He shore will." And Lilly, growing angry on the instant, turned his attention to the second party at the bar.

Trono was smiling in the tight malevolent way of a man enjoying himself over a victim. He was a short and burly creature with immense shoulders and arms; a thick, columnar neck supported a face that was as swart as any Indian's; but here the resemblance stopped, for his chin was of the outthrust, cleft kind and he had bulging green eyes. Somewhere he had been engaged in desperate fighting, one mark of which ran across the high bridge of his nose and up in to the half-bald bullet

11

head. Undeniably he was of the cattle range, and he was taking a cowman's attitude toward the nester. He lifted his own whisky glass, speaking in a rumbling, husky voice.

"We'll drink to the sudden death o' all nesters. Down she goes."

"Well, I dunno's that's perlite," protested the other. "I'm a peaceable feller, a-mindin' my own business."

"Mean to say yuh won't drink with a man?" roared Trono. "That's the sorta insult that don't go down in this country! Why, you—"

"Oh, I'll drink if it'll soothe yer feelin's any," said the nester, raising his glass.

Trono was grinning. And when the nester was about to drink, one massive arm swept across the intervening space and slapped the glass to the floor. The nester spewed the liquor from his mouth and wiped his eyes. His flat chest rose and fell with an excess of outraged feeling, but in the end he spoke quite mildly. "Seems to me you be tryin' to pick trouble. I want these fellers to know I ain't startin' no trouble. It's a free country."

"Free fer anything but bugs," broke in Trono, working himself to a rage. "Y' know what we do with bugs, mister? We bash 'em! Better take warnin' an' clear out."

"No, I don't guess I'll give up," said the nester. Tom Lilly inwardly applauded the man's courage. It took nerve to stand in the midst of a crowd of cowpunchers and declare himself. Even more nerve to say what he went on to say. "Pilgrim Valley wa'n't created jes' purposely fer the Octopus an' his JIB ranch, though you seem to think so. I'm holdin' my land by gov'ment consent. Mean to prove it an' farm it."

"Oh, you *do?*" muttered Trono, bearing down on the final word.

The nester hastened to take the sting from his pronouncement. "Ain't no reason fer you folks to git sore. They's aplenty land left to run cows on. Shucks, I'm only holdin' a half section outen three-four hundred thousand acres."

"Bugs breed," replied Trono. "Leave one alone an' he hatches a hundred more. No, that ain't no argument. Hey, where you goin'?"

The nester had started to back off. Trono's right hand dropped half way to his gun and the nester's whole body stiffened; he, too, made a gesture toward his coat pocket, only to throw both arms free of his body as if to show he meant no trouble. It was a cruel ordeal and the mark of it appeared on his lean face in deep furrows and fine beads of sweat. Tom Lilly sighed to relieve the pressure of his accumulating anger. First and foremost he was a cowman, with most of the prejudices of that class. But he fought fair, always, and now his sympathies were entirely with the nester who was being badgered. It bore hard on him to stand back and watch this quarrel being trumped up by Trono; for there could be only one end to it. It was obvious that Trono meant there should be but one end.

"I'm goin' about my business," muttered the nester, rubbing his lips with a trembling hand. "I know you, Mister Trono. You figger to cause trouble. You've allus tried to haze me off my claim. Well, if I was a younger feller I might stand up to you. All I ask is to be let alone. It's a free country and they's plenty o' room fer all o' us in it. I'm gettin' along in years an' there's nobody to take care o' me when I break down, so I want to make a little stake afore I die. Now you leave me be."

Lilly checked an impulse to step forward between the men. His sharp eyes caught the stiffening muscles beneath Trono's coat and the sudden flare of fire in Trono's eyes. The killer instinct was there; he had seen

13

such a light before. But, on the verge of acting, he took hold of himself. It was not his quarrel and nobody had asked him to interfere. The strictest kind of unwritten rules guarded such an affair and held him in his place. Even so, as he watched Trono gather himself, he had come to a decision. Trono's voice droned throughout the room.

'Callin' me a trouble maker, you damn fool? Come back here an' drink!"

What passed in the succeeding moments was something that only swift eyes might see. Trono's arm dropped and seemed to waver. It was only a gesture, yet it might have been the first move to draw his gun. The nester, badgered until his nerves were torturing him, saw that gesture and copied it. But where Trono had been clever, he was only clumsy. He could not feint. One paw started downward and could not stop. After that it was murder. Trono's gun gleamed in the light; the room rocked and roared and someone cried out a warning. That was Tom Lilly's voice, though he never knew it. His eyes, passing from side to side, saw the nester struggle with his weapon and stand a moment; then like a man crushed by a burden, he buckled at the knees and fell forward. The life was out of him before he struck the floor. His lean, bewildered face stared dumbly through the trailing gun smoke. Not a soul in that room moved, not a word was spoken until Trono's harsh voice broke the spell.

"You boys saw it. You saw he went for his gun. I'd 'a' been plugged cold if I'd waited. Plain self-defense, understand? Such actions is about all you can expect from a nester." And he swept the crowd with a hard, cold glance. For one instant his attention was fixed on Tom Lilly; then he walked from the place. Lilly rubbed his hands along his coat edge and tried to clear the unreasoning, white-hot rage from his head. A kind of whistling sigh passed over the onlookers and the bartender's carefully indifferent words reached him.

"Some o' you gents lug him into the side room. I don't want my floors all bloodied up."

Lilly turned away from the sight and built himself a cigarette with unusually awkward fingers. One of the men at the near table shuffled a deck and spoke philosophically. "Well, that's another chalked up to Theed Trono in behalf o' the JIB. God-darnit, why didn't the fool stay clear o' Trono?"

Lilly bent forward, speaking with a sharp rise of voice. "Does this Trono hombre run this JIB rancho?"

The group at the table turned toward him and spent some time in a carefull inspection. He was rewarded finally by a brief word. "Not exactly, stranger. Though I'd say he had a-plenty to say about it. Fact is, he's old Jim Breck's foreman. Who is Jim Breck? You shorely must be from distant parts. Jim Breck is chief factotum o' Pilgrim Valley."

"And where might that be?"

"South thirty miles or so. It's behind the string o' Buttes you might see from here of a day. Though if yore lookin' fer a job you won't have to ride that far."

"I'm han'somely obliged, but I mistrust my ability to work under that Trono gent," said Lilly. "I take it this here nester occupied unhealthy soil."

"Well, you can read the picture an' title fer yourself," answered his informant somewhat briefly, and turned away. Lilly understood the meaning of this perfectly. Trono, he decided, in a wave of disgust, had Powder buffaloed. He said as much in an audible phrase that was addressed at nobody in particular. It was meant to provoke attention and it succeeded admirably. The group turned on him with sharpened interest and the spokesman put a direct question. "Who the hell are you, amigo, to tell us what the trouble is? You a candidate for the unpopularity contest?"

"I'm just a simple creature," murmured Lilly, "that never learned the a-b-c's from any book. But I was always taught murder was a crime."

"Mebbe you'd like to try yore luck with Theed Trono."

Lilly ground the cigarette beneath his boot heel and stared at a group with a cold directness. Ice edged his words. "You can bet your last chip, fellow, that if I ever do, there'll be more'n one bullet fired. That's information for general publication." He swung and left the saloon, knowing that every soul within the room had heard his last statement. Knowing, too, that in time the challenge would reach Theed Trono. He had meant it as a deliberate challenge; etiquette had kept him out of a poor nester's trouble, but there was nothing in the books that forbade a man starting an entirely new quarrel if he was so minded. As he walked somberly down the dark street he had a clear picture of Trono's savage, bullying face. Why, the man had committed the coldest kind of murder and these fellows stayed glued to their seats! It was enough to rouse the spirit of an Eskimo, for a fact. What sort of a fool was this Trono and what kind of an outfit was the JIB to allow such free-handed killing?

He paused in front of the livery stable, sympathies more and more engaged in the affairs of the dead nester. There was a volcanic upheaval inside him and he stared narrowly through the dark, recalling the sage words of Joe Breedlove. "I nev' yit did know a red-headed gent that wa'n't burnin' to right the wrongs of thisyere unjust world." Well, that wasn't exactly so. He, Tom Lilly, wasn't going around with a chip on his shoulder, but there certainly was such a thing as fair play in the world.

The stable roustabout ambled out of the doorway and murmured. "Ain't the flesh pots lured yuh yet?"

Tom Lilly built another cigarette and began delving for information. "Once upon a time there was a nester—"

"Yeah. I heard that shot in the saloon. The ways o' man are plumb mortal."

"Where might that nester have had his claim, anyhow?"

"Jes' inside Pilgrim Valley, offen the road to the JIB about four miles. They's a nice cold spring on the place, which shore has been poison bait fer many a foolish feller."

"In other words," said Lilly, "the JIB has sort of illegally swallowed a lot of gov'ment entry land along with its rightful range an' objects to a man peaceably settlin' thereon."

"If yore askin' fer an opinion I ain't got any. If it's a question o' facts, then I guess you don't need no correction on the foregoin' statement."

"Well, it's an old game," murmured Lilly. "But mos' usually a cattle outfit will draw the line at cold murder. Pilgrim Valley, I reckon, is exclusively JIB territory?"

The roustabout happily fell upon a remembered phrase. "The memory o' man runneth not to the contrary."

"Sho'," approved Lilly, glowering at the shadows. A vague excitement gripped him and he felt a sense of personal injury. Theed Trono was taking in too much territory and so was a ranch that tried to keep settlers off government land. Boiled down, it amounted to nothing more than a curtailment of his own liberty, for if the nester was shooed off, then they'd shoo him off too. No, that was a situation hardly bearable. He threw away the cigarette with a hunch on his shoulders. "Ain't there a land office here?"

"Over the gen'ral store. See the yaller light? He sleeps there, too. An old dodo bird that come out here to die an' ain't been lucky at it yit." As Lilly drifted away the roustabout sent a warning whisper after him. "Don't you be a fool, amigo."

"It's a man's born privilege," replied Lilly, crossing the street. "A privilege I shore do exercise a lot, too," he said to himself, climbing the stairway. He steered for a door emitting a single beam of light through the keyhole and knocked once. A grumbling invitation was evoked and he entered a room that was both an office and a kind of living quarters. On an army cot behind the counter—a counter heaped with record books and plat maps—was stretched an ancient fellow with tobacco stained whiskers and a parchment skin. Amber eyes moved fretfully toward Lilly. "What you want?"

"Aim to file on some land."

The old fellow stroked his faded whiskers and grinned a toothless grin. "Wal, my conscience is clear, friend. Takes a lot o' people to make the world. Don't never say I encouraged you."

"Cheerfulness," opined Lilly, "is a priceless thing. Don't get up if it hurts you, though I'd like to have you show me one particular spot on yore maps."

The old man groaned and hoisted himself an inch at a time. "Ain't there nothin' I can do to restore sanity. Le's see; have you got a thousand dollars, a copper lined stomach, the strength o' a horse? Have you—?"

"Yore makin' that up," interrupted Lilly. "Just state gov'ment requirements."

"Upon which portion of this earth's crust do you aim to take root?"

"Why, there was a claim relinquished half an hour ago

by a gentleman in Jake Miner's place. It's over in Pilgrim Valley an' it's got a spring on it. I don't doubt but what you recall the spot."

The answer came quickly enough. The old man's face drooped a little and he made aimless figures on the counter with his pencil. "If the advice of a friend is worth anything, my boy, *you* don't want land there."

"JIB got you buffaloed, too?"

The other shook his head. "I'm too far along to mind bein' shot. It'd be a blessin' to die that sudden. But they wouldn't tackle a government official. You watch your step."

"Show me this place," insisted Lilly. And the old man, displaying visible reluctance, turned the book to a certain page and with traveling pencil point indicated the homestead. "Hamby was a nice feller, too," he opined. "I thought it was jes' an ordinary shot when I heard it. Well, you understand, there's formalities to go through with before you can file. If you want to squat until then it'll be all right. Better take lots of cattridges."

Lilly turned toward the door. "Consider me as bein' entered, then I'm here to stay." He walked out, going cautiously down the stairway. There was a matter of supplies to take care of, but these could wait until later in the evening. Right at present he felt inclined to return to Jake Miner's place; he had laid an egg there that by now ought to have hatched something. Poised in the doorway he heard voices floating through the darkness and by and by Theed Trono came into the small reflection of the hotel light. There was another man with him —the tall, horsey-faced type familiar throughout the cattle country. England was stamped all over the long, out-thrust chin and the prominent nose. Only for a moment were they suspended in this yellow beam. Lilly tarried thoughtfully, mind revolving around several pieces of information he had gathered. What he now proposed to do was enter Pilgrim Valley and challenge Theed Trono's attention; Theed Trono, who was a killer foreman walking under the protection of the JIB, and its owner. Men seemed to be reluctant to speak of the owner of this ranch. The roustabout had mentioned his name—it was Jim Breck—casually and with no desire to go on. And the nester had called him an octopus. Fitting title.

"Well, if Breck instigated the shootin' the devil will shorely pay him for it."

With this reflection he advanced on the saloon and pushed through the door and into trouble. Trono was at the bar, his eyes quite hard and bright; when he saw Lilly advancing he put his whisky glass carefully on the bar and thrust his bullet head forward as if wishing a closer view of this new specimen. Once again Lilly was aware of the pervading silence of the expectancy half-veiled in men's eyes. The Englishman, he noticed, had not entered the saloon.

"Amigo, I been hearin' things about yuh."

It was Trono's voice, unpleasant and blunt. Lilly inclined his head, eyes pinned on the burly one. "Always been my policy to declare myself," he admitted. "Whatever you heard about me goes."

"Uhuh. Pass some remark about more'n one bullet flyin'?"

"That's correct."

"Ain't you a little previous with them rash words?" growled Trono. He closed the fingers of one hand as if to show Lilly the power that was in his arm. "Usually a gent don't go huntin' fer trouble."

"Fatal error of my education," admitted Lilly.

"It's apt to be fatal, shore enough," said Trono, displeasure growing. "I think I got an apology comin' from you. Gettin' pretty bad when a man can't perform his chores 'thout bein' libelled. I'm listenin'."

"You'll listen a long, long while, hombre," replied Lilly. He had a hard struggle with the flame of outraged anger that blazed up. "To shorten this palaver I will add that I don't like yore methods or yore manners. I hear you don't allow nesters in Pilgrim Valley. Tomorrow mornin' I'll be on my way up there. You'll find me squattin'. Better change yore style, mister, before you try to run me off."

Fighting talk. A cooler head would not have invited trouble in such a way. But Tom Lilly's sympathies were in control and he was willing to force the issue. He saw quite clearly that sooner or later he would clash with this Trono and he was willing that the fight should come and be done with. Trono seemed plunged in deep thought, studying Lilly with a long, deliberate glance. Evidently the swart foreman saw something in his adversary that bade him move carefully. Lilly was no half-broken nester. That gun butt was placed in the careful manner of a man who had experience.

"Well," he muttered, "if yore lookin' fer trouble, they's folks that'll oblige yuh. Personally I'm a peaceable man—" He seemed to feel that he was losing ground, so he finished with a huge roar. "But I'll give yuh twenty-four hours to pull freight! After that I'm shootin' at sight!"

"A large and clear statement," observed Lilly and turned squared around. It was fifteen feet to the door and at each step he expected to hear a warning shout. None came. He reached the street with mingled regret and relief. "I shore played my cards to the limit that time. Joe Breedlove wouldn't scarcely care for such sword-swallowin'."

There was another question in his mind and he re-

21

traced his steps to ask it of the roustabout. "Say, tell me somethin' more about this Jim Breck."

The answer rolled solemnly out of the doorway. "Sooner or later, amigo, he'll cross yore path. An' you won't never fergit it. That's the old Octopus."

The meeting of Lancelot Stubbins and Theed Trono had been very brief and very private. Only by a moment of carelessness had Stubbins permitted himself to be drawn into the patch of light near the hotel. It was here that Lilly had seen the man's English features, and in turn Stubbins had caught a glimpse of the newcomer. The next moment he had pulled Trono into the shelter of the shadows, grumbling at his own negligence. "That was foolish. Well, I'll turn into this alley. Trono, I wish you could hustle things a bit."

"Tomorrow night is plenty soon, ain't it?"

"How's Breck now?"

"Seems like he's losin' his grip faster ner usual. He don't get around like he used to a month back."

"His kind goes down all in a pile," observed Stubbins. "I don't believe it'll be long now. Then you and I can do what we want to."

Trono was dubious. "You got to consider the girl, Stubbins. She's a fighter like her daddy."

Stubbins laughed. "Trono, I've got a way with women. Don't let that worry you. It's only old Jim Breck I'm afraid of. He's stung me too many times when I thought he was licked. We can afford to wait. Tomorrow night, then, at the usual place."

"Uhuh," said Trono, started toward the saloon. Stubbins looked back toward the hotel and saw Tom Lilly advancing also upon the saloon. But the stranger made no particular impression on Stubbins, whose mind was filled with other things, and thus preoccupied he slipped between buildings and rode from town.

II

THE OCTOPUS

"This bein' a bad man is shorely a tough job, fer sooner er later they's bound to come a leetle bit badder man who's honin' to shoot off the tie."—Joe Breedlove.

AT FALSE dawn Tom Lilly was away from Powder, heading south toward the Buttes. By sunrise he had crossed the railroad tracks and penetrated a land that boasted neither house nor windmill nor fence. It was strictly cattle country and for the greater part of the morning he traveled across it, marching directly upon the high bluffs and then paralleling them until the road swung sharply upward and passed through a gap into a kind of elevated valley. This, Lilly had discovered from the maps, was Jim's Pass and the only entrance to Pilgrim Valley from the west. He turned his horse up the side of the gap and stopped on a commanding point. What he saw caused him to whistle softly and build a cigarette in deep meditation.

The valley, ringed on three sides by the Buttes and merging into a pine forest far to the south, was a self-contained, almost inaccessible land. No such thing as a fence was needed and since it was a great deal higher than the country outside and below the Buttes it drew more moisture and was visited with a cooler air. The buffalo grass, just turning yellow, covered the valley in a solid mat as far as his eyes could reach. It was an astonishing contrast to the dead area stretching west and north. No wonder Jim Breck, the octopus, wanted to keep out interlopers. The sight of its explained a great many things to Tom Lilly and as his eyes wandered out upon the plain below him he recalled stray gossip he had pumped from the reticent roustabout.

That road, for instance, which drifted away before it reached Jim's Pass and vanished into the desert. He had learned that it led to the 3Cross, an outfit owned by an Englishman called Stubbins. Stubbins, the roustabout had cautiously implied, ruled the country outside of Pilgrim Valley and had even tried to penetrate the JIB domain. But old Jim Breck had fought him to a standstill, using the heavy-handed methods common to the country. Ever since they had dwelt side by side in an uneasy attitude of peace; just two gents, the roustabout had indicated, trying to cut each other's throat and alike only in the manner they hazed unwelcome newcomers out of the country.

Lilly pinched out his cigarette and threw it away, turning down into the valley. Five miles farther on he reached a small trail that darted from the road toward the pine forest and this he followed for something like an hour when of a sudden he dipped over a ridge and came upon a shanty nestling between three or four young cottonwoods. The soil had been broken around the house and corn was coming up; a piece of fence had been built and a plow stood idle in the yard. Tom slid from the horse, took his sack of supplies and pushed through the door.

Typical bachelor's quarters. The dead Hamby had spent very little time in housekeeping. A long row of nails stretched around the walls from which hung most everything capable of being suspended. A pine table, a bunk, a chair, and a stove well filled the place. All there was of food stood on the table and Lilly saw at a glance that the nester had allowed himself to get very low before venturing to town. The man must have understood his danger and put off the trip as long as possible. The thought revived Lilly's sulphurous anger and on sight of a rifle hanging above the doorway he walked over and took it down, sliding the bolt thoughtfully.

"Well, old fellow, I sure can't help you any, but I can show this JIB crew a few things about land rights."

That reminded him he meant to pay a visit. So, after watering his horse from the spring at the rear of the shanty and eating a can of cold beans, he swung up and rode east. Somewhere beyond the grassy ridges was the JIB home quarters. What he meant to do was state his intentions to the so-called octopus and withdraw. After that it was a case of listening for the thunder to roll across the sky.

He smiled grimly at the thought of turning nester. Twenty-four hours before he would have taken the idea in great and unbelieving humor. Why, he hardly ever turned around unless on the back of a horse. And as for struggling behind the handles of a plow—"Joe Breedlove shore would laugh," he murmured, closing his eyes against the glare of the day. "Oh, I know I'm hot-headed. It's been proved plenty times enough. But, by the Lord, that shootin' would make a wooden Indian cuss. If this ain't a free land it's high time somebody changed things."

And as he was thus plunged deep in a study he crossed a ridge and saw the many buildings of the JIB ranch stretched before him. The place took him back forty years to the time of the Indian wars. Once upon a time there had been a stockade stretched around the place, an occasional mark of which still was visible. Within this stockade they had built the dozen or so houses in the shape of a square, with the main house sitting in the middle of the great yard thus formed. All were built of logs and the center house, a single storied structure sixty feet long, had elbows built at each corner with rifle embrasures cut through; atop a sod roof a cupola likewise hewn of logs commanded all angles of the yard. A porch ran the length of the place, upon which at intervals opened heavy oak doors.

Men moved slowly about. Dust rose out of a remote corral and a horse sunfished upward through the haze with a man weaving perilously in the saddle. At another corner several Indians seemed busy around a fire. As Lilly drew rein before the main house he was hailed by a rumbling voice.

"Sit an' light."

Tom had to look around a pine pillar to see the man, and at once knew him to be the redoubtable Jim Breck. He was sprawled in a chair, his massive body overflowing it—a body that even with the accumulated layers of fat displayed something of the tremendous muscles that once must have stretched across the shoulders. The head was square and seemed hewn out of so much granite, each feature chiseled roughly and generously. The Octopus, someone had called him. Well, it was a good nickname. Even so Lilly was not prepared exactly for the rest of the picture. Here was an old man, a sick man; one who sat very still and listened to the sound of his own heart as it labored toward the end of its journey. A gray, dust-like pallor was on the face and the lips were almost colorless; a strange and depressing spectacle of a mighty frame going to pieces. Still, there was fire in those grim eyes. It flashed out now, fitfully.

"Come out o' the sun, young man. We'll eat shortly."

At this moment an ancient, skinny Indian slipped

26

around the corner of the house and reached for Lilly's reins.

"No, I don't believe I will, thanks. It ain't right to traffic on a man's hospitality. I take it yore Jim Breck. Such bein' the case I don't reckon I could eat comfortable at your table."

One mighty shoulder rose and fell. "Knew somethin' was itchin' you when I saw you comin' over the rise. Say it, younker."

"I'm settlin' on the three-sixty over at the spring. I aim to stay, notwithstandin' yore foreman. Just wanted to declare myself."

Jim Breck sat motionless, his eyes exploring Lilly. After a long interval he answered almost gently. "The fightin' kind, ain't you? Somethin's roused yore sense o' justice. But it's too late, Red. They's a nester on that place now. A fellow by the name o' Hamby."

Tom shook his head. "Yore foolin' me, Mister Breck. You ought to know better."

"What's that?" asked Breck with an increase of energy.

"Yore foreman bullied him into a fight. Shot him dead." Lilly was unable to keep the anger from his words. "About as dirty a piece o' work as I've seen in my time. Don't you draw the line at anything?"

"So," muttered Breck. His chin fell forward and he fumbled in his pocket for a cigar. He looked wistfully at it, then with a defiant gesture put it in his mouth. "So that's got you excited. Hornin' in on another party's misfortune. 'Tain't a safe game, son. But yore kind don't care about playin' safe. Reckon you've got me gauged as a hop toad, eh?"

"Yore reputation is on public record," said Tom.

"Well, that's so," murmured Breck in a gentle voice. "But I was raised in a hard school. Had to fight my way.

27

Don't this ranch look like it was built to stand siege? If you observe them logs you'll see bullet marks a-plenty."

"That ain't no answer for shootin' a nester."

Fire gleamed in the eyes again. "Mebbee 'tain't. When a man gets to the end o' the road an' looks back he sees plenty things different than he used to. Well, I like yore spunk. I could shorely use a fighter on this ranch. Want a job?"

"No," said Lilly. 'I'm obliged, but that's not my politics. The world ain't goin' to be large enough for Trono an' me, let alone a ranch. Anyhow, I'm camped off yonder an' I wanted to let you know."

"Pleased to know a man's real feelin's," agreed Breck. He started to add something, but was interrupted. A door opened and a woman's voice broke in. "Dad, are you disobeying the doctor? You give me that cigar."

"Damn the pill peddler," muttered Breck, irritably. "If I got to die, I got to die. But I'm goin' to have a leetle fun."

Lilly turned in the saddle and without knowing just why, removed his hat. She was a girl of perhaps eighteen or twenty; a sturdy supple figure dressed in riding clothes. In the shadow of the porch her eyes glowed and there was a rose-pink color on her cheeks. She took the cigar from her father in a quick, defensive movement. "You won't help yourself, so I must treat you like a baby." Then she saw Lilly and a smile flashed out. Her black eyes passed from man to man and the quick, open-handed hospitality of the West prompted her to speak to the newcomer. "Won't you stop for dinner?"

"I'm han'somely pleased," said Lilly, "but I've got to get back to my place."

"You live near here?" she asked, puzzled.

"Yes'm. I'm taking up the homestead by the spring."

He saw friendliness vanish and resentment spring up.

Old Jim Breck's chuckle followed him away from the place and far along the road home.

"Spitfire," he murmured. "She's got every bit of her daddy's temper. But, by Godfrey, she's pretty! Now look what I'm into."

The rest of the journey was made in heavy silence. This meeting had greatly puzzled him. If Breck were so heavy-handed, why hadn't the man challenged him on the spot? Instead he'd been offered a job. Was the Octopus the kind that spoke softly and struck in the dark? This affair was getting complicated and that was a fact. There was only one thing he could depend on for a certainty—Theed Trono's outright enmity.

Back on the porch, Jill Breck spoke her mind. "He certainly has got his nerve riding deliberately over here to tell us that. Did he mean, Dad, he was going in with Hamby?"

"Hamby died," answered Breck, staring into the bright yard. "The lad's goin' to take over the homestead."

Jill fell silent for a moment. She was a loyal girl with an immense pride for everything concerning the JIB. Nor was it her fault that she did not know the seamier side of her father's affairs. She had always thought that every acre within the valley was owned in fee simple and she could never understand why nesters dared to trespass. She had asked her father about this once, but the reply had been so vague and technical that it only served to strengthen her belief that her father was, in a kindly way, trying to shield the lawless nesters. For she had never seen other than kindness in her father. What he had been in his younger days she never knew, and was never told. The stories of the range wars came down to her as so much legend and whatever the trouble occurring between JIB and 3Cross in later years, it was carefully kept from her, just as it was kept from the outside world.

"Well, I'm sorry the man died. He was old and goodness knows how he made a living, but he shouldn't have come on our land. And I don't see why you allow this red-headed cowpuncher to defy you like he did. I'll bet he's a Stubbins' man. A nester doesn't wear clothes like that, or ride like that."

"Uhuh. Jill, you go see about the grub."

When she had disappeared inside, Breck spoke to the Indian who had held Lilly's horse. "Pattipaws, you git Trono for me. Tell him I want him."

The Indian was away on the run, leaving Breck a morose, silent figure. "Seems there's a lot o' things passin' on hereabouts I don't have wind of lately. Trono's forcin' my hand. Well, I allus knew what sort of man he was. If he's tryin' to out-nigger me, it's my own fault."

Trono rolled around the corner of the house, a surly indifferent man built in the same mold as his boss. Breck, eyeing the foreman, concluded that was the reason he had kept the foreman so long. Here was the image of himself as he had been in earlier days—huge and tireless, without compunction, a hard driver. If Trono, in addition, had the handicap of being without loyalty and was a dirty fighter in his rages, Breck had shut his eyes. Trono had accomplished the necessary and unmentionable JIB chores; that was the service he had required. But now Trono was assuming too much; he was becoming intractable.

"Well?" muttered the foreman.

Breck closed his great fists. "Who told you to kill Hamby?"

Trono smiled. "How d'yuh know?"

"Don't trim with me, you yellow-belly!" cried Breck. "Ain't I told you to leave Hamby alone?"

30

"Well, that's all the good it did yuh. If yore goin' to call names, I'll call a few myself. Yore gettin' chicken-hearted. Losin' yore grip. I tried to use peaceable means on that nester, but he was pigheaded, so I killed him. Since when've you changed idees on that subject? Wa'n't long ago when you sent me out with a gun fer those fellas."

The gray color swept down into Breck's collar and his hand pressed at his heart. "The world ain't the same to an old man, Theed. Was a time when the whole valley wasn't elbow room enough. Well, I'm more peaceable now to'rds neighbors. Y'see, about all the land I'll be needin' is a strip six feet by three."

Trono ripped out a short and ugly word. "I killed Hamby fer my own pers'nal satisfaction like I used to do certain jobs fer you. An' I'll kill any other gent that tries to squat on that spring."

"You got my orders on that, Trono," said Breck, speaking in a dead level tone. "Mean to disobey me?"

Trono was grinning. It was the same tight, malevolent grin Lilly had witnessed the night before in Jake Miner's place; the man was riding his victory high and wide. "Who's talkin' about obedience? I'm a free man, Breck."

Breck leaned forward, one trembling forefinger tapping the arm of his chair. "Listen, Theed. Nobody ever crossed me yet an' got away with it. Which applies to you. Yore my foreman. I picked you outen trouble an' I give you a job when other folks wanted to tie you to a limb. Now, boy, don't try any rannies or I'll bust you. I'll bust you, hear? You do my orders an' you do 'em on the jump. What's more, keep away from the spring. They's a new man there and he's welcome to the place. I suspect he's more'n a match fer you, at that."

Trono's features suffused with a purplish red. "That

31

redhead eh? So he come tellin' you tales. I give him twenty-four hours to pull out an' by Godfrey he'd better take the warnin'!"

"You got my orders, Trono!"

"To hell with you, Breck. I'll do as I please. You start a fight with me an' I'm apt to show you a few surprises on this yere ranch. Think that over!"

He wheeled off toward the bunkhouse. Breck saw him stop, whisper something to one of the hands and jerk a thumb toward the porch, nodding his head derisively. The old man relaxed in his chair, breathing hard. A grinding pain ran from his neck down his left arm and a cold sweat covered him from head to foot. Of a sudden he was very weak and the world grew dim and distant. He seemed to be apart from his body—watching himself die. Well, he had a few regrets. He had lived his share of years, lived them up to the hilt and had all the fun any man could have wished. A few things, perhaps, he would like to have the power of undoing. But life wasn't that way; once a man played his hand there was no recalling it.

No, it wasn't for himself, but for his girl that he worried. Trono had the upper hand now, and Trono was a disloyal, self-seeking dog. Why hadn't he considered this long ago when he could have crushed the man with his fist? What would happen to the place after he died? Jill was a hard-headed little kid with a world of spunk, but she couldn't run a cattle ranch without help and she couldn't buck Trono if he was of a mind to make trouble. And the foreman meant to make trouble; the man's last warning indicated as much. There were a dozen ways in which a ranch could be stripped, ruined and made unbearable for the girl. Breck gripped his hands together, feeling the sweat roll down his sleeves. This helplessness was something new, something terrible.

32

"I'm of a mind to kill him, by the Lord!" He groaned, and he thought of getting his gun and calling Trono back. Shoot him cold. Once he would have had no scruples, but the stomach was out of him now, just as the foreman had said.

The day grew dimmer and the sunshine turned to shadow. In the dim borderland which is passed by man but once he found himself thinking of Tom Lilly. There was a fighting heart and an honest face. He had seen men like that before. He had ruined men like that before. Ruined them and laughed. But there was no laughter in him now. "Jill," he muttered, "Jill! You send for the pill peddler. And bring Pattipaws to me. I've got one more shot in the barrel yet."

Tom Lilly ate his supper, rolled a cigarette and sat in the doorway watching the sun go down over the Buttes. With the lengthening shadows came a breeze that soughed through the cottonwoods and lulled him to a lazy, dreaming peace. There were plenty of things to think about, but for a time he let his fancy roll where it pleased. It was a mighty queer feeling, this, of being perched high above the heat of the desert and watching the world turn around from his own doorstep. Of course, it wasn't really his yet, but it would be. He meant to camp. The rolling stone had found a mighty fine place to grow a little moss.

"Joe Breedlove would shore laugh," he murmured. Tom Lilly a nester. Well, worse things had happened. Clerking in a store, for example, or doing roustabout's work in a stable. And this land suited him right down to the grass roots. He ran his eyes along the unfinished fence with a professional interest and he began to calculate the amount of hand labor that lay before him. There was plenty of it—but there was plenty of time, too. First

33

and foremost, he would be busy with the JIB and its efforts to remove him from the valley.

So he sat until it was quite dark. Then he rose and lugged his saddle to a ridge a hundred yards left of the house and returned for his pony. It wouldn't do to sleep in the shack this night. Unless he was greatly mistaken there would be visitors along to see him. He picketed the buckskin in a hollow and rolled himself in a blanket, staring upward at the inky sky. It was very strange, this feeling of restfulness that took hold. Most usually he was always wanting to go on, always wanting to see the land beyond the ridge. He chuckled. "I'll have to tell Joe about this."

He wondered how much the girl knew of her father's affairs. By George, but she was a pretty one, and with her little head plumb full of fight! Those black eyes had changed powerfully quick from friendliness to resentment when he announced himself. "I wonder if she understands what her daddy and that Trono person have been up—"

The question was pushed to the back of his mind. The ground was telegraphing him the beat of many hoofs coming rapidly across the swelling valley floor. He rolled from his blanket and touched the butt of his gun; the rumbling grew louder and presently a party swept over the ridge and toward his house. He heard them stop and made out the murmur of voice. A match flared and by it he saw the dim blur of a face. According to the noise of the horses there must have been a half dozen in the party and they appeared to be waiting. A horse blubbered softly and a stray word floated over the still air. "Late."

This was interesting. Lilly gathered himself and crept down the side of the ridge until he made out the faint outline of men and beasts. In a few moments he heard

34

the rumbling of another rider and he stopped, plastering himself to the ground. The newcomer spurred out of the east and reined in with a jingling of gear. A heavy, grumbling voice that was quite familiar to him floated across the black gulf of space. "Hey, Stubbins, this is a hell of a place to stop. They's that red-head around here. He's took up Hamby's claim."

A ripping, explosive oath. Men dropped out of their saddles and circled around the house. A match flared again and by it Lilly saw someone move in and out the door of the shanty. "Well," announced a voice, "he ain't here now. Guess he got cold feet an' departed. Whyn't you let me know this before, Trono?"

"Wasn't able to get away. Been a lot o' thunder raised at the rancho."

"Old man gettin' ticklish, eh?"

"I told him where to head in," muttered Trono. He was in the saddle again, moving toward Lilly's position. "And I give this red-head twenty-four hours to vamoose, but he's plumb bull-faced an' won't scare. Can't have him puttin' his long nose into our affairs, Stubbins."

"Well, if he meddles he'll get badly scorched," replied the Englishman. "No great worry about that. You're always issuin' some sort of a challenge, me lad. Better salve yourself. And I wouldn't cross old Jim. He's a tough fellow. Easy does it."

"Pussyfoot," snorted Trono. He was within ten feet of Lilly, turning from side to side in his saddle. "That don't get you nowhere."

"Sometimes it does," countered the Englishman. "The trouble with you, me lad, is that you fail to understand when a soft word will do the work of a hard one. I have no scruples about violence, you mind. But I'd rather take the easy path than the hard one. There is trouble enough in this country without creating more. Well, let's haze these brutes out of the timber before daylight. Onward."

The party drifted around the shack and were lost in the rising ground to the south. Lilly rose and returned to his blanket, piercing together diverse bits of information. Trono was a JIB man and Stubbins ran the 3Cross. Why all this fraternizing when the two outfits were in a state of armed truce? The answer was simple enough. Trono was knifing his boss. This night party was making a raid on JIB stock; they meant to break the old Octopus who was no longer able to fight for himself. Lilly shook his head in disgust. "I'd as lief sleep with a skunk as have any business with Trono. The doggone doublecrosser! If he ain't even loyal to his own outfit he ain't fit to be shot." Perhaps old Jim Breck was unscrupulous, but it was plain dirty to knife a man when he was down. And so he drifted off to a light slumber, mildly sympathizing with the man he had not long before defied.

He had trained himself to wake at the slightest sound. Yet when he did wake it was at no sound, but rather from a sense of danger close by. Even before his eyes opened the nerves at the back of his neck sent a chilly warning through him and he groped for his gun, rolling swiftly aside from his blanket. Gray dawn had come and at his very feet, crouched, was the skinny Indian buck who had held his reins the day before, Pattipaws. The Indian had crept within five feet of Lilly without betraying himself and now as he saw Lilly rising up in self-defense he held out a hand, palm to the front, and the inscrutable copper-colored visage moved from side to side. "Pattipaws a frien'. You come with me. Boss he want to see you now."

Lilly studied the Indian with mild indignation. "You shore had me in a hole, Smoke Face. First time I was ever trapped like that."

"Indian way," said Pattipaws briefly. His faded, murky eyes played across Lilly's face for a long while. He put out his hand. "We frien's. Come."

Lilly saddled and swung up. The Indian trotted over the ridge and reappeared on a flea-bitten paint pony, riding bareback. Together they galloped eastward toward the ranch. Rose dawn suffused the sky and the light, cold air carried the heavy aromatic smell of the sage. Lilly bent toward Pattipaws. "This a peace talk, Smoke Face, or are we raisin' the hatchet?"

"Plenty peace, plenty trouble," said Pattipaws, his moccasined heels banging at the paint pony's flanks. "Boss, he dyin'."

And when they reached the ranch and entered the house Lilly found old Jim Breck lying in bed, the massive face turned to the color of old ivory. But there was still a gleam in the heavy eyes; when he saw Lilly he smiled in a grim sort of way at his daughter and an elderly man who bent over him. "I'm playin' my last card," he muttered and for a moment was silent, collecting his energy. Short, clipped words issued from his strangely immobile lips.

"Red, you come to this country lookin' fer trouble. Well, you're goin' to get it. I'm passin' out. You take my cards from now on. I'm makin' you foreman on the spot. Ain't time to tell you what to do, or what to watch for. But—you'll have to fight Trono. He's bent on bustin' the JIB. Act as if this place belonged to you. Jill understands. Take care of the kid. You promise?"

The elderly man, who appeared to be a doctor, leaned over to mark Breck's flagging pulse and shook his head in warning. Lilly, plunged in a profound and wondering study, saw the girl fasten a sharp glance on him that had all the effect of a blow. Then she dismissed him with a pressure of her lips and turned toward her father, her hands tightly clenched and her whole body rigid. "Father, what is it you are doing?"

"Yeah," assented Lilly. "You don't know me."

"I've seen yore kind afore," muttered Breck. "Know you right down to the ground. I'm bankin' on you, Red. It's a go!"

"It's a go," said Lilly in a gentle voice. "But there'll have to be a showdown with Trono. You don't know half o' what he's up to."

"I can guess," replied Breck, grimly. His chest filled and swelled under the bed covers. "Damnation I'd like to be strong fer five minutes. I'd break him with my two hands!"

"That," broke in the doctor, "is no way to leave the earth. You'd better get a little charity in your system, Jim. You'll need it."

"I ain't no hypocrite," said Breck. "A man can't change himself in the last five minutes." His face turned toward Pattipaws who stood silently in the background. Of a sudden the room was filled with a guttural droning of the Bannock dialect, at the end of which the Indian stepped between Lilly and the girl, laying his hands on both and in turn tapping his own heart. Gratitude crept over Breck's face—a strange emotion for that heavy, granite countenance. "He'll stick when all the rest are gone," said the old man, pointing toward the Indian. "I fought this buck's tribe forty years ago. Made friends with 'em and quartered 'em on the ranch. They'll be leavin' now, but Pattipaws said he'd stick. He knows a few things that may be helpful when the shootin' starts. Now, Jill girl, I don't want you to feel harsh to'rds yore paw fer what he's told you in the last couple hours. When a man plays with a deck that's been marked by crooks, he's got to do the best he can. Doc, gimme a cigar."

But the cigar was of no earthly use to him. He died before it touched his mouth. Pattipaws turned sharply and darted out; in a moment there was a long subdued wailing from the Indian quarters and when Lilly left the room he saw the Bannocks filing slowly away toward the pine forest, their travois raising dust in the fresh morning air. One by one the cowhands began to collect in front of the porch, staring at Lilly in the manner of men not pleased by what they saw. The Octopus had departed and with him went the iron discipline surrounding his name. Trouble brewed, even as the doctor emerged and spoke briefly. "He's on his way, boys. Said he wanted to be buried before noon. You know what to do."

III

SHOW-DOWN

"When a gent figgers to pick a quarrel with yuh, don't watch his eyes ner his gun arm. Keep yore orbs plastered in the middle o' his chest. He'll telegraph his nex' move from there."—Joe Breedlove.

IT WAS A hurried, brief funeral and of all the crowd only Jill, the doctor and Pattipaws seemed to show grief at the old Octopus' passing. The doctor, standing beside Lilly as the grave was dug—on a knoll near the house— spoke sadly. "He never was a hand for sentiment. Never gave any and never expected any, except with Jill. There ought to be a parson to say a few right words, but he wouldn't have it that way. Said he wanted to be out of the road so he wouldn't be cluttering the affairs of live folks. My boy, there was iron in old Jim!"

It was wholly a man's affair. Jill had taken leave of her father in the bedroom and after that vanished somewhere in the dark recesses of the house. One of the hands who was something of a carpenter made a coffin and presently they were lowering it, with its great burden, into the earth. All of the crew stood about, with Theed Trono in the background. Lilly, turning his eyes on the foreman, saw nothing of sympathy in the hard, coarse face, nothing of regret. Rather, there was a kind of sardonic, illy-concealed triumph on his countenance as the coffin vanished from sight. It was an expression that, in varying shapes and degrees, could be seen among the others also. The doctor, conscious of his lack of Biblical knowledge, stooped and took up a handful of soil, letting it trickle beneath his fingers.

"There ain't nothing I could say to speed Jim along," he murmured. "There ain't much he'd want me to say. He always figured he could fight his own way, here and hereafter. He never needed help, he never turned color when he was in a hard fix. It was always up and a-doing. He took his medicine and kept his mouth shut. He was hard, but he never double crossed a friend and he never pretended to be something he wasn't." The doctor pressed his lips tightly together and surveyed the crew with a defiant, unfriendly glance. "You won't ever see another like him—never. Good hunting, Jim."

That was all. Pattipaws stretched his skinny hand toward the west and turned away. Trono stepped to the fore and pulled his gun, firing once into the air. "That was the sound he like best to hear," he explained and stared at Lilly from beneath his heavy lids. The newcomer met the challenge with a brief glance and followed the doctor down the hill. On the porch he tarried, building himself a cigarette and watching the crew drift

40

slowly toward the bunkhouse. The doctor went inside and presently came out, looking very glum. As he climbed into the saddle he swept the ranch with an arm and spoke.

"You got a job, boy. I don't envy you. But you better be straight to the girl or I'll have something to say."

With that warning he galloped away, his little black satchel flopping from the pommel and his coat-tails streaming in the wind. In a moment he was beyond a ridge and out of sight, leaving Lilly to his problem. The crew had disappeared and the yard baked under the hard noon-day light. A Sunday's stillness pervaded the place, but it was not the silence of peace. Lilly could feel a threat in the warm, lazy air, a warning of trouble to come. Still, he smoked on as if serenely unconscious of impending danger. Perhaps he put more of negligence in his bearing than he felt, for he knew that from the windows of the bunkhouse he was being surveyed by many pairs of eyes.

"If the old man had wanted to get even with me," he reflected, "he shore couldn't have picked a better way. Here I am plumb in the middle of uncertainty with nine chances out of ten that I'll get my head shot off before sundown. A pleasant prospect. If I got any value on my hide it'd be better for me to take a good long pasear and never come back."

But he was only kidding himself. He was in this fight up to his neck and he had no idea of backing out. Meanwhile time rolled on and there was something being hatched over at the bunkhouse. It would do no good standing here and letting them get the bulge on him. He had to get busy. So he tossed the cigarette into the yard and went through the door to the main room. It was dark and cool in this long, low-beamed parlor and for a moment his eyes, dilated by the sun, saw nothing.

He stood there on the threshold sweeping the dark corners until he made out a figure huddled in a chair. A silent figure who stared at him with hot, mistrustful eyes. She had been crying, he could see that; but the tears had dried, leaving her with somber, unpleasant thoughts. Lilly guessed that Breck had told his daughter many things about the JIB she had never known and that she was struggling now to reconcile them with her father's kindness and with her own sense of loyalty. He hated to break in, but he knew very well he had to come to some understanding with this girl. He could not begin unless she supported him, and already he felt he had in some manner aroused her antagonism.

"Ma'am," said he, still on the threshold. "It's a hard time to palaver, but we've got to thresh a few things out. What I want to know is: Are you acceptin' me as foreman o' this ranch?"

He thought she had not heard him, so long was the silence. In the end she moved her head slightly. "You heard what my father told you."

"Yes, I heard. But I ain't heard what you think about it. We've got to work together if we work at all."

The dam broke all of a sudden. "Who are you? What do I know about you? What did my father know? He saw you twice and then trusted you with the ranch—and with me. Am I to believe you are the only honest man in the county?"

"As to that," said he, "I don't know. I'm not claimin' any particular virtue for myself. But yore daddy appeared to be in trouble and he thought I could help you. Give him a little credit if you can't trust yore own eyes. That's about all I can ask. Maybe there's lots of honest men hereabouts, but there's also a considerable number o' crooks—a few of which are on this ranch at the present time."

"How do you know? You rode into this country yesterday and now you say you are quite honest and that the crew is not. That's taking in a lot of ground."

"You heard what yore daddy said. I'm no prosecutin' attorney. I've been given a job to do and I got to have yore help to do it. If yore goin' to buck me I might as well roll my blankets."

"You know the way out," she reminded him. "You can quit now if you want."

"I can," he admitted grimly, "but I won't. I give my word and I'll keep it. Yore old enough to know better. Don't be so foolish. I don't love this ranch, ma'am, and I don't hone to assume any responsibility for its past misdemeanors. But we're in a hole right now and we've got to pull together." He saw that he had spoken more sharply than he meant so he tried to soften his words. "There ain't any reason why you should jump on me."

"Oh, I know it! But can't you see—my father told me things—! Everything is crooked, everything is opposite what I've always believed it to be. Now you come and ask me to trust you. How can I know that the men here are not loyal, or that you are any better than they are—if they are not loyal?"

"You better believe me on that subject," said he. "And come to a decision."

Again a long silence. There was a rumbling of voices outside, a short distance from the house and the girl seemed to see the tightening of Lilly's face muscles. "Well," she admitted, "I'll do what my father asked. You are the foreman. But remember I have the final say. I won't have you discharging men who have worked here for years."

"We'll strive to please," said he, though he disliked her assumption that she was doing him a favor. "But there'll have to be a show-down between Trono and me. Unless I'm plumb wrong, one of us has got to go. We'll know in a minute, for I think I hear a committee."

When he reached the porch they were grouped around the steps—every man who had been at the funeral. It was not a committee, it was the whole crew and they were led by Trono who was standing with his shoulders squared and a light of trouble in his eyes. The man was reaching out now to new heights of recklessness. The only power that had ever been able to check him was gone and he had come to the point where he might work his own will, whatever it was. Lilly understood instantly that Trono regarded him as only a straw to be blown away, and at the thought he scanned the crew with a careful, hopeful glance. But if he hoped for supporters he was to be mistaken. The character of the JIB cowpunchers was written quite plainly on their faces. With the exception of one or two, they were the sort of men to be found along the border, one jump from Mexico; restless, unscrupulous men who hired out their services to the highest bidder. They were not the type that ran a peaceful cattle ranch. Lilly did not fail to note their white hands and the way their gunbutts swung forward; the new foreman guessed that they were better with the gun than with the rope.

Well, it was none of his business if this was the kind of a puncher old Jim Breck had needed in his business. Many and many a ranch had to have its professional fighters if it were to survive the encroachment of other ranches. Still, this kind of warfare was dying out; cattlemen used more peaceful methods and it was something of a surprise to Lilly that the JIB still carried its full complement of feudists. It would make his job the more difficult. He stood immobile, trying to gauge the extent of their hostility toward him; and while he was thus groping for the right word to say Trono took the bit in his mouth and issued his challenge.

"Don't yuh believe in signs, amigo?"

"Depends on the sign," replied Lilly amiably.

"Well, yuh heard my statement the other night. Yore twenty-four hours is about up. I ain't a man to go back on my word. What yuh doin' around here?"

Nothing could come of the delay or soft speech. Trono was not the kind to understand it. So Lilly spoke his piece.

"I'm foreman here now, Trono. Yore out of a job. My orders are to give you a job as top hand if you want it. If you don't want it, roll your blanket and walk."

Trono had not looked for such an attack. It took the belligerent words from his mouth and he stood with his head craned forward while the ruddy blood rushed into his face. The green eyes were unblinking. "Who told yuh that?"

"The old man."

Trono's reply was short and unmentionable. He took half a step forward, his arms swinging wide. "Yuh lie! Bring Jill out here a minute an' I'll talk to her! Don't fool me, Red."

From somewhere came Jill's voice. "That is the truth, Theed. You have your choice."

Trono looked from window to window; but Jill had vanished again and in the silence Lilly tried again to find a friendly face in the crowd. "Well, we might as well get this straight. Are you working for me or are you pullin' out?"

"Work fer yuh? Hell, I wouldn't take yore orders if I starved. Yuh ain't gettin' away with that, Red. As to pullin' out, I dunno about that, either. Misdoubt if you got any right to hire or fire."

Lilly looked to the others. "You boys have yore choice. It's me or Trono."

45

There was no answer. None was needed. Lilly understood his situation thoroughly. These were Trono's creatures, they would fight at Trono's nod. The new foreman, watching Trono with a steady, cautious glance, wondered why that nod didn't come. If the man was brash enough to force the issue now was the proper time. Trono's face was settled in reflection and there was a slow evaporation of his belligerence. Again, as in the saloon, he hesitated, seeming to weigh Lilly. In the end he turned and spoke briefly to the men. "We're pullin' out. We ain't workin' on no ranch run by this jasper. If the old man wanted him so bad that ain't no skin off our nose."

The whole group turned and walked toward the bunkhouse. A quarter hour later they were galloping over the ridge and out of sight. Lilly watched them go, both relieved and puzzled; it was hard to understand Trono's mildness, hard to fathom why the man hadn't made a stronger bid for control.

"It shore looks like he's backed down from his bluff about me leavin' the country in twenty-four hours. Yet, somehow, it don't seem Trono would give in that easy. Must be a nigger in the woodpile."

Rolling a cigarette, he settled in a chair and watched the sun dip westward. Life on the ranch had come to a full stop. Nothing moved in the yard, no sound came from the corrals. It was as if Breck's passing had withdrawn the JIB's driving force; as if Pilgrim Valley had shrunk and shriveled and like many another deserted cattle ranch would forthwith be a place of memories. Well, perhaps the old man in his sickness had been too suspicious, too willing to believe in trouble and disaster. Anyhow, it was a serious matter to usurp authority without sufficient reason. Perhaps Trono had realized it and ridden away to other fields.

Here was a job for a man to do. Somehow or other, he had to get a decent, faithful crew and start the ball rolling again; prepare for the fall roundup and patch up any number of things. It took but a brief glance to see that Breck had let things sort of slide. Some of the top rails of the corral were down, the barn doors sagging on their runners. The Indian quarters were strewn with trash piles and the sod roofs of all houses were badly shaken. When the fall rains set in there wouldn't be a dry spot in any of these old structures.

"If it's this way on the home stretch," he mused, "what will it be like out on the range? How many cows am I goin' to find?"

Considering the night party that had passed by the homesteader's shack, it looked as if he wasn't going to have much rest. Well, he could put a stop to rustling and he could make a sweet-running place of it, providing he could find men. There was the rub. Being a stranger in the land, knowing nothing of ranch politics or of men's sympathies, he was going to have difficulty in collecting six or seven good top hands.

Studying this from all its angles he was interrupted a couple of hours later when a pair of riders dropped over the ridge and galloped down the slope toward him. Within fifty yards he recognized them to be from Trono's party and he stood up, suddenly wary. They whirled before the house and dismounted, each looking to the other until one took up the burden of explanation.

"It's like this," said the spokesman looking the new foreman squarely in the face. "We couldn't nowise break away from Trono here on the ranch. We ain't his kind, y'understan'? But a fella has got to watch his p's and q's. Bill an' me is square an' we like the JIB. So we sorter told Trono we was a-goin' to ride up in the pines to have a look-see. When the boys got out o' sight we come foggin' back here. If yuh need help we'd be right pleased to throw in. They'll be gunplay sooner or later, yuh bet."

Lilly worked his thumbs through his belt and stared at them with a mild, disbelieving countenance. "If you weren't Trono's men how does it come you worked under him?"

"Hell, a man's got to eat, ain't he? Now, amigo, let that ride. We didn't bust into this jes' cause we liked to be shot at. The old man was white to us. We been here a long time—before most o' those jaspers Trono hired on his own hook. Yu' see? Better make peace an' take what help yu' can get, which ain't goin' to be plenty. Trono'll scare cowhands away from here an' yu' ain't able to turn this job by yoreself."

"Lads, it's too good to be a real yarn. I'm obliged but I don't hire on Tuesdays or Fridays. Just run back an tell Trono it didn't work."

The pair looked mournfully disappointed. The spokesman shook his head and observed that you never could tell which way a red-head would jump and wasn't it a fact. "Amigo, what's bit yu'? Yu' asked for help an' now yu' won't take it. Tell a man!"

"I've changed my mind. It's goin to be a new deck. I'm obliged but the road out is over yonder—"

"They can stay."

It was Jill speaking. She had come from the house and stood with her back to the logs, tight-lipped and somber. "I know these men. Billy and Slim have always been good hands. My father spoke highly of them. Hang your saddles in the bunkhouse, boys, And thanks for coming."

The two made off, but not before Slim, the spokesman, had gravely assured Lilly he didn't hold anything against him for the refusal. "A man can't be too careful these days."

Lilly waited until they were well out of sight before speaking. "Ma'am, why do you suppose they come back? Don't you think they'd of stayed when I asked for 'em to choose between me and Trono? Their yarn is full of holes. They're Trono's men shore as shootin' an' they'll only make trouble—of which we've got a-plenty right now."

She was bitter-eyed, resentful; and when he had finished she laid down the law to him in no uncertain terms. "Remember, you are the foreman. Nothing more. I told you I would do the firing. As for those two I know them better than you do. How is it that you, a complete stranger, insist that all this crew is untrustworthy? I might use the very same words to you."

He rubbed his hand slowly along the back of the chair, watching her as the anger seemed to mount. Perhaps he would have washed his hands of the affair then and there, have taken his horse and ridden over the ridge—if the saving grace of humor had not helped him. She was a spitfire and no mistake! But he knew, or thought he knew, what was behind those hard words. Her pride and her loyalty had been shaken by Jim Breck's confession of fault and in the after hours of tragedy when she was trying to rebuild something from the wreck, trying to regain her own self-respect, she had unconsciously laid the blame on the nearest man. Which happened to be himself. "She hates to have me see her humbled like this," he reflected. "She thinks I'm passin' judgment." Well, that would pass and she would be sorry for it. He could bear it. If she didn't change he would still stick until the trouble was averted and then pull freight. He hated a shrewish woman.

So he turned her accusation aside. "Well, if you

think they're all right that settles the matter. Maybe I'm wrong. I've always been taught to be suspicious until I was shown otherwise. Now, ma'am, if you don't mind I'd like to see yore daddy's books. I've got to understand his business before I can start working."

She turned this over in her mind for some time and Lilly thought she was about to refuse him. "I guess you have a right to that," she admitted. "His office was at the end of the house. Look for yourself." "Look for himself," he judged was going to be his motto on the JIB. Entering the old man's office—which was a bare room with only a great roll-topped desk and pine chair to relieve its emptiness—he sat down and tried to find his way through the mass of letters, catalogues and bills of lading. Everything was in confusion and according to the dates of the letters nothing had been filed for six months. The drawers and the pigeon holes were jammed full of unrelated things as if the old man, suddenly tired of seeing the top of the desk so cluttered, had swept it clear with his fist.

It grew dark long before Lilly had reduced anything to order or had found what he most wanted to find—the tallies of the spring roundup. Abandoning the job for the day he strolled to the porch. A light burned in the kitchen and he saw the girl bending over the stove; her white, strong arms moved swiftly and once as she turned Lilly thought she looked somewhat happier. She had forgotten for the moment the troubles of the day. Work did that, Lilly reflected, strolling across the yard. Many a time he had plunged headlong into any kind of labor to keep himself from thinking. Dusk fell across the land in gray, swirling waves, bringing with it a cool night breeze. There was a light in the bunkhouse and he heard one of the hands singing a doleful ditty about Sam Bass.

He moved by the corner of an Indian house and started toward the corrals. There was a slight, hissing sound to his rear and the crunch of a boot. He turned swiftly, arm dropping toward his gun; but he was too late to save himself. A loop fell over his shoulders and tautened with such a force that it threw him to the ground. In the dusk he heard a man breathing heavily, advancing on the run; and when the fellow stooped to take another hitch in the rope he saw it to be Slim the spokesman. Slim grunted his satisfaction. "Yu' damn rascal! I knew I'd ketch yu' if I waited long enough. Quit that squirmin or I'll bust yu' to aitch! Hey, Billy—come on now. I done snared him!"

Slim was on his knee, one arm planted in Lilly's chest. Lilly bent upward and with one desperate wrench of his shoulders butted the puncher beneath the chin, throwing the man off balance. A stream of profanity followed and though Lilly tried to pull his hands clear of the rope he failed. Slim's fist shot through the shadows and took Lilly in the temple. "Yu' damn fool, I could smash yu' fer that! Now git up an' travel to'rds the bunkhouse!"

"Here," said Lilly, "what kind of a game are you playin'? Just what's yore profit in this?"

Bill, who had joined Slim, chuckled. "You'll have to ask Trono that, amigo. Hey, Slim, it's the smokehouse we want. Yeah. All right, fella, back in there an' hold yore nose."

Lilly could not see where they were putting him. A door groaned and Slim's hand went rummaging through his pockets for knives and sundry weapons. The gunbelt dropped from his hip and he was shoved none too gently across the high sill of a shed no more than three feet

51

square. Then the door closed and the hasp fell over a staple, to be locked. The two men, retreated speaking softly. By-and-by Lilly heard three shots near the main house. Three shots evenly spaced—the ancient signal of the range. Within ten minutes he heard many men riding into the yard. Trono had returned.

IV

LAW

"The picture o' a gal blindfolded an' holdin' a pair o' scales is shorely a fine sentiment as regards equal justice to all. But sometimes the lady ain't blind. Sometimes she's cross-eyed, which is shorely sad."—Joe Breedlove.

TRAPPED. Neatly put out of the way in a place so small that he could touch all four walls without moving. Above his head was a sharp steel hook; from below a current of air scoured through an aperture in one corner of the hard-packed floor. Long seasons of meat curing had impregnated the pine boards with a sharp, woody smell and left heavy layers of soot. His exploring fingers found it everywhere; found, too, an occasional rafter charred from the heat. Still, it was not an unsubstantial prison for when he put his shoulders against the door it did not give. The old man had built this house as he had built all others—solidly and meant to endure.

His head ached from the blow Slim had given him on the temple; blood trickled down his jaw. But that didn't matter. What really hurt was to have been so easily captured and put into Trono's power. What would the old man say if he knew what was going on? Lilly saw Breck's heavy, fighting face scowling at him through the black pit. This was not what he had expected of the red-headed stranger. Lilly reached for his makin's, growing impatient with himself. What he ought to have done was to have kicked those two agents off the ranch in spite of Jill's say-so. After all, he was responsible for her—responsible for the JIB. She wasn't the one that had to do the fighting.

"Well," he muttered, "this ain't no time to hold postmortems. Every minute I stay here means money in Trono's pocket. That gent used his head proper. Instead o' bein' bull-headed and shootin' it out he saved himself the trouble an' snares me like a rabbit. Oh, fine! That's what I get for not followin' my original idea. The question becomes, what does he aim to do now that he's got control?"

It was very puzzling. Not that a man couldn't wreck a ranch and make it thoroughly unprofitable for the owners to stay on. Between Trono and Stubbins, Jill couldn't hold her own. By sundry devices, most of which were illegal, they could haze her off. Just bring the pressure to bear hard enough and she would have to quit. It was a matter of rustling JIB cows, of sending 3Cross stock in to graze on JIB territory, of preventing cowpunchers from working for JIB. Threats—and actual violence. Oh, the road was wide enough for them to follow and no doubt they had examples set them by old Breck himself in earlier days.

Still, what was their next move? Having control, what would they do with him? They couldn't kill him outright. That would—or it should—create a stink in the country. Probably they'd escort him down the line and see that he didn't get a chance to come back. What would they do with Jill? Lilly shook his head and drew a deep breath of cigarette smoke. There was one girl they'd have to treat with gloves. She could fight and she might be able to draw enough sympathy to her throughout the county so that both Trono and Stubbins would find it entirely disagreeable. So, if they figured to do the thing neatly they'd have to keep Jill from getting where she could make herself heard.

But they couldn't keep her prisoner forever. That would leak out. What they ought to do was withdraw from the ranch and do their dirty work from the sidelines. If he was Trono and in that kind of a game it would be his tactics.

"Followin' which train of thought," he mused, "they got to put me out o' the road. Then, if they've got the county buffaloed, which it seems they have, it's only a waitin' game before the JIB is busted. Tom Lilly, my boy, it's yore move, even though you only got four feet to move in."

Someone passed near the smokehouse, feet shuffling on the hard earth. Lilly flattened himself against the door, listening. Presently the sound died. The crew appeared to be in the bunkhouse and in a happy frame of mind. They were making the rafters ring with "Arizona Boys and Girls," with now and then a gun shot to punctuate the rhyme. Lilly, crouched on the floor, opined they must have found a quart of whisky somewhere to induce all the hilarity.

"The boys in this country, they try to advance
By courtin' the ladies an' learnin' to dance—
An they're down, down, an' they're down!"

"You'll shore be down if ever I get out o' this mousetrap," muttered Lilly, enraged. "A fine specimen, I am!

Supposed to be protectin' the gal an' here I sit, of no more use than two-bits worth of canary seed!"

He waited until the crew had embarked on another verse of the song before butting the door with his shoulders. It gave slightly and he tried it a second time, hearing the hasp grate against the lock. Someone moved outside and he stopped quickly, gathing himself in a corner. As before the sound vanished, leaving him perplexed. Were they guarding him? And what about Jill? Were they keeping watch over her? Lilly had a vision of Trono smiling in his tight-lipped, sardonic manner; smiling at the girl with his immense shoulders humped forward. He would ride his victory high, this one-time foreman; would probably exult at his dominion over the possessions of old Jim Breck. He was dangerous—dangerous because of the uncertainty of his temper and of his mind. There was no telling when he might take it in his head to use violence; Lilly had read the ruthlessness, the killer's instinct in the green eyes and he well knew that a time might come when Trono would tire of playing safe.

The thought moved Lily around in his black cubicle and set him to exploring again. He dug his fist down into the vent hole at the bottom of the house. This was the flue by which smoke was sent into the place from a near-by oven. If he could enlarge it—dig his way through to the outside. A few attempts at crumbling the hard-packed ground discouraged him. It would take hours to make any impression and unless he mistook his man very much, Trono would be up and doing before long. Probably the burly one was mulling over the situation now in his clumsy mental processes. Lilly stepped back a pace and hurled himself at the door once again. There was a long groan of the hasp and a sharp splintering of a board, followed by those soft, shuffling steps outside. This time they came nearer and stopped. Someone was fumbling with the lock and as Lilly crowded himself in a corner, ready to spring at whoever crossed the sill, he heard the hasp give way. The door came open, inch by inch. As he poised on his toes the soft, guttural voice of Pattipaws floated in. "Huh. You come now."

He slid outside, to be met by the Indian's outstretched hand. Gun and gunbelt was there, not his own, but one that did quite as well and felt extremely satisfying as he strapped it about his waist. The Indian whispered. "You go get girl. I fin' horses. Put 'em by barn. *Hyak*."

The singing had diminished. Of a sudden the light streaming from the bunkhouse was shut off by an emerging figure. A figure that rolled unsteadily along for a brief time on the path of the yellow beam and then turned directly toward the smoke house. Pattipaws dissolved in the shadows, leaving Tom Lilly rooted in his place. The advancing puncher stumbled over his own high heeled boots, swearing immoderately and presently he was directly before the house, swaying a little, his tall, lanky figure but an outline in the night. Lilly tarried, not quite sure of his future course. But here was a temptation too great to be passed by. Thus, when the man stretched his arm forward and put one hand on the open door Lilly drew his gun and reversed the butt, lifting it high. It was a moment of uncertainty until Lilly heard the puncher's breath whistling inward as if preparing to send out a cry of discovery. That cry was never uttered; Lilly crossed the intervening space at one stride; the gun came down, not with full force, but heavily enough to send the wandering puncher to the ground senseless.

Lilly worked quickly. He untied the man's neck piece

and gagged him. With his own handkerchief he tied the fellow's hands. Then he lifted him into the smoke house and closed the door, propping it shut with a stray piece of wood. This was all makeshift, he well knew; at the most he had no more than fifteen minutes to warn the girl and effect an escape before the puncher would rouse himself and struggle free. Turning, he tiptoed across the yard to the house, coming to a halt at one end of the porch. He had meant to save time and enter by one of the front doors, but the gleaming tip of a cigarette told him he would have to circle around to the rear. He could see the man, but it took only half a guess to surmise who sat in Jim Breck's rocker. Trono. Trono mimicking the habits of the old man and flattering his own vanity by the performance. Temptation beset Lilly once more; this time he shook it off. The odds were too much against him. Possibly he might surprise and take Trono stowing him away as he had the fellow in the smoke house. But there were a good dozen men in the bunkhouse and he could not hope to dispose of them in the same manner. So, foregoing the pleasure, he retreated, circled the house and came to the kitchen door. It stood ajar, leading into a darkened room. Listening for a moment, he finally groped through it and opened an inner portal; this was a hallway leading he knew not just where. But he could hear the creaking of a rocker out on the porch and presently a man coughing. Nowhere could he see a light until he turned about and looked at the other end of the hall; then he made out a faint yellow beam creeping beneath a doorway. On his toes he crept toward it, listening. No sound.

Undoubtedly it was the girl's room since all the rest of the house was dark. She was in there, waiting for trouble to break, grieving for what the day had seen. Well, it was a poor time to spend in grief. Right now self-preservation was foremost. He put his hand on the knob, very much wanting to announce himself but afraid of having her challenge him and thus arouse Trono. Half turning it, he felt the latch give and at a single movement opened the door, swung himself inside and closed it, coming face to face with Jill.

She was in a chair and she had a gun trained directly on him. The color had partly left her face, but he was never to forget that flash of eye which fell fully upon him and then, after what seemed a long, long time, fade before relief. She had been expecting someone else— had posted herself there to stop that someone. Lilly put a finger to his lips and crossed the room. "Fix up. We're pullin' out. Quick now."

She nodded, keeping the silence, and rose. Whatever of resentment Lilly had felt against her for withholding trust in him vanished. She was a thoroughbred! She asked no silly questions, wasted no time. A small bundle of papers went into her coat pocket, papers she had no doubt salvaged from her father's office. Then she clapped on a battered hunting hat and turned to him as if asking his approval. And for the first time he saw friendliness in her face. The color had returned; something moved in the depths of her eyes as she held out her hand, offering him her gun. He shook his head and beckoned. Together they stepped into the hall, closing the door behind, crossing to the kitchen and threading its cluttered space to the back. The night breeze struck Lilly's face and the fresh, sage-scented air was as a call to adventure. Up above, the sky was metal black, pricked by a dozen dim stars. Beyond this cluttered yard and its garrison of lustful, over-weening men was freedom. Southward stood the shadow of the pine forest. Lilly felt the girl's hand slip into his; with a swift up-thrust of reckless pride he closed his calloused fists about her small fingers and led her across the yard toward the corrals, venturing a husky phrase.

"We'll beat 'em, my girl. Don't you forget it."

They had only passed the smoke house when a strangled cry emerged from it—a cry that woke every echo on the ranch. Boots struck the bunkhouse floor, the hum of speech ceased. Trono's bull voice boomed across the area. "Who's that?"

"Shucks," grunted Lilly. "I didn't hit that hombre nowise hard enough. Comes o' bein' chicken-hearted. Now we've got to leg it. Hold tight, girl."

The crew rushed pell-mell out of their quarters and, directed by another muffled cry, bore down upon the smoke house as Lilly and the girl slipped away from the yard and circled the corrals; Pattipaws waited somewhere ahead, obscured by the heavy shadows. Fury was behind. The crew had found and released the imprisoned puncher. Lilly, chuckling softly, observed he hadn't impaired the man's voice. It rose toward the sky in outraged accents. "—An' I gits a strangle holt on 'im an' he breaks it like I was a leetle chil'. Belts me acrost the coco a terrible wallop! Boys, I'm all busted up! Somebody gimme a drink! Oh, Gawd that was a dirty blow! I'll rake him across his face with m' spurs! Yeh, I will! Say, gimme a drink!"

"Pattipaws," breathed Lilly, coming to a halt. They were behind the corrals, groping into a small hollow. "Injun, where are you at? By the Lord Harry, I hope he got the cayuses. Listen to Trono yell!"

Trono had done some exploring on his own account and found the girl missing. He was thundering furiously at the crew. "Jill's done gone. That red-head missin', too? Well, you damn fools, don't stand there chatterin' like a cage full o' monkeys! Git yore hosses! They ain't

far away! Two-three you boys gallop aroun' the premises! On yore toes now! We're shore sunk if they ain't
rounded up!"

"I'm shore glad to hear it from his own mouth," muttered Lilly. "Pattipaws— Oh, that you?" The Indian
slipped up to them and grunted briefly. He was leading three horses. Lilly helped the girl into a saddle,
hearing someone running around the corrals, rapidly approaching. "Injun," murmured Lilly, "you lead off to'rd
the hills, savvy? Walk along easy for a hundred yards,
so they won't hear."

The Indian was in front, the girl in the center and
Lilly at the rear. They climbed the far slope of the
hollow and pointed south, going at a slow and silent
gait. The exploring party had gone on to the back of
the corrals, missing the hollow by a few yards. Elsewhere was the creaking confusion of men saddling up in
the dark. Trono's bellicose voice rose and fell, cursing,
threatening, lashing at the crew as so many convicts.
Quite gradually these sounds grew less distinct and
mingled to a kind of rumble. Lilly spoke to the Indian.
"All right. Let's stretch out now. We'll have to clear this
place before they begin to circle around. Hustle."

Jill had not uttered a word all this time. And now as
they swung toward the towering shadow of the pine
forest she was equally silent. The leather gear creaked
beneath them and the steady breathing of the horses
made a kind of rhythm as they covered the miles. Behind them was the one clear beacon of the sky, the
North Star. Elsewhere a dusky veil covered the count-
less twinkling lights; a soft breeze fanned them and
presently the aromatic smell of the sage was blended
with that of the trees.

It was a sober, thoughtful caravan that fled from the
JIB. Once only during the night were they in danger.

Lilly halting the group got down and put his ear to the ground. Somewhere in the near distance was a pursuing party. He published it briefly. "Find us a hollow or arroyo somewhere, Injun. We'll anchor a minute." The Indian grunted and turned his course until they were traveling back toward the ranch. The ground grew rough and in five minutes dropped from them. Here they stopped and waited until the rumbling of hoofs could be distinctly heard in the clear, quiet air. Presently a cavalcade swept by with a great clatter and groaning, to vanish westward. Lilly waited some length of time and then signaled the Indian to move on. As near as he could judge, Trono was sweeping the land in widening circles from the ranch.

Midnight passed and they stopped for a brief breathing spell. Toward morning they reached the first trees and began climbing, penetrating deeper and deeper into the recesses of the pines. Daybreak found them high above the valley floor. Lilly, seeing the weariness on the girl's face called a halt. But she was quick to dissent, saying, "If you're stopping on my account, I won't have it. I can travel as long as needed." And Pattipaws made a vague gesture forward, at which Lilly gave in. So they went for perhaps another hour until the pines suddenly made a small bayou and revealed a cabin. There they stopped.

It was an old, mouldering trappers' cabin. On all sides of the little clearing the ground rose in rugged layers and the underbrush sprang up quickly between the trees. Not a great deal farther ahead Lilly saw the base of a half bald peak and he marked it as a place from which he might scour the valley below. Meanwhile there were other things to consider. Rest and food—and a plan for the future. For all her splendid endurance and courage, the mark of the night's ride was on the girl as she slid from the horse and looked uncertainly to Lilly.

"Well," said she, "what are you planning now, Red?"

Lilly grew unaccountably warm at her use of the name. The last twelve hours had revealed many things to her; she accepted him now. Drowsiness weighted her lids, but still there was a frank friendliness in her eyes, and unreserved trust.

"First off we'll fix up a place for you to get a little sleep," he replied. "But not in that shack. If they pick up our trail—and I think they will—they'll have a look at it. I'll spread the saddle blankets up in the brush for you. As for anything to eat, it appears as if we went on a water diet for a few meals."

She waved that aside as unimportant. "I've been hungry before." Then she flushed a little, still holding his eyes. "I'm—I'm sorry. Most of this is my own fault. But Slim and Bill were two of Dad's trusted men. Even Trono was always kind to me. I had no idea—"

"Yore dad," he reminded her, "was a powerful man. Nobody tried anything on him. They toed the mark and jumped at his word. But you can never tell what a fellow carries around in his mind. That crew puzzles me. A fine bunch of bandits! I'd think yore dad would have known what they were like."

She was struggling to keep awake. "I think he did. You see Trono picked quarrels with some of our old hands and they quit. Usually there'd be a new man the next morning. Dad didn't like some of them—I could see that, though he never told me—but we had to have help and Trono always recommended them. So Dad took Trono's word. Now that I think of it, Trono seemed to do a lot of things, these last few months, that Dad used to do himself. Dad—was getting sick."

"Uhuh. Trono packed the ranch with his own private bunch. Prob'ly bought Slim and Bill to his own side o' the fence. It's an old story. Well, it looks like a running fight for us. We'll do a lot of dodgin' before we can hit back."

"You're the boss, Red. I'll not speak out of my turn from now on."

That gave him courage to say what was in the back of his head. Through the long night ride he had come to a plan that he thought would work. "All right. We'll sleep on it. Then, this afternoon we'll dodge into Powder and leave you."

He was not quite prepared for her sudden awaking. Dissent flashed in the dark eyes. "What will I do there?"

"Just wait until I get things in order."

"And where will you be?"

"Roamin' these hills and sort of scoutin' until I lay a few traps. Don't you worry, girl. Inside of three-four days I'll wash these bad, bold hombres off the map."

"Leave me in town, doing nothing while you're up here fighting? No! I won't do it, Red."

"But look here. I've got to leave you in a safe place. This is going to be a rough job."

She was looking at him with a curious intensity. There was something of her father in that sharp, weighing, penetrating glance; something of the same forthright recklessness in the way she threw back her head and pursed her lips together. The rich color rose higher in her cheeks. "I'll ride with you. Do you think I'm a coward? This is my country and I'll fight for it. Oh, I know what you're thinking! How will I stand up! Don't you worry about me. And I don't care a rap what anybody thinks! Maybe I can't be of any help. Maybe I'll even hinder you. But I'd die in Powder. I'd feel like a shirker, thinking about you doing the hard work and me doing nothing. No, we'll ride together, Red."

She spoke her mind and turned half away, as if afraid to see the effect on the man. Lilly fumbled for his cigarette papers, disturbed profoundly. This was not at all as he had planned it. What could she be thinking of, anyway? In the midst of these troubled reflections he caught her eyes—and his uncertainty vanished. She was a fighter, like her daddy. And she had forgotten, it seemed, that she was a woman. He doubted if she realized what a curious, gossiping world would have to say.

"Red, I know what you're thinking. Never mind me. I don't belong to any social clubs and so they can't kick me out in disgrace. It's my business. I'm not an infant—and I *will* fight for JIB!"

He nodded. "All right. That's settled. We'll get along somehow. Now for a siesta. Come along."

He took off the saddles and appropriated the blankets, leading her well into the thicket. It was a rough bed, among the rocks, but when she settled down she was already half asleep. Lilly bent over and folded a loose end around her shoulders, wondering if ever a girl had been fashioned quite like Jill Breck. The dark hair was all tousled, making her strangely boyish. Yet no amount of sun or rain or rough riding could conceal the beauties of the clear white skin of her neck or the pink flush on her cheeks. She had a drowsy, warming smile for him. Then she was plunged in profound slumber.

Lilly walked down the slope to where Pattipaws crouched against the side of the cabin, warming himself in a patch of sun.

"Old-timer," said Lilly, "I've got a chore for you to do."

"Um. Pattipaws do."

"It's a long trip. Sleep first."

The Indian shook his head. "Pattipaws no need sleep.

Sleep for young bucks. You fix'm."

Lilly found a pencil and piece of paper in his pocket and after staring thoughtfully at the ground wrote a very brief message, signing his first name. He folded it and passed it to the Indian who tucked it in a pocket. Thereafter for three or four minutes Lilly carefully explained the contents and delivered his instructions. In the end the Indian rose, jumped on one of the horses—scorning a saddle—and pushed through the brush. Lilly watched him go and listened until he could no longer hear the rustling of leaves and the click of hoofs on the stony ground.

One more chore he had to do before finding himself a moment's rest. Hiding the horses deep in the forest and likewise caching the saddles where they could not be seen by prying eyes, he started toward the summit of the peak. It was a long, weary climb and more than a half hour elapsed before he reached the top. Once there he was rewarded by a magnificent sight of the whole valley. It lay before him as a map unrolled on a table with each depression and each knoll visible under the hot summer sun. Here was an isolated kingdom, elevated above the burning desolation of the desert outside the rimming Buttes. And in the center of it huddled the buildings of the JIB. He could see them as so many dark specks against the yellow earth.

But as for moving figures, he saw none. Not a thing seemed to tenant the valley. No tell-tale wisp of dust kicked up behind a traveling cavalcade. Trono had buried himself; Lilly, venturing a shrewd guess, believed the foreman was already in the pine forest seeking his erstwhile prisoners. The thought hurried his inspection and he turned down the slope, plunging through the trees. By-and-by, he heard a sound and he stopped dead, searching the brush with cautious eyes. It came but once and after a few moments he proceeded onward, using a great deal more caution. A warning had come to him, not anything tangible that he could put his five senses to, but still a warning that stayed his feet when he reached the edge of the little clearing again. Heavy silence pervaded it, broken by the sudden heavy beating of a grouse's wings. Far off, he thought he heard the click of rock against rock.

Very still, very peaceful—yet a quick, unfathomable excitement took possession of Lilly and, without displaying himself he withdrew and he circled higher in the brush, aiming for the girl's covert. He crossed a small alley of trees on his stomach, crawled over heavy boulders and half fell into the pit formed by an uprooted pine. And of a sudden he was looking at the very spot he had placed Jill. The ferns and smaller brush were trampled down on all sides, the blankets thrown carelessly aside. And the girl was not to be seen.

She had vanished without warning. But at the end of twenty fleeting minutes Tom Lilly read the story all too well. Trono had traced the hoof prints this far—Trono and a party of four others. And he had found the girl. There was the mark of struggle in the manner the brush had been beaten down; Jill had not surrendered without a fight, though it puzzled Lilly that she had not sent out at least one cry. The pine trees made a vast sounding board and would have carried her warning well up the slope. Perhaps she had—and he had been just beyond the range of hearing. At any rate, struggling had done her no good. Trono had taken her and made his escape.

The horses were still tethered where he had left them. That, too, was peculiar. If they had sought through the underbrush for the girl and found her, how was it they had not discovered the horses?

Lilly extended his radius of search, combing the rocky slopes and the long avenues between trees, coming at last to the conclusion that Trono had been satisfied with his single capture and was not in the vicinity, waiting to ambush him. Quickly saddling a horse and letting the other animal go free, he struck downward, following the trail. It was a clear trail in places, showing the homeward bound prints of Trono's horses. At other places it grew dim and was lost on the rock surfaces. Lilly pursued it as rapidly as his sense of caution allowed, at times striking into the woods and skirting such points and ledges as might form a decent place for a surprise.

When he arrived at the edge of the timber he found the trail of the party diverged from the route leading to the JIB and swung westerly on a path that led directly toward the homestead and Jim's Pass. The thought that they were taking Jill away from her own house to some unknown hiding place enraged him beyond measure. He struck the flank of his horse, swearing softly.

"Damn 'em, they can't get away with it! They can't do it! By the Lord Harry, I'll kill the man if he hurts her! I'll run the legs off him!"

He spurred along the trail, growing reckless. During the fore part of the morning he had been very careful; the farther he traveled across the undulating floor of the valley the less heed he took of his own safety. He kept recalling the old man's last words. "You take care o' the gal, Red." What a fine job he'd done so far! For all the good he'd accomplished he might as well be in China. Then he kept seeing her as she was in the covert, her black hair tousled, her sleepy eyes smiling upward at him. The fighting rage welled up and flowed over. Rising in the stirrups he scanned the ground ahead.

Once, toward noon, he thought he saw something moving along the skyline near the homestead and he turned toward it, quickening the pace. Up and down the rolling slopes he galloped, the wild temper overmastering his caution. Once indeed he drew rein to give his horse a brief rest and in the breathing space he recalled Joe Breedlove's sage remarks about the unnecessary trouble red-head gents brought down upon themselves. He threw the thought aside and went on. "Joe never got into a jackpot like this," he muttered, squinting against the hard, glittering light. What good came of holding back, of caution? He had been careful and see what had come of it! "I ain't made on that plan," he reflected. "Better stick to my own method o' fightin'. And by the Lord Harry, I'll nail Trono's hide to the wall!"

The long chase was rewarded at last. When he reached the top of a swelling ridge he saw the homestead shack nestling in the cottonwoods a hundred yards away. Around it were three horses, and loitering in the shade were three men. They saw him the moment he came in view and, as he was against the sun, mistook him for one of the JIB crew. That was all the favor he needed. Drawing his gun he raced down upon them, seeing Trono's massive frame rise slowly and then come to astonished attention and swift recognition. The bawling voice broke the silence.

"Hey—it's the red-head!" And his big fist-swooped downward.

Lilly stopped him with a shot that furrowed the sand. "Cut that! You other two boys put 'em in the air! Nev' mind edgin' to'rds the door! I ain't in no good humor right now." His attention snapped back to Trono. "You dirty pirate, what'd you do with Jill?"

Trono, hands half raised, looked toward the man on his left and winked broadly. "Hear him," he grunted. "That's a big bluff for certain. Red, yuh oughta know where she is since yore the one that took her away. Here, yuh be careful o' that cannon! Goin' to shoot me cold?"

Lilly, shifting his glance toward the others, realized they were both strangers; neither were JIB hands. The one to whom Trono had spoken had a pair of cold gray eyes and a clean shaven face that at present wrinkled in puzzlement. Trono broke in, "Yuh fool! Tryin' to bluff it out now? it won't wash. This yere's the sheriff an' he's lookin' fer yuh. Better put down yore gun. Yuh can't bluff the law, kid!"

Lilly slid from the saddle advancing on Trono. "Listen," said he, checking the volcanic eruption of anger, "I'm of no mind to be played with. Yore goin' to tell me what you did with Jill Breck an' yore goin' to do it sudden. Hear that? I'm a white man, but by the Lord Harry I'll use Injun methods if you stand there an' fool me! Know what that means, don't you?"

A side glance into the cabin had told him the girl was not around the homestead; and the three horses likewise indicated there had been a shifting of the original party. As to this stranger being a sheriff, that was a bluff. Even so the man did not bear the stamp of Trono's breed. He looked honest. Meanwhile the JIB foreman shifted his weight and, seeing the expression on Lilly's face, he began to sputter.

"That don't get you by! If you touch me you'll live to regret it!"

Lilly was on the point of replying when the man with the honest face broke in, speaking quietly and with a certain clear assurance. "Put yore gun down, boy. I declare yore under arrest." With that announcement he hitched his shoulder in a way that threw his coat aside, displaying a star.

"Arrest me?" demanded Lilly. "And what for?"

"Kidnappin' Jill Breck," announced the official. "When the doc got back to Powder he said the situation out here was in poor shape, so I rode over. First thing I found was you'd gone off with the gal an' the whole ranch was lookin' fer you. That's a ser'ous offense, my boy."

"Yore takin' Trono's word against mine?"

The sheriff seemed to have some certain mental reservations. In the end he shrugged his shoulder. "Yore a stranger here. All the JIB boys stick to the same story. Deliver me yore gun."

Lilly was shaking his head. "Don't propose to do it, Sher'ff. They may have you deceived, but they ain't got me that way. If I got to buck the law to find Jill Breck it's plumb too bad. But I aim to wring a confession out of Trono or cripple him in the attempt."

There was a movement of the sheriff's eye and a sudden relief on Trono's sweating face. At the same time a cool voice spoke from Lilly's rear. "Yore covered. Drop the gun."

Lilly stood immobile for one long, desperate instant. In the end he nodded briefly, passing his revolver to the sheriff and locking his lips to keep in the flood of bitter disappointment. Trono, relieved of danger, sprang forward with an upraised fist. "Now who's goin' to do the cripplin', you—"

"Back off," said the sheriff, coldly. "You'll do nothing to this man. He goes to Powder."

"He oughta be lynched here an' now," muttered Trono. "If the rest o' my crew was around you'd have a hard time gettin' him off safe."

"So?" grunted the sheriff. "Trono, you don't talk sense."

Another man moved into view, the one who had caught Lilly from behind. He, too, was a stranger, and doubtless of the sheriff's party. "Good thing," said he, "I happened to stray off."

The sheriff motioned Lilly to get in the saddle. Meanwhile he and his deputies found their animals and mounted, leaving Trono alone. The heavy man was frowning deeply and the sheriff, catching sight of his temper, stopped to issue a warning. "Don't get it in yore head you can raid the jail, either. There'll be no lynchin' in my bailiwick."

"You goin to let him go off 'thout tellin' where he's got the gal!" bawled Trono.

"That will develop," said the sheriff, cryptically and started on. The deputies fell in behind. They rode as far as the main trail through the Pass before Lilly roused himself to speak. "So this is justice in Robey County."

"Sometimes," stated the sheriff, "justice don't show her face completely to the onlooker."

When Lilly turned to look at the sheriff, the latter was smiling slightly. That smile engrossed Lilly's attention all the long weary ride into town and puzzled him even when he had been locked behind the cell door.

V

TRONO VERSUS STUBBINS

"Hark to me, amigo: a woman may shorely be a weak vessel but she's got more ways o' fightin' than a man ever heard about. It ain't because o' chivalry a man don't want to hit a lady—it's because o' fear o' gettin a fine lickin'. You bet.'—Joe Breedlove.

71

JILL BRECK had fallen asleep instantly in the hidden glade. But it was not a dreamless sleep; the long ride and all the discouraging, tragic incidents of the day had bruised her profoundly and left unforgettably vivid pictures in her mind. So she dreamed; terrifying dreams that at times brought helpless, cries from her. It seemed she was being led away from the JIB, that the house and quarters were going up in flames. She was being roughly treated and each time she protested a vise-like fist closed around her throat. She was driven to a strange country—to the chasm of a river she could not recognize. Above the roar and rush of water she heard a heavy fist closed about her wrist and someone spoke ironically.

"What yuh shoutin' about, sister?"

She woke with a scream in her throat. Trono, his face beet-red and glistening with sweat, was bending over her, grinning in his tight, triumphant manner. "If yuh aimed to hide yuh shouldn't be caterwaulin' in yore sleep. Come up girl, we got to be movin'. Where's that red-head went?"

"Take your hand off me!"

"Oh, don't talk sassy. Yuh'll live to regret it!"

When she pulled back, resisting the force of his massive arm, he grew suddenly enraged and yanked her forward at a motion. She struck at his leering face and left her mark; roaring, Trono slapped her with the palm of his hand, shoved her through the bushes and into the clearing. Half a dozen of the JIB crew were scattered around the cabin, guns out, moving warily. "Yuh goin' to tell me where the red-head went?" demanded Trono.

She felt the cruel pressure of his grip and gave up her attempt to get free. "You will be paid for this, Trono! Don't you know what the men of the county will do to you for treating me like you do?"

"If there's any pay comin' I guess we'll get it all right," muttered Trono, hoisting her into the saddle before him. "But I guess we'll ride that down. As fer the men o' this county they oughta know better'n to tackle me or my men. Stop that squirmin', yuh little spitfire! Ain't your own crew good enough fer yuh? Think yore awful smart, sidin' in with this waddy. Well, we'll learn yuh manners."

"What are you going to do with me?"

"Wait an' see. Come on, boys. We've lost the redhead, I guess. It won't do fer us to let him take pot shots from the bush. Anyhow, we've got Jill, which is plenty. We're ridin'."

"If my father were alive he'd skin you."

Trono chuckled. "Yeah, he shore would. Or I'd skin him. The old man was afraid o' me. Never had the nerve to gimme my time. Didn't know that, did yuh? Well, I had the dope on him. I'm a-tellin' yuh. I ain't no church member, but yore dad wa'n't a Methodist elder by a long shot. Come on, boys.

She closed her lips, venturing no more. Trono was a desperate man, and the recent turn of events had unleashed the everpresent strain of lawlessness. Authority, he had never held in great esteem. More than once he had openly flouted it, though he perhaps did not quite understand that the county left him alone because he had the protection of Old Jim Breck. In his overweening pride he considered that it was his reputation they were afraid of; he believed he was the one who had made the JIB formidable. Stubbins would have told him otherwise, but on this morning Stubbins was not present to give his cautious advice. The girl wisely held her peace, uncomfortable in her precarious seat, thinking of Red and wondering what had become of him.

They reached the open country and instead of going

toward the ranch, curved westward, dropping into an arroyo that put them below the horizon. Much later they reached the homesteader's shack and stopped for a rest while Trono sent out men to skirmish. Jill, half asleep in the house, heard one of them ride hurriedly back some time later and presently the word "sheriff" revived her hopes. It was swiftly quenched. Trono hailed her, half hurled her up before another of the party. Then they were away, riding in great haste, leaving Trono behind.

She grew so weary that she lost trace of time. Once they stopped in a depression, the men whispering to one another and keeping watch over the surrounding land; later they left their shelter and struck rapidly toward the Pass, crossed it and dipped into the burning plain below. Jill closed her eyes and for long stretches of time was oblivious of her surroundings. She never knew how long she rode; but toward sunset she was roused by a man speaking and she looked up to see the 3Cross ranch-house directly in front of them. One of the party rode ahead. By-and-by the cavalcade reached the porch and stopped before Stubbins.

Stubbins smiled courteously, but Jill understood him well enough to know there was little hope of help here. Still, she protested as much as her flagging strength permitted.

"Mr. Stubbins, are you making war on a woman? For shame, but you will never live it down! I'll fight back—you'll never keep me long!"

"Ma'am," said he evenly, "don't put it that way. We're only rescuin' you from your enemies. Consider yourself my guest, nothing more. All right, boys, the lady rests here."

She slid gingerly to the ground. "Rescue! Fine words.

But, then, you never were a hand to speak the truth. You were afraid of my father, Mr. Stubbins. You never had the courage to face him. So you waited until he died —and then began to fight *me!*"

Stubbins reddened. His thin lips folded beneath the bear-like nose and he motioned her inside with a gesture abrupt and impatient. "You take advantage of a man, knowin' he can't strike back."

"Fine reasoning," she retorted. "What excuse have you for taking advantage of a woman?"

He half pushed her down a hall, into a bedroom. Without a word, bowed himself out. She heard the key turn and when she crossed to pull down the shade at the window she saw a puncher negligently stroll across from the bunkhouse and take up his station. A prisoner of the 3Cross! She dropped on the bed to cry, but instead, fell asleep.

Though transplanted from his native land—or, more properly, driven from it by an outraged family—Stubbins had never foregone its leisurely, formal customs. It was quite dark when he knocked on the door and announced supper. "I am waiting for you, of course. We must not let the meal get cold. Come, now."

Awakened, Jill debated on self-imposed confinement. But that passed, for she was not the kind to sulk. Hers was the temperament that took the fight to the enemy; in this case she considered it the better part of valor to break bread with the Englishman and talk him out of his ideas. So she rose, washed some of the dust from her face and stepped forth to meet him. He had recovered his perfect urbanity and led her into the dining-room, seating her with a studious politeness. Jill looked about her with considerable interest.

The man lived high and took pains to bring as much

of England into the desert as he could. He had fashioned the dining-room, which was the living-room as well, after the fashion of a manorial hall, its ceiling extending a story and a half up. Trophies studded the four walls and bear rugs quite entirely covered the floor. There was a great fireplace, surmounted by a mantel filled with pipes, tobacco and a litter of purely masculine bric-a-brac. A long gun rack stood to one side, the row of oiled weapons glistening dully in the lamp light. And somewhere he had picked up some magnificent oil paintings of the West—a Remington's scene of a bighorn on the high ledges; a thorough-brace stage coach tilting perilously down a mountain road done as Russell alone knew how to do.

He enjoyed her unspoken compliment and said so. "You see, I surround myself with as many comforts as I can. Really, the old Westerners are grand fighters, but they don't understand the gentle art of living. It takes a gentleman of the old country to show them."

Jill shrugged her shoulders in dissent. A Chinaman came silently in and they ate through four sedate courses, conversing in desultory phrases. The Englishman proceeded quite as if he were entertaining an honored guest and Jill, for all her distrust of the man, conceded that he was a far more polished specimen than she had ever before known. He made a ritual of supper and, when they had finished, drew her to the glowing blaze. The Chinaman came in with coffee; over the cups Stubbins smiled expansively and touched on dangerous territory.

"Jill, it has been unfortunate that your father and I never struck it off. A fine gentleman. One I was sincerely sorry to see go."

The girl stared at him somberly. It was a direct lie; she saw as much in his eyes. Stubbins spread his hands outward in a symbol of frankness. "All this warfare has been exaggerated. True, we fought sometimes, but usually it was our crews that collided and caused the rumpus. What I'm getting around to, is that you must not harbor ill will toward me on account of a fancied feud. I—most assuredly do I say so—am your friend."

"What are you getting to?" demanded Jill, using her father's bluntness.

Stubbins shut his mouth suddenly and breathed through his nose. "Ah, you disbelieve. My dear girl, you must understand that this world is a dreadful place. Men fight each other over nothing at all, bear tales that are untrue and so go on weaving a web of animosity. It's this I wish to break down, betwixt you and me. We must stick together."

"By all means," said Jill. "Even if you must lock me in my bedroom."

"Only because I was afraid you would run away before I had a chance of putting the situation before you in its proper light. Now, look; here you are entirely alone and very much in trouble. What are you going to do about it?"

"I am going to scratch your eyes out, Mr. Stubbins," said she, quite earnestly. "Once I get the chance."

He pondered over this, not quite knowing whether she meant it literally or figuratively. The girl made herself clear. "Don't take me for a baby. Trono is quite crooked—and you are behind him. You mean to make life so miserable for me that I'll be glad to give you the JIB."

"Who told you that?" he asked, drawing the question through his nose.

"It's to be seen."

He put his cup down, growing slightly red around the gills. "That newcomer filled you with that yarn. You sh'd have known better than to've trusted him."

"How is it you know so much about him in so short a time?" she countered. "Evidently someone has been keeping you informed."

The Englishman studied her at some length and at last came to a decision. "Well, if you want the cards on the table, I'll not deny I've been interested. But I'm a little better than you give me credit for being. Truth is, I have long cherished a notion."

"Yes?"

For so stolid a temper, he displayed unusual signs of nervousness. Rising, he kicked back the log of the fire, aligned the pipes on the mantle, and jammed one hand in his coat pocket. "Jill, you can't go on alone. Who ever heard of a woman running a cattle ranch? Now, look; I'm a substantial man. I own a great deal of land and stock and I can command a fair size of money. I'm not so old and, bless me, I do know how to enjoy life. But it is plagued lonesome batching in this house. Here—I'm getting into deep water! Will you throw in with me, Jill?"

"Marry you?"

"Well, it's a pleasant idea."

He was not expecting the torrent of laughter that followed. Indignant refusal he could understand, but laughter! Ridicule! The rosy color stained his long, horsey jaws from temple to cleft and he stood very quiet, waiting for her to stop. "What would you be marrying me for?" she asked, catching her breath.

"Why, devil! What does a man marry for? Companionship."

"And land and cattle," she added ironically.

"You are refusing me?"

"Of course. Do you think you are so profound that

you can't be seen through? Now, let's talk sense. When are you going to stop this piracy and let me go? You will find you're keeping a white elephant. Sooner or later there will be trouble for you."

"I had thought you owned a little solid wisdom," he muttered. "I see you are but a giddy thing. I'll teach you better. Ay, I will."

She rose. "I give you warning you will learn more than you teach, Mr. Stubbins."

Stubbins watched her vanish toward her bedroom, his hands locked behind his broad back. He was scowling heavily in the heavy outraged manner of a man who has found his charitable intentions trampled under. Like many another of his kind he lacked humor; not the small incidental humor that causes a man to laugh at incongruous things, but the deep, rich vein of amusement rising out of self-knowledge. He was, in truth, a grave ass who thought he was doing Jill Breck a great turn. Naturally, he expected to profit from it. The fact of the matter was he did care somewhat for the girl, but this curious affection had been nourished almost wholly on the assumption that in marrying her he would be master of Pilgrim Valley.

Deprived of this manner of acquiring territory he became distinctly dangerous. Cautious, disposed to use a soft word where it would do the work of a hard one, he nevertheless always pushed toward the main object, never allowing himself to be shunted aside. He had feared Breck as he had feared no other living man; that alone kept him humble. But Breck was gone and, like Trono, he felt a weight removed. From now on he would be less cautious.

So he stood before the fireplace, pipe clenched in his teeth, studying his problem. Possession of Jill was no simple matter; he knew he had most of the county officials beneath his thumb and he likewise knew that with the 3Cross crew and the JIB crew—the latter chosen by him through Trono—he could stand off a good sized posse. Even so, it was a dangerous situation. Once a sentiment thoroughly took hold of the country it swept men along at a tremendous rate. If Jill's captivity should become general knowledge it would do nothing but harm to him.

"Trono," he muttered, "was a cursed fool for making this move. He should have taken the girl back to the JIB and held her there. Then nobody could say she was being kidnapped—on her own ranch."

Trono, as it had often turned out before, was the stumbling block. The man was forever doing the wrong thing, the bull-headed thing. Always butting into trouble. Trono didn't know that you could only push a community about so far; after that they rose and wrought destruction.

"Well," he said to himself, "she made a bad bargain when she turned me down. I may look soft but I'll not let her turn me. Gad, I will not! She chooses to take pot luck. All right. I'll use a man's weapons on her. That I will."

Jill, meanwhile, had gone storming to her room with mixed emotions. In the darkness—there seemed to be no lamp—she stood quite still, listening for the lock to turn; but Stubbins had not followed her and she felt more relieved than she could express. Stubbins had made his bid and in doing so had disclosed his mind. Here was another of those men who would stop at no point short of his destination. He used a little bluster, he was quite the suave gentleman when it pleased him; that made him the more formidable. Jill, on tiptoes, went to the window and peeped through the blind. A cigarette tip glowed in the darkness, warning her that she was still guarded.

It heightened her feeling of desperate resistance. Catching hold of the door knob she turned it until the lock clicked ever so slightly. Inch at a time she slipped it open; down the hall the boards glowed from the reflection of the fire in the big room. That way she could not go without crossing Stubbins' vision. The other way, then. Slipping through, she closed the door with equal care and slid into darkness, not knowing where this black alley led. Dishes rattled from the kitchen, a patch of light fell athwart her path, then a draught of air. Luck! She was on the sill of an open door that led into the back yard of the house.

The glowing cigarette tip was just out of range around an elbow of the house. The barn loomed against the sky, a landmark on which she unconsciously set her course. Somewhere she'd find a horse and get clear of this Englishman and his plans. But Red, where was he? Jill, setting her foot into an unexpected hollow, bit her tongue and wistfully wished for the comfort of his presence. Her father had judged right at first sight—Red was a man!

The barn's shadow engulfed her and Jill, fearful that Stubbins might now be discovering her absence, moved faster. She brushed a post, lost her balance in the sharp turn and unexpectedly kicked over a bucket, waking what seemed to her every echo on the ranch. To the right, the bunkhouse door suddenly opened and a figure stood silhouetted in a gush of yellow light. Someone drawled, "That you, Bill?" Hard on this, she heard Stubbins' mealy accent bark across the yard. "Ashbey, where the devil have you been? She's given me the slip! Roust out!"

At that she ran faster, circling the barn, seeing the

man spring from the bunkhouse in hot pursuit. She collided against the sharp bars of a corral and said "darn!" in an aggravated, rising tone. She could not turn back, so she started to climb over; but that, too, was fatal. Boots thudded near by and an ungentle hand hauled her down from her perch. "Honey," said a soft, southern voice, "you got spunk, but yore buckin' the wrong brand."

She marched meekly back to the house and into the light of the big room. Stubbins stared at her with a hard, glowering gaze. "Get to your room! Don't try that again, hear! I have men on guard around this house and they're ordered to shoot."

Jill said, malice in her voice, "I told you, Mr. Stubbins, you'd have trouble keeping me. I'll scratch your eyes out yet." She went quickly to her room, this time hearing the key turn. There was another sound, too. Hoofs drummed on the hard ground outside and a man challenged, evoking a rumbling, familiar reply. "Oh, put up yore damn gun. Yuh'd think this was an army. It's me—Trono."

The interview between Trono and Stubbins was very brief, as usual. The two men seemed to find little comfort in each other's company, for all their common crookedness. Trono strode across the room in long, aggressive steps, stopping directly in front of Stubbins.

"Well, you got the girl. Now what you goin' to do with her?"

"That's something you should have considered before you brought her to me," answered Stubbins. "It was a foolish thing to do. Supposing this gets out? Why, I'll have a fight on my hands. You should have left her at the JIB and seen to it she stayed right in the house until she was ready to pack up and leave the country."

"Yeh? Yuh always got a better idea, ain't yuh?" grumbled Trono. "I brought her here because the sher'ff was roamin' around the Valley. Then that damn Red was causin' trouble. We pinned his ears back an' led him to the calaboose fin'lly. But yore the boss, so you tell me what yore goin' to do."

"Mean to say the fellow is in jail? Oh, the devil! Now he'll spread the story and stir the county. My Godfrey, why didn't you put him out of the way?"

Trono took the rebuke with ill grace. "Say, do yuh think I'm Jesse James? I been havin' plenty o' trouble the last thirty-six hours. Now I'm sharin' some o' it with you. It's yore job, anyhow. You jes' mix in an' do a few licks yoreself. As fer the red-head, the sher'ff's got him booked fer kidnappin'. I think he'll have a hard time."

"Kidnappin'? Hm. That sounds interestin'," Stubbins studied his ally. "He ought to be put out of the way, my lad. He's a dangerous critter."

"How about this?" said Trono, leaning forward. "We'll jes' hide the girl some place an' then take a bunch o' the boys down to Powder an' lynch him fer doin' the deed. Then he won't give us no bother."

Stubbins nodded. "Now you're thinking what you should have thought some time ago. But I can't have her here. Somebody's liable to drop in and see her. Got to put her in some other cache."

"Thought you had a way with wimmen." Trono grinned.

Stubbins pressed his lips together and looked angry. "You take her, Trono. Now. Over the mountains to the last line rider's cabin. Grub there. Then in a couple days I'll see to it a lynchin' party starts for Powder."

"So I'm to pull the coals outa the fire again?" Trono

was sullenly intractable. "Why don't you do it yoreself? Supposin' I get caught?"

"Afraid?"

"Hell! I'll go. But what you goin' to do with her after that?"

Stubbins hadn't decided that. Truly, Jill was becoming a burden to him. But he didn't say as much to Trono; the burly foreman was given to spells of ridicule that Stubbins disliked. So he dropped his head significantly and said, "That will take care of itself. This newcomer must be fixed first. I'll get the lady."

He roused Jill and escorted her into the hall. Trono grinned sourly at her and winked portentously at Stubbins. "Jill, we got to go fer a little ride. Don't you be afeerd, though. It's all right."

The girl lifted her shoulders. She knew, in a half certain way, what they were about, thought she didn't understand that it implicated Tom Lilly. Resistance was utterly useless. Mustering her courage she lifted her clear, oval face to Stubbins. "I'm already becoming a burden to you, am I not? All right, Mr. Stubbins. You'll find that a woman has a thousand ways of fighting back you never heard of. And, remember, I'll scratch your eyes out before you are finished with me."

Trono led her into the yard. In a few minutes a 3Cross man led around a second horse and presently the girl was traveling again. This time southward. She had managed to smile somewhat at Stubbins and assumed an air of triumph. Here in the utter darkness, bound for an unknown destination, this triumph deserted her.

"Oh, Red, where *are* you! I wish you'd come!"

VI

IN POWDER'S BASTILLE

*I'm a peaceful man. Fightin' I don't like. But here
I am, now who do I shoot?"—Joe Breedlove.*

POWDER sweltered under the baking, midday heat; Powder shivered with the midnight cold. It was a town of violent extremes, living in a state of suspended animation for long periods of time until the cowboy and his money rode furiously in to spill the red paint. Life here was indolent and easy until the slumbering passions flared up; then it became cruel, raw, unjust. Such was Powder as it appeared to Tom as he surveyed it from the second floor of the sheriff's office during the two days of his confinement.

There was nothing much to divert him, save his own thoughts and these were not of a kind to guarantee peace. He was never the man to play possum; he had no easy-going philosophy to console him when things went wrong. Rather his quick temper fed upon his injuries and the injuries done to others, growing greater, more volcanic. So it flickered and flared under pressure, ready to burst forth at the first opportunity, making of him an extremely dangerous character. The sheriff, visiting now and then, saw this and in an easy-going way tried to humor him.

"Now it don't ever help a man to hold his breath until his lungs cave in," he warned. "That's what yore doin'. You'll bust yore G string and be plumb out of harmony if you don't just float with the tide a while.

Sing yoreself a sweet little ditty an' pretend yore takin'
the rest cure."

"That," muttered Tom Lilly, "is what Joe Breedlove
would say. Yeh, 'Take it easy' is his fav'rite motto."

"Yore friend has got plenty of sense," said the sheriff.
"An oiled wheel lasts longer than a dry one."

"Hell! I'm not built that way. Yore a fine fellow to
come round here talkin' like Santy Claus. It ain't no
skin off yore nose that they's a bunch of wild men up
in the hills pickin' the JIB to pieces."

He couldn't quite understand the sheriff. The man
draped himself against the door, smiling down his
pipestem. There was apparent honesty in his eyes and
a certain stubborn fearlessness in the cut of the grizzled,
middle-aged face. "Seems to me you didn't have any
friendly notions to'rds the JIB when you went into
Pilgrim Valley," said he. "Why all the concern now?"

"I hate a double crosser," said Tom. "It natcherlly
makes me riled."

"Well, you're buckin' some powerful gents, my son.
Take the advice of an old campaigner. Slick does it
in this country. Don't go around announcin' your intentions. Just sing low until you're ready to slam in
with the artillery."

"Fine to say," grunted Tom. "But do you realize they's
a girl bein' held somewhere in those hills? By the Lord
Harry, it ain't nothin' to smile about! That's what gripes
me. I'd kill somebody for that."

The sheriff stared long and intently at Tom Lilly.
His forehead wrinkled thoughtfully and he removed
his pipe, tapping it against the grating. "Wherever she
is, nobody's treatin' her too bad. Them boys ain't forgot
they're gentlemen—of a sort."

"What boys?" demanded Lilly.

The sheriff merely grinned. Lilly stood up. "Say, you

seem to know a powerful lot. When do I get tried for this awful crime I didn't commit?"

"Soon enough," said the sheriff. "As for knowin' things, I'll admit it. That's why I hold my job. You have to mingle politics with duty in this country, Red."

Lilly heard him creaking down the stairs and call to somebody in the street. A short while after a rider cantered southward from the town—Lilly saw him go from the back window of his cubicle. The sheriff, too, got aboard his sorrel and ambled leisurely away from the smothering heap that was Powder. The day droned along; night came and with it the sounds of reviving pleasure. Supper came. The piano in Jake Miner's place sent forth its stuttering off-key harmony. Boots clumped across the sheriff's office below him. Evidently that worthy was back from his ride. Lilly rolled an after supper cigarette and reflected on many things. Considering the seriousness of the charge placed against him, it seemed the sheriff maintained a mighty friendly attitude toward him; nor did he seem greatly exercised at the thought of Jill Breck having disappeared. There was mystery behind this. Was the man in league with Trono? On the surface it appeared so, but Lilly could not imagine double-dealing behind the sheriff's square, frank face.

Darkness had long since fallen. Below, there was a murmuring of voices, two or three of them. Then the stairway squealed under a heavy body and a vague shadow appeared beyond the grating. A key scraped the lock and a soft voice—a voice that had a sweet and laughing timber to it—floated inward.

"Yeh. The sheriff said this was where he kept his star boarder. 'Iron bars do not a prison make.' Shore enough. Mister Lilly would you be so kind as to step forth where I c'n shock myself with yore unholy mug oncet more?"

Lilly sprang up, checking a shout of delight. Joe Breedlove! Pattipaws then, had delivered his message. He shoved the door open and with an effort spoke casually. "You old wampus cat."

"Yeh. Same to yuh an' many of them. It shorely seems natcheral—me gittin' yuh outa jail oncet more. I'm allus gittin' yuh outa some mess." A firm hand closed on his shoulder. Breedlove's tall, square body stooped toward him. "I'm a man o' peace. I hate to fight. But here I am, now who do I shoot?"

"Easy, boy. What'd you do with the sheriff?"

"Oh, Moses an' I sorter sauntered in like we wanted to converse with him an' gits the drop. He's down talkin' religion to Moses now. Only it's hard fer a gent to talk with his hands tied."

"You brought the boys along?"

"Eight simple-minded men o' the open spaces. We rolled our blankets five minutes after yore telegram come. Hopped a freight at the water tank an' had a right nice journey. Railroad men c'n be awful accommodatin', when they got to be. The Injun was at the Junction waitin' fer us. Guess he knew all about yuh, fer he leads us thisaway. I left the boys outside so nobody'd get excited."

Lilly groped down the stairway and opened a door into a side room. A lantern emitted feeble rays through its smudgy shield, revealing the sheriff neatly tied to a chair and a sad-faced, loose-jointed person standing near him, speaking in polite solemnity about the weather. The sheriff seemed not to mind his position; he grinned with cheerful humor when Tom Lilly entered.

"I was wonderin' when your party would arrive,"

said he. "Better turn down that lantern a little. Some-body might peek in that door."

"Huh?" asked Lilly. "How did you know I asked for help?"

"Shucks, man, give me a little credit. Ever' time a sparrow ketches a worm in Robey County I know it. How? That's my own business. What's your next move?"

"Now look here," interrupted Lilly. "Explain yoreself. I don't arrive at you atall. Are you for me or agin me? If yore for me, why did you put me in the jug? If yore agin me, what's the idea o' actin' as if you'd found yore long lost brother?"

"I'm for justice, Red. That's a-plenty. But sometimes I've got to use devious means to arrive at it. Now, I pinched you to keep Trono and his fine assassins from tyin' you to a tree, which they honed to do. As for lookin' proud in these close-embracin' folds of rope, what good would it do me to cuss? You got me. Now go on an' peddle your papers. Though I'm more'n half glad you rustled up some good men."

"Don't it beat hell?" grunted Lilly. Joe Breedlove was smiling, his tall, husky frame slightly bent over. His was the countenance of a man well disposed toward the world; from his sandy yellow hair downward he made a picture of an easy-going, shrewdly-observant character. Sadness had touched Joe Breedlove; he had never had a home. Once, he had seen himself double-hitched and running his own small ranch. But that was only a memory now. Out of all this he could still smile that sweet, charitable smile, looking at the world with eyes that were sometimes thoughtful, but never embit-tered.

The sheriff seemed to find him worth studying. "Tell that red-headed friend of yours how it is when you get a chance. You savvy, don't you?"

Breedlove nodded. "Uhuh. Tom might, too, if he wa'n't such a dog-goned ser'ous nature. Y' see, he's all fight."

"So I can see. Well, where you bound for now?"

"I'm goin' to rake Pilgrim Valley with a fine comb," said Tom Lilly.

"It's plumb empty," replied the sheriff. "Turn your attention to the 3Cross. You'll find something interesting there."

"Well, by the Lord Harry," exploded Tom, "if you know that much, why haven't you collected a posse and gone after 'em?"

"Because I couldn't find ten men I could trust. Somebody'd squeal and when I got to the rancho I wouldn't find a thing."

"Well, we'll surprise 'em this time," said Tom. "You better come along."

"Nope," objected the sheriff. "There might be some violence done and I'd have to take official cognizance of it. What I don't see I don't know. Just tie me tighter in this chair an' shove me in the corner. Then turn out the light, lock the door and be on your way. Good luck."

Joe Breedlove, chuckling, stepped forward to do as the sheriff asked. The two exchanged glances, they understood each other quite well, for they were of the same type. "I'd admire to drink with yuh some day," said Breedlove.

"Well, that goes double," replied the sheriff. "When your vacation in the hills is finished drop back."

Lilly shook his head. "You shore beat me, Sher'ff. Well, let's be goin'." They slid out of the office and, hidden by the shadows, ducked through an alley to the back of the town. A hundred yards off they collided with a waiting party. Muffled words of greeting floated upward, the rough and apparently unemotional talk of men glad to see another.

"Here's the ol' hoss."

"Drunk er sober? Hey, remember when we had t' pull him outen that scrape at Box Canyon?"

"He don't git no tamer."

Lilly fired back. "Same old pack of gossipin' gran-ma's. Hope you brought yore tattin' along."

They had journeyed into the country without horses or gear. Yet here they stood, eight of them, each mounted, and with an extra animal for Lilly. Mounting and leading away to the south, he put a puzzled question. "Where'd you collect these scarecrows from, Joe?"

"Why, we borrowed 'em from the town's stable. The gent in charge is out in one o' them empty sheds, reflectin' over the sinfulness o' this world."

There was a suppressed chuckle. The H-II crew was having a glorious vacation. Lilly settled into a stiff pace and led them toward the 3Cross. "Well, have a good time while you can, amigos. There's shootin' work ahead. Don't forget it." Leather creaked and spurs jingled. A black veil shrouded the sky and left the world in utter darkness. Somewhere, a coyote sent forth his quavering, lonesome cry; the smell of sage was in the night breeze.

"Ease up," said Lilly in a muffled voice. The cavalcade dropped to a slow walk, crawling southward. "We're pretty close to the 3Cross now. I can smell it."

"Do we pay 'em a visit or a surprise?" whispered Joe Breedlove.

"A surprise. It's a fightin' game now, Joe. I want you to take four of the boys and corral the bunkhouse. I'll picket a couple around the house an' one at the barn. Me, I'm goin' in to find this horse-faced Englishman and pluck his eyebrows out, one at a time."

"Sounds bad," murmured Breedlove; he was chuckling. "The boys'll enjoy this little holiday."

Blacker shadows in the thin, morning air. Lilly halted, the cavalcade colliding with him. Soft warning ran from man to man and there was a slight groaning of leather and the muffled sound of hands sliding across holsters. "We walk from here," announced Lilly. "Joe, I'll give you five minutes to get that bunkhouse located. When yore ready, let out a whoop and a shot as warnin' to me."

They slid down, leaving the horses. Indian file, they slouched forward behind Lilly until the ranch-house barred their way. Silently, Joe Breedlove touched the four nearest men and, together they disappeared. Lilly whispered directions to the remaining three and waited until they had slipped off before advancing across the porch of the house. As with all Westerners, Stubbins scorned to lock his doors and Lilly raised the latch and opened the portal an inch at a time. A single coal gleamed in the fireplace; stale pipe smoke filled the room. Lilly groped his way over the rug-strewn floor, touched a table and stopped to orient himself. This room was quite silent; but he heard the heavy snoring of a man come out of some near-by room. He skirted a chair, entered what felt like a hallway to his exploring fingers and stopped at a sudden opening. The sleeping fellow's breath rose and fell, alternately sibilant and droning. A heavy sleeper, this one. Lilly felt certain it was Stubbins and moved over the threshold, approaching the bed. There was a window directly beyond the bed and by the patch of gray shadow relieving the opaque dark of the room he saw the crooked figure sprawled beneath the blankets.

Closer he dared not go. So he rested, bringing up his gun and waiting for the signal from Joe Breedlove. Treacherous silence pervaded the 3Cross. The sleeping figure strangled and turned, relapsing to a more normal breathing.

The signal changed all this. There was a high, "Eee-yippy-yippy-yip!" and the flat explosion of a revolver. A door was smashed in and instantly a dozen voices and another gun shot answered the challenge. Lilly had no opportunity to follow Joe Breedlove's fortunes; his own man had risen bolt upright in bed, silhouetted by the gray patch of the window, and was swearing broadly. "What's that—what's that?" he grumbled. A better comprehension came to him when Lilly stepped up, speaking in a soothing voice. "You stand fast, brother Stubbins. I recognize that beef-eatin' accent. Boost yore hands. Boost 'em!"

The bed springs screeched. Stubbins flung himself backward and smote the woolen head of his couch with terrific force. Lilly saw a hand go around in a semi-circle and knew the man was reaching for his gun. He brought the barrel of his own weapon down, smashing Stubbins across the head. Thereupon, the master of the 3Cross grunted and temporarily passed from the scene. Lilly's exploring hand reached and appropriated Stubbins' gun and holster hanging on the bed post.

A rear door opened with a clatter and boots came tramping down the hallway. A voice said, "Hey, Stubbins! What the hell—?"

He was pouring words through the bedroom door; but his senses told him something was wrong and he drew back with a challenge. "Who's that there? Speak up or I'll plug yuh!"

"Same to you, brother," announced Lilly and stepped aside into a deeper patch of darkness. An orange-purple flame ran out and was met by another; a water jar trembled in its bowl, the acrid odor of burnt powder swirled high. A gun dropped, a body slid down with

93

a surprising sigh. Somewhere to the rear a Chinaman's voice was flinging weird, wild words about like so many pitched knives. Over this bedlam he heard the drawling voices of one of his own men, Moses. "Well, how's it stand?"

"I plugged somebody," announced Lilly. "The main guy is here on the bed where I plastered him."

"Fifty-fifty," announced Moses in a bored tone. "I ketched me a person at the front door. Seems like he was on guard, but I reckon he fell asleep till the noise jarred him some. He's chewin' at the knots I took in him. Say, that Chink is apt to bust a lung if he don't take a few cinches in them gosh-awful words."

"Light up," said Lilly. "I think Joe's rounded his critters."

He had followed the sound of struggle in the bunkhouse but intermittently during his own activity; and by now the shots had ceased and there was only the hum of voices like the buzzing of bees in a disturbed hive. Breedlove sent his gay announcement across the yard. "Say what, Tommy."

"Good enough here."

"Well, what'll I do with these boys? Never saw so many punchers fer one ranch. I count fifteen."

"Hobble 'em an' come over."

Moses had found and lighted a lamp in the main room. He carried it into the bedroom and inspected the man Lilly had dropped at the door. Blood streamed down his face, but it seemed to be something less than a mortal wound. Moses put the lamp on the floor and ran an investigating finger over the fellow's head. "He's grazed, Tom. Sorter knocked him cuckoo. I'll put a han'k'chuff aroun' it an' he'll be good enough."

Stubbins on the bed, was coming out of his enforced sleep; coming out in a fighting mood, twitching his arms. Lilly waited until the Englishman opened his eyes and shook the mists clear of his head. Anger glinted in the pale blue eyes as he stared toward Lilly. "What's this confounded banditry about?" he growled. "I shall hold you for this, friend. I'll have your scalp for it, believe me."

"What have you done with Jill Breck?" demanded Lilly.

"Oh—that's it, eh? It would please you to find out, wouldn't it? Well, she's not here, Red. She's far away." Then it seemed to occur to him that he had forgotten himself. "Why, you damn pup, *you* know well enough where she is! I'll have you back in jail within six hours. Watch you hang, too, by Godfrey!"

"Yore out of date," said Lilly. "Things have happened since you went to sleep. Yore gang is hog-tied. I've got a posse here that'll string you to a tree if you lie to me. Time's past for foolin'. I've got enough on you this minute to send you to the pen."

"What's that?"

"Some of the JIB boys have been tellin' tales," offered Lilly. "Some of the JIB cows have been found in yore herds, too. We know Jill Breck's been here. Now, you talk turkey an' talk fast."

It was all guess work, but based on good evidence. Lilly watched the Englishman's face settle and to further upset the man he ordered him up and into the main room where Joe Breedlove and three or four of the H-H crew were lounging. "It's all off with you, Stubbins. You tell the truth. We've got six men who'll turn state's evidence against you. Where's Jill Breck?"

"What if I tell?"

"You'll get an even break," promised Lilly.

"What if I don't tell?" shot back Stubbins, his thin mouth disappearing beneath the great nose.

"You'll be hung in an hour."

"Eh? Oh, no. You wouldn't dare that. I'm too big a man in this country."

"So? Say, when this leaks out there won't be a man, woman or dog in Robey County but what won't want to take a piece out of yore hide. No, you ain't got a foot to stand on. Now, where's Jill Breck?"

Stubbins thrust a long, cool glance around at the H-H men, then rose and filled one of the pipes on the mantel. Behind a cloud of tobacco smoke he deliberated. For all his villainy, there was something in the man to evoke admiration. Here he stood, with all his plans crashing down around his head, with three or four grave charges against him—charges that would inevitably lead him to the penitentiary or worse; he had no means of knowing whether this posse would take his life or not, or if they let him go, whether an outraged county would be as lenient. Still, he smoked imperturbably, as if deciding no more important a thing than whether or not to hire another hand for his ranch.

"Yore house is made of cards," broke in Lilly. "As long as old Breck lived, he and you could buffalo this county. But it's too big a job for you alone. A dozen good men can bust any sort of range piracy, and we're goin' to bust you. Times are changin', amigo. You'll change with 'em or go down."

Fretfulness invaded the horsey face. "Damn the man," said Stubbins testily. "Damn Trono. He was the one I always mistrusted. You can't play with a bull-headed fool. Now, he shouldn't have brought—" There he stopped, finishing the sentence to himself.

"Anybody's a fool to trail along with Trono," broke in Lilly. "He'll saddle murder to you yet."

"What's that?" demanded Stubbins, jerking up his head. "Murder—murder?"

"It's the kind he is," replied Lilly. "I know him. He'll go bugs an' shoot anything in sight."

Stubbins appeared to be seeing unwelcome visions. "Ay, I know that. Look; what do you mean by an even break?"

"Stolen goods returned and no questions asked."

"Ah. What goods?"

"Jill Breck for one. Later Joe and I will hold a roundup of yore stock and pick JIB critters."

"And no tales told!"

"None but what naturally leak out, amigo. Of course, yore goin' to lose some of them nice cut-throats you've got hired. Joe's goin' to see that they get started north after breakfast. I'll send the JIB bunch over to you, seein' they're yore men anyhow. Now, let's shorten this palaver."

"Devil," muttered Stubbins. He shot a glance at Lilly. "My boy, you ain't scarin' me, understand? I do this of my own conscience. No man's big enough to scare me."

"Have it yore own way," said Lilly. Joe Breedlove dropped a wink at his partner, which Lilly answered.

"Well, then, Trono took Jill Breck, the night before last. I told him to stop at a line rider's cabin." He marched to a book case and found a map of the country, running his finger along its surface and pointing for Lilly's benefit. "There you are. It's twenty miles southeast. In the fringe of rock and trees. Welcome, my lad."

"And you let that lout take her off!" cried Lilly, his temper rising. "If she's harmed I'll kill you for it!"

Stubbins returned a hard, obstinate stare, growing red around his heavy neck. He was about to make some rousing answer when he caught Joe Breedlove's usually mild eyes anchored on him with such an intent, weighing glance that he forebore. Instead, he asked a question.

"You mean to kill him?"

"One of us goes down," retorted Lilly.

"It's all the same to me," said Stubbins. "You or him." With that he dropped in a chair and smoked furiously.

"Moses," said Lilly, "find me a fresh horse." He walked into the pale light of false dawn, Joe Breedlove close behind. The big man's arm rested lightly on Lilly's shoulder.

"Well, this is yore fight, Red, so I ain't goin'. But watch yore rear. An' say, yuh wouldn't have hung Stubbins, even if he'd refused to talk."

"I guess not," said Lilly, "but I shore would've done somethin'. He's slick, that boy. Know why he told on Trono? Because he knew one of us won't come back, which is just right for him."

"Like hell it is," growled Breedlove. Moses was returning with a saddled paint horse. "If yuh don't show up in five-six hours, Mr. Stubbins is like to have an accident. Meanwhile, we'll take care o' this crew."

Lilly swung up, gripped Joe's outstretched arm, and spurred away. Dawn was just below the eastern rim; toward it he traveled, going as fast as the horse would stand.

The sun rose in its arc, glowered from zenith, and fell westward, growing more wrathful, more sultry. The vast plain shimmered under the heat and above the undulating barren spaces queer, phantasmic shapes formed and dissolved. To all this Tom Lilly was unconscious. He traveled with Stubbins' map firmly fixed in his head, and an unreasoning hatred in his heart. It was Trono, always Trono who interposed his unlovely, killer's face into the images that passed and re-passed Tom Lilly's vision. Trono was a bad Indian; and never would be a good one until dead. Where had the man got all this vindictiveness of spirit? What could he hope to profit from his course of lawlessness? Well, he was an outlaw by nature; made the more so by his training under old Jim Breck in the days when the Octopus had given him hard chores to do. Evidently, he had formed connections with Stubbins—probably would be a chief heir of the looting of the JIB.

"Even if there wasn't a cent to be made he'd be a renegade, though," opined Lilly. Reviewing the course of events he slapped one hand against the saddle skirts, saying, "It's him or me. If he's laid one o' his dirty paws on Jill—"

He could not, for all the glaring sun, keep her clear, oval face from his eyes. She was like no other woman he had ever known. Old Jim Breck had given her a good measure of his sturdy spirit and some of his uncomplaining fortitude. Never, in that long night of flight, had she whimpered. Never had she traded on the fact that she was a woman; seemed, in fact, reluctant to admit that she couldn't do all a man could do. And she had smiled at him in such a manner when she rolled up in the blankets, the rosy color tinging her cheeks and some unfathomable emotion moving in the sleepy eyes.

He swerved, climbed the bench on his left and presently was threading his way among the pines. Shade here, but no coolness. He struck a trail that slanted upward into deeper recesses of the forest and of a sudden all things immaterial to the chase left his head. The tracks of two horses were in the sandy course before him. Not fresh tracks, but recent enough to still show a clear imprint. These he followed, resorting to trailing tactics, for he had followed men before and understood their slyness.

At intervals he left the trail and dived into the trees, going a hundred yards or more before reappearing. Sometimes, confronted by a barrier of rock or dead-fall, he made a considerable detour and came to a halt, sweeping the vistas, listening for out of the way sounds. But the forest was silent, save for the drone of heat and small insects. So, he pushed on until his eyes saw a thinning of the pines directly ahead and when he dismounted and crawled forward flat on his stomach, he saw a miniature meadow in which sat a cabin and a small corral. Lush grass stood ankle-high; a small path was beaten through it from the trees to the door. And on the threshold of the door, squatted down like a massive, sullen spider, was Theed Trono. The sun slanted against his face, bringing into bold relief the cleft chin, the columnar neck; shaded by the wide hat-brim his upper features were obscured. A cigarette dangled from one corner of his mouth and he played idly with his lariat, making loops on the ground.

He seemed so much off guard, so little expecting danger that Tom Lilly tarried a while in his covert, shooting glances to all corners of the clearing, seeking some manner of a trap. But though he waited a good ten minutes, he could find nothing to justify his caution. The girl was not to be seen; doubtless she was inside the cabin.

He parted the grass before him, gun forward, and rose to one knee. "Trono," said he, in a quiet voice, "you'll stay right there. Hoist yore hands."

Trono's body stiffened. The hand holding the lariat stopped its circular movement and the Stetson jerked upward, revealing the flash of his green eyes. By and by he dropped the rope and hunched his shoulders, moving his big arms above his head. Lilly stepped from his shelter and walked half way across the meadow. The burly one watching him from half closed eyes; an almost lifeless tone emerged from his enormous chest—the tone of a man discouraged and defeated.

"Knew yuh'd git here soon er late. Shore a persistent fella, ain't yuh, Red?"

"Expectin' me?"

"Yeh." The green eyes flared. "I've had too much time to think. Thinkin' ain't good fer a critter. A fack. Bust outa jail?"

"That's right," agreed Lilly, watching his man closely. "No fooling, now. You know what I'll do."

"I reckon," said Trono, wearily. "Nex' time Stubbins c'n do his own chores. What a hell of a time I've had. Well, le's git this over with."

Looking beyond the man, Lilly saw Jill Breck half-risen, dimly visible, in the semi-darkness of the cabin. He saw some movement of her lips and shook his head at her; whereupon she disappeared, leaving him with his great problem. Trono was smiling slightly. "Don't yuh know what to do with me, kid?"

"I see trouble in yore face, Trono. Turn around, face against the logs. I came here to get you—bear it in mind, amigo. If you want to take the chance, all right. I'm just warnin' you."

Trono turned, muttering, "Oh, I've had plenty. I been thinkin' Stubbins double crossed me. What would I do with this gal, anyhow? Ain't it a hell of a chore fer a man? Him a-sittin' back an' lettin' me run the danger. No, I won't raise a rumpus. I'm a-goin' back with you an' turn state's evidence on that beef-eatin', mealy-mouth fool. A fack."

"Change of heart, eh?" grunted Lilly, moving closer,

distrusting all this talk. Trono was a bundle of dynamite; a vicious cross-grained man who liked to lull an opponent and strike unawares. So he moved cautiously, arm reaching out for Trono's revolver.

"Well, call it that," said Trono, his great body as straight and rigid as he could carry it. The massive shoulders seemed to fill and threaten the seams of his coat. "But what'd happen to me when a posse got on my trail? I'll go with yuh, an' be thankful it ain't a worse proposition. That gun don't slide out easy, Red. Pull hard. Oh, pull harder!"

Lilly, his fingers touching Trono's gun felt the big body tremble. He had jammed his own weapon into Trono's back. But the feeling came over him all of a sudden that the man meant to make a play; desperate as the case was, Trono had decided to fight. And so, dropping his fingers, Lilly stepped back. Trono waited an instant then swung about. The change in his face was striking. Sweat poured down his swart cheeks and the glitter of evil was in those green, sparkling eyes. Once more he carried the high, triumphant, gloating grin.

"Nerve a-failin' yuh, Red? Caught on to my leetle trick, eh? All right, I'm a-tellin' yuh, I won't go."

"I can't shoot you in the back, Trono," said Lilly. "And I'd have to if you turned on me like that."

"I knew yuh didn't have no nerve," said Trono. "What yuh goin' to do?"

Lilly nodded his head. "Walk over there ten yards. I'll give you an even break."

"Fight it square?" bellowed Trono.

"Fight it square, or drop yore gun belt," announced Lilly.

Trono, without a word, backed away from the log house and stopped. "Red, I shore take my hat off to yuh. But I ain't goin' to go back, see? Say when."

"Drop yore arms, slow, until they're to yore belt. All right, that's good. Now I'm puttin' my gun in the holster. We're even." Lilly's hand rose clear of the gun butt. "Last warnin', amigo. You'd better give in."

Trono only shook his head. He was a sinister figure, this man, with his thin lips but a white line in the dark face and the nostrils contracted from inner excitement. Beads of sweat stood out on his upper lip; he was swaying slightly, leaning forward, arms spreading away from his body. Lilly felt the full impact of that deadly gaze and there flashed across his mind the picture of a rattlesnake coiled and about to strike. Trono the killer stood forth in full panoply.

"No signal," said Lilly. His own nerves had jangled a moment and then stopped. He was cold—very cold in this bright sun-drenched clearing. Cold with the premonition of death. All his senses focused themselves on the bulky figure ten yards away; he heard nothing but the drone of his own words; saw nothing but a patch of Trono's shirt where his eyes had centered; felt nothing but the flexing of his right arm. "No signal," he repeated. "Go to it when yore ready."

The world was remote. Time ceased to be. Trono seemed to grow larger, bulk tremendously against the light. The patch of shirt wrinkled and the man's right arm dropped. Lilly had no notion what his own gun arm was doing; it appeared to be detached from whatever mental motor guided it. Fretfully, he wondered why he wasn't matching that swift, cat-like draw. The blue metal barrel gleamed in the afternoon sun. As from a distance he heard a heavy explosion—no, there was a double explosion and instantly the world and all its bustling noises, its cheerful warmth, its grateful light, flooded back. Trono was squinting across the space, the tip of his gun slightly deflected. Lilly, watching the weapon with a queer fascination, saw it dip, jerk upward, and dip again. It dropped to the ground and Trono began to droop. The starch of life was going out of him; quite slowly at first he sagged, then, as if his will power had snapped, he collapsed and lay sprawled, face turned toward Lilly. His thin lips were fashioning words.

"I'll cash my chips, mister. Yuh c'n never tell—what a redhead will do."

He was dead. It seemed altogether ridiculous to Lilly until he looked down and saw his own gun in his hand. Why, he never knew he had drawn, never had felt the recoil of firing! He returned it to his holster and in a moment of thoughtfulness extended his arm to full length. It seemed ice-cold; not a tremor moved his fingers.

"Tom Lilly didn't fire that shot," he murmured. "I guess the Lord shorely is providin' protection."

Jill Breck's voice issued from the cabin, high and electrical. "Red—Red, did he touch you?"

Tom was at the door at one stride. "Lord bless you, no. I'm a fool meant for a different end. Why, what's the matter with you?" Rage jumbled his words together. "Did that swine hurt you?"

Her voice was of a sudden faint. For a moment he saw only an outline in the semi-darkness. "No, Red. I'm all right. All right. But he's kept me tied to this bunk most of the time."

His eyes, becoming accustomed to the shadows, saw that she was half sitting, half lying on the bunk. Her feet were loosely tied to the frame and her hands were bound behind her. She could move two or three feet, no more. Lilly got his knife and cut the rope, his hand beginning to tremble. Her arms went around him and he lifted her up as if she were an invalid. It was then his opportunity came and again his guiding angel helped him to do something that he would never have been able to do otherwise. In short, he kissed her, called her "Jill kid!"

Her body quivered. She was saying over and over again, "I thought you'd never come. I knew you would, but it was so long waiting. It was so long waiting!"

Dusk had settled around the 3Cross. Close harmonies emerged from the bunkhouse, that is to say, harmonies as close as the ensembled voices of the happy H-H crew could manage. It had been a full day and a satisfying one; now they reclined on alien bunks, sustained by 3Cross chuck. In the main house Joe Breedlove was playing a close game of checkers with Lancelot Stubbins, his mild eyes holding no greater care than a concern for the next move. Stubbins seemed to have forgotten his own tangled, troubled affairs. Pipe smoke curled high in the room and the mellow light of the fireplace shimmered over the floor. Remington's bighorn looked down from his high perch with a smug, defiant glance of safety.

"Checkers," observed Joe Breedlove, "is a pastime from which due observations regardin' life might be made. Yuh advance, then yuh stop. Mebbe yuh are taken. But yuh don't go back unless yuh reach the king row. Same in a man's life—only they ain't no king row."

"Mf," said Lancelot Stubbins. "D'ye know, you're a queer cuss."

"It's been told me before," replied Joe, "only in less elegant terms. Don't I hear hawsses?"

He abandoned his game and went to the door. And when he saw Jill and Tom advancing out of the night he began to smile that rare, sweet smile. He saw them dismount and observed the careful manner in which Lilly lifted down the girl. At that he turned back. "Guess JIB will have good management from now on."

The pair came into the room. Tom Lilly walked straight over to Stubbins. "I'll keep my promise, amigo. Yore free as the air. But I'm yore nex' door neighbor from now on and you'll shoot square with the JIB."

"I guess," said Joe, "us boys won't have much more to do in these parts."

"Oh yes, you will," replied Tom. "Yore goin' to conduct a roundup on 3Cross an' ketch JIB critters. Also I'll be needin' a man to go to Powder an' have the sher'ff come out. He'll find Trono in the line rider's cabin."

"Is that all?" asked Joe.

"No, you son o' Satan, it ain't. Yore hired permanent as foreman o' the JIB. I'd like the boys to stay with us, too. We got to run the present crew off the range. Then we got to make a skookum ranch of it. What'd you do with Mr. Stubbins' men?"

Stubbins slammed down the handful of checkers he carried and rose, exploding a brief word. "Ran them to the county line, by Gad!"

"Fair enough."

"Is that all?" persisted Joe, smiling.

Tom Lilly looked to Jill soberly; she had nothing to say. "Well, you can be best man," he replied.

Joe's arm fell across his partner's shoulder. Nothing was said, but a glance passed between the two of them such as only loyal abiding friends would exchange.

RIDE OUT!

I

A MAN'S WAY

ON ENTERING Buffalo Crossing, Bill Maude rode directly to the hotel and slid from his saddle with a coupled ease that was in considerable contrast to the long, loose-jointed frame he carried about. Going through the door, his hat peak scraped the top and he rolled up to the desk with a mutter of irritated good nature. "This joint," said he to the clerk, "was built for a race of stunted tobacco chewers."

"If you aim to talk with me," retorted the clerk, "lean over so I won't get a crick in my neck lookin' up to you. Trouble is, you're too accustomed to walkin' through barn doors."

"Train in yet?"

"No, it's late."

"Good enough," reflected Maude. "I never like to keep a lady waitin'."

"What lady?"

Maude grinned. "Pause and observe before you a duly constituted squire of dames. The new school mistress of NoNo district arrives on that train and I'm to be queen of the may, mother. I, in person and without injurious substitutes, take her home."

"You got competition," said the clerk.

"As how?"

"Tom DeLong was just in to meet same lady for same purpose."

Bill Maude had a lean face upon which serene humor ordinarily dwelt. But it could harden swiftly enough and it did now. A speculative gleam glimmered out of his gray eyes. "Ain't that odd now?"

"What's odd about it?" asked the clerk. "He's a director of your school board, too."

"Which is why it's odd," grunted Maude. "And if you don't know anything about NoNo politics you're well off. I'm goin' out for a minute and if she comes meanwhile, tell her by all means to wait for a fellow with kind eyes and a handsome figure."

"Would you make a liar out of me?" objected the clerk, and ducked.

Bill Maude strolled leisurely from the hotel, to find a rider with ruddy, reckless cheeks waiting beside the porch. On seeing the man he grinned again. "Hello, Link."

"I observes this undernourished, dodder-headed specimen of a cayuse a-droppin' here," said Link casually, "whereupon I knows the kingpin of the Cross Iron is carousin' inside. Come over to the breakin' pen, Bill. We got a lulu there just itchin' to bust yore Injia-rubber neck."

"Nice," applauded Bill Maude and swung to the saddle. Side by side the two passed part way along the main street, cut through a right angle thoroughfare and went down Railway Avenue, paralleling the transcontinental tracks. It was apparent Buffalo Crossing knew Bill Maude very well, for his hand and his drawling voice kept answering men on the walks. But presently Railway Avenue became a dust road leading toward corrals while the buildings of town dropped behind. Immediately Bill turned sober.

"You did it just right, Link," he said. "Whenever we meet in public it's got to seem accidental and without any mark of a business transaction. What's your answer?"

"I quit my job. Got drunk to make the thing seem real enough. Now, I'll work for you."

"Fine," said Maude. "I been after a wildcat like you for a long time. But I won't want you to come over to the ranch as a regular rider. Right now I've got more men than any ordinary outfit carries. If I added you, folks would begin to guess. So I want you to get yourself a sack of grub and ride off in the hills like you was prospectin' for somethin'. But keep in touch with me regularly and when the play comes I'll give you the signal to be on the job."

"Things as bad as that?" queried Link.

"Bad enough," agreed Maude. "And I'll warn you now, the job is full of grief."

"My meat," was Link's brief answer. "That's why I'll work for you. Judas, look at the cyclone in that breakin' pen!"

The breaking pen, which was one of a series of corrals beside the track, emitted a vast cloud of dust. A pair of hoofs flashed above the corral's rim and fell back; and along the top bar a crowd of idle rail birds offered gratuitous advice to some violently blasphemous man down in the thick of the trouble. Climbing to a point of view, Bill Maude discovered a brillantly black horse plunging around the snubbing post, trying to shake free the cramping saddle and to burst the rope that held him. A long figure clung to the loose end of the rope, dodging the beast's tempestuous assaults.

"This mebbe is yore idee of a good time!" he yelled. "But how in hell am I goin' to let go?"

"Ain't he the fire-eater?" muttered Link. "Never had a saddle on him till now, and I don't see anybody yearnin' to climb the deck, either. Twenty bucks to you, Mister Maude, if you amalgamate the situation."

"Took," agreed Maude, whose attention was momentarily diverted by the long, wailing blast of an engine's whistle. Out on the prairie a white column of steam rose against the sunlight and the flowing line of the morning trail rolled nearer. "But it's got to be sudden," he added. "I'm to meet that train."

"Oh, it'll be sudden enough," predicted Link, and followed Maude to the center of the corral. Link took the snubbing rope from a weary puncher while Maude advanced cautiously on the nine hundred pounds of fighting animal. Suddenly the beast changed tactics and stood still, feet braced and every muscle rigid. Maude advanced with soothing speech.

"So you want me to come on and bust my neck, Coaly? You're tellin' me it can't be done, that it? All right, I never learn till I'm shown. Just remain in status quo a minute. Maybe I'm right and maybe you're right. We'll debate it." His hand brushed the horse's withers tentatively, gripped the pommel. At a single surge he reached the saddle and kicked his feet into the stirrups, reaching down to take hold of the taut hackamore rope. The horse seemed to flatten in every part.

"Let go, Link, and run like sin," Maude said. Link obeyed, scrambling for the corral's side; and suddenly the horse, opening the battle with a magnificent rage, shot toward the sky.

At that moment Maude, looking directly between the brute's ears, saw the sun. Then the saddle appeared to sink away from him and the impact of the horse's front hoofs striking the earth had the effect of stunning Maude's spine and of twisting him internally. Swaying to keep balanced, he found himself turning in a violent circle. More shocks ran up through the beast to daze his brain. A kind of roar came from the horse and it rose on its hind feet again and walked the full diameter of the corral, shaking its body at every step. Maude felt the menace of the corral side in time to lift one leg free of the stirrup as the horse plunged against it, trying to scrape the maddening burden from him. Unsuccessful, it launched into a terrific, stiff-legged pitching and turning, and twisting—a half a ton of sinew and bone convulsed in a series of mad, volcanic explosions.

Maude, taut with the strain of balancing himself, felt the yellow dust fold around like a blanket. From far off he heard Link's shrill cry of warning and he felt, too, the straining of his vital organs. There came another belch of sound from the horse and another terrific sweep toward the sky. The shadow of the corral's high side loomed suddenly and Maude, feeling disaster, brought his feet from the stirrups. The horse struck the pole barrier dead on with a report like a cannon shot. Half prepared for this, Maude partially saved himself by flinging his shoulders sidewise, and thus he went careening through the air, to ram the base of the corral with the back of his neck.

He heard, in a state of half consciousness, somebody say: "He's dead. Oh, my, my, my!" And a flood of irritation passed through him that anybody should be so silly. At the same time he realized the black was a killer and he twisted himself around to avoid an attack of hoofs. But there was no such attack, nor even the trace of a sound from the beast.

Rousing himself, Maude saw punchers swinging down from their roost and advancing on him. The horse lay dead on the ground. Considerably shaken and still a little dim of mind he did the instinctive thing, climbed the corral and straddled the top bar. Sitting there he accumulated himself together by degrees; the cloudiness passed away from his eyes and he reached for his cigarette makings.

Link looked up from the fallen horse. "A born killer, Bill. He busted his neck clean tryin' to get you. Judas H. Priest!"

Maude shook a jot of tobacco into the creased paper with fingers that were a little unsteady. But the fire had stopped burning in his stomach and there was a touch of wind on his cheeks. He managed a grin. "Well, he blamed near busted mine. But I rode him till he quit, didn't I? You owe me twenty dollars, Link."

A woman's clear, cold voice said: "It isn't the horse he cares about. Killing an animal makes no difference to him. It's the money he worries over. Quite a fine gentleman!"

Maude spilled the tobacco in turning around. For the first time he saw that the train had drawn alongside and halted short of town. A Pullman window abreast him was open; through it he saw a man of the traveling salesman type, and a woman whose face was turned out. Her eyes were fastened on him—on Bill Maude— and they seemed scornful. The man in the other seat muttered something about the cold nerve of a rider who thus risked his neck, which brought another tart reply from the girl.

"If he rates his life so cheaply, why should anybody grieve if he loses it? Apparently it isn't worth any more than he considers it to be."

Link, who had the almost solid wall of the corral bars between him and the train, started to climb with fire in his eyes. "What fool female—"

Bill Maude pushed Link urgently to the ground,

never letting his attention stray from the girl. He doubted if she was more than twenty-three, but at that point his doubts ceased. The rest of the picture was clear. She had dark hair and eyes that snapped. They went right through him and left him for the moment speechless. Then the train bell clanged and the cars moved slowly on toward town. The girl's shoulder turned slightly to keep sight of him; afterward she let the long glance drop with an impatient shrug.

"Who in thunder said that?" exploded Link. "Some gal that never was spanked enough, I'll bet a cooky. And there yuh sat like a bump on a log and never said a thing."

"I'm talkin'—to myself." Maude grinned and dropped outside the corral. He went to his horse and mounted, Link coming behind him. But he warned the puncher tersely. "We can't afford to be seen together too much. Ride for the hills as soon as you can —and keep in touch with the ranch at all times."

Maude followed the road back to town, observing the train halt a-straddle Railway Avenue and drop its passengers. There was the usual scattering of people and the usual confusion, but when it had cleared and the train moved on, he saw the girl standing in the deep dust beside her suitcase; and he was near enough to observe that Buffalo Crossing made no favorable impression on her. Her face seemed to drop and her shoulders fell a little. Presently, she lifted her suitcase and trudged down the short street. Following at a discreet distance, Maude saw her turn into the main street and when he came around that corner she was on the point of entering the hotel. Instantly an enormous thought struck him.

"The school teacher! Great jumpin' grasshoppers, now what am I going to do?"

But his mind was soon made up for him. Tom DeLong, the school board man the agent had mentioned, crossed quickly to the hotel and entered; and at that, Bill Maude drew alongside the porch and marched through the door with a poker face. DeLong, a red-eyed and disheveled man with little civility about him, was making himself known to the new teacher. "I'm DeLong what had all the correspondence with you regardin' the school. Speakin' as chairman of the board I'll sure say we drew a peach this time, and no mistake, little girl."

"My name," said she, "is Louisa Cherry, if you please." She had a firm chin, sturdy shoulders, and there was distinctly a level, "stand-away" look in her eyes. Her clothes stamped her as Eastern but the cool competence of her carriage belied the softness an Easterner was presumed to have. Maude, content to stand back by the door for a moment, began to feel irritation at DeLong's rough, clumsy manners.

"I been wantin' to ask you a question ever since I got your application to teach," pursued DeLong. "Whut in thunder brought you clean out here from Ohio to struggle with kids when they must of been plenty schools there?"

"My private life is my own," said Louisa Cherry.

"Oh, sure," was DeLong's hasty rejoinder. "I don't want to scare yuh away. We like Eastern teachers. Adds style to a school. It's just that I couldn't figger how you'd know anything about NoNo Valley away back in Ohio. But it don't make any difference. I'll drive to the depot and pick up your trunk in my rig. You're boardin' at the Lee Colter ranch this fall. All our teachers lodge around like that."

Maude came forward, for the first time noticed by the other two. DeLong scowled. Louisa Cherry's mouth came together. Under this handicap, Maude managed to maintain his sleepy smile admirably. He bowed and announced his name. "Also a member of this board. I was delegated by the other honorable members to meet you and give you the keys to the valley, even though none of them would probably fit. DeLong, what's the idea of crampin' my style?"

"I took the notion to come in," grumbled DeLong. "My rig's ready for her."

"Well," reflected Maude, "I was given this duty and I'm a great hand to obey duty's clarion call."

"I spoke first," snapped DeLong. "Ma'm, I'll get your trunk."

Louisa Cherry studied Maude critically. "I shall accept Mr. DeLong's invitation. Thank you."

"Sorry," said Maude. "I'll not intrude."

"Mr. DeLong," said the girl, checking the man's departure. "I have already arranged for a place to stay."

DeLong's brows arched. "As how?"

"Do you know of the Will Slover homestead in NoNo Valley?"

Something happened internally to DeLong. He shot a hard glance at Maude, stiffened, put himself on guard. "What about it?" he demanded, an edge in his words.

"Is it close to the school?"

"Couple miles," muttered DeLong. "But that's out. Forget it. You can't stay there. The house is a wreck. Place ain't fit for humans. You'll stay at Colter's like I said."

"I don't believe," was the girl's quietly definite answer, "that you understood me. I'm staying at the Slover homestead."

115

DeLong shot a blunt question at her. "What do *you* know about that place?"

"I own it."

"Own it?" echoed DeLong incredulously. Maude's attention, likewise, sharpened.

"Will Slover," explained the girl, "was originally from my home town. He went West, and later came back to die. He deeded the place to my father. It became mine when father died. I wanted to come West, looked up the schools around here, and found yours was near the homestead. So I applied for the position. Your mystery is solved."

"You can't stay there," insisted DeLong. "It ain't fit, that's all. The place is a wreck. House all shot to pieces. No wood, no water. A barren bunch of acres. Nope, you can't."

"You are really too kind and protective, Mr. DeLong. But I shall live there."

Thick-skinned as he was, DeLong flushed. His lantern jaw protruded like that of a balky horse. "I know this country. Seems as though a tenderfoot would take the word of an old hand. Why, ma'm, the place is—is haunted!"

Louisa Cherry smiled faintly. "And I suppose you believe in fairies, too? Let's not argue the point. If you'll get my trunk I'll meet you on the street. I have some shopping to do."

"Let that wait," grunted DeLong. "There's a store at the Settlement you can buy from."

"Is it on the road to my place?"

"We-ell, not exactly. About four miles beyond."

"Then I'll shop here," said the girl. "I'll be in that big store across the street when you come from the depot."

DeLong was thoroughly angry. "Seems like you make

it a point of not acceptin' the good and true advice of a man."

"I have found," said Louisa Cherry, "that the advice of most men is neither good nor true."

DeLong ambled morosely out of the hotel and the girl turned a glance on Maude that was as disconcerting as it was direct. "I suppose you have advice to give also?"

But Maude's faint smile remained fixed. He slid back his hat, shook his head. "Not a syllable, ma'm. I seldom ever burn my fingers twice the same day. Good luck to you." Louisa's inspection wavered a little, and when he turned through the door, his height altogether blocking it, a flush of color came over her cheeks.

Outside, Maude went to one end of the porch, debating with himself and losing the cheerful aspect he had carried around most of the day. He was thus engaged when Louisa Cherry came from the hotel and went across to the general store. A cavalcade came loping through the street, raising heavy folds of dust and Bill Maude's idling gaze swung and rivetted itself on the leader of that party.

The man had a wide and heavy body with a sweeping mass of shoulder that threw all his features out of proportion. For that matter, he was striking in other respects as well and particularly as to neck. He seemed to have no neck. A great head sat like a knob on the torso—a head of heavy bones, an out-slung chin that brought lower teeth and lip far beyond the upper line, and jet black eyes placed well back in protecting sockets. A dark and unbreakable man, such was the instant impression. And to Bill Maude, who knew as much about Ike Lang as any person in the country, the impression was more than idle fancy. Lang, meanwhile, had caught sight of the girl and his restless, swift glancing eyes flashed a queer smile at her. Passing by, he lifted his hat, bowed, and laughed outright. The next moment he saw Maude, and the laugh died, to be replaced by a sullen stare. Galloping on, he led his men around into Railway Avenue, out of view.

Maude's indolence vanished. Moving rapidly, he returned to the hotel, passed through a side door to a saloon, scanned it and walked to the street again. Crossing, he entered another saloon, left it by a rear exit and cut through the gloom of a stable, once more on the street. DeLong was coming back from the depot, driving a rig. In front of the general store another rig stood. A few horses waited at the adjoining racks and a few loitering punchers clung to the shady side of town. Mirroring a certain dissatisfaction, Maude started into the store and paused.

The girl was there, busy at the counter, but she had no part of Maude's interest this moment. Rather, he watched a family standing in the darkened rear —a family consisting of a faded, wistful woman, three silent children and a fellow who swore with half-hearted stubbornness.

"What of it?" he was arguing. "What if Ike Lang is in town? I'm not goin' to pick a fight. I'm goin' to get my wagon, put my folks and provisions in it and drive home. He can't do nothin' to me. I'm peaceable. This is a free country, ain't it?"

"You just wait here till he goes, Joe," pleaded the woman.

The storekeeper looked up from his business with Louisa Cherry to interject a bit of advice. "That's best, Meek. No use provokin' Ike. Lay low."

Meek was old and stooped and skinny and his hands trembled. "I'll be everlastingly condemned if I hide like a rat every time he shows up! I'm no coward!

I got rights! I'm goin' to get my wagon! Stay here, Minnie, till I come around with it."

"Joe, he'll be bound to hurt you!" cried the woman.

But Meek went doggedly out, passing Bill Maude with deeply troubled eyes. He went directly over to the stable and there Maude saw him pass out to a rear compound. A few minutes later, with Maude still standing on guard by the store entry, the man drove around a corner and started down the street. As he drove abreast one of the saloons, the granite figure of Ike Lang appeared, blocking the street by his very bulk and threat. The turn of events seemed to be expected, for silence and a sudden halt of movement came to Buffalo Crossing. Watching Lang with a sharp regard, Maude was aware that the girl had started from the store counter, bound out. As she reached the door, he dropped his hand across it and thus barred her exit. Instantly he was challenged by a coldly angry demand.

"Take your arm away, please! I want to leave!"

But Maude only shook his head and motioned at the developing scene.

II

THE WEST BARES ITS FANGS

TURNING she saw the whole situation instantly. A wagon and team stood in the middle of the street about thirty feet away, and beside it was the man Meek, who had left his family in the store. Apparently he had jumped from the seat, for the reins were trailing on the ground and he himself was a good yard off from the vehicle—motionless, face drawn and a little pale, and staring straight at the great hulk of a man planted athwart his path. This was the one who had smiled on her and this, she knew, was Ike Lang. The hot sun deepened the blackness of his face, intensified his rocklike strength. He was scowling at Meek and the girl felt, in a sudden wave of pity, that to the old man the scene must be a terrifying nightmare. Ike Lang spoke again, brutal and impatient.

"I'm askin' you a question. Ain't I warned you before?"

Meek nodded.

'Carryin' a gun on you?"

"Yes," whispered Meek.

"Want to settle with me now?"

"No—no," said the old man. "I've got nothing against you, I'm peaceful."

"You're a liar, a fool, and a coward," growled Lang, each word coming across the space to fall on Meek like the lash of a whip. "Will that induce yuh to fight?"

Meek shook his head, face showing the mark of the hunted beast.

"I will put both arms behind my back," said Lang, "and lock 'em together. Will that be handicap enough for you to draw?"

No answer. The girl's throat ached; she felt faint. All along the deeper niches of the street she saw people standing very still, looking on as she looked on, not daring to move. Life in Buffalo Crossing had ceased, while a man fought to exist and another strove to kill. Looking to Maude beside the door, she found him watching Ike Lang with a sober concentration, and her original resentment toward him deepened to something almost like hatred. He stood by and feared to move.

"You're a skunk," droned Lang. "You're the lowest thing that walks and breathes. You run like a rabbit when I'm in sight, you hide behind walls and other folks and petticoats. You ain't even a man."

"I want no trouble with you," said Meek, voice breaking. "All I want is to be let alone. I'm mindin' my own business as I always have—"

"Shut up!" bellowed Lang. "Why, you yellow, degraded rat you're too yella to do anything else! I want everybody on this street to know how pitiful small and rotten you are! If what I say won't make a man claw for his gun there's nothin' in him but putrified flesh!"

Meek stood as if in a dream, swaying a little. Ike Lang swore a bald, unprintable oath. "I see you won't fight. Nothin' can make you fight. Now I've told you for the last time—get out of my country. I'll say it no more. And maybe this will make you understand."

He walked forward, reaching into his pocket. When he came to the team he had brought out his knife and in a half dozen slashes of the instrument he cut the near harness to useless bits. He was then facing the store and his eyes, rising from the brutal chore, fell on

121

Maude. For a moment that seemed everlasting to the girl these two stood and measured each other, neither speaking, neither moving, neither changing so much as the twitch of a muscle. Abruptly Lang broke the deadlock, crossed to the far side of the street and rolled into a saloon.

Old Meek staggered to his wagon and leaned against it, physically sick. Maude dropped his arm from the door and nodded at Louisa Cherry. "Sorry. No offense meant. Didn't want you stepping into possible bullets."

The girl swung on him with both fists clenched. "You stand by and let that happen?"

"If," was Maude's quiet reply, "I tried to mix in all the unjust quarrels of this country I'd never be through."

"Is there a better thing than fighting for what's fair and right and decent?"

"Yes," drawled Maude. "Mindin' your own business. Much better and much harder."

"I can understand fear," shot back the girl.

"I suppose you can," agreed Maude, and studied her at length. "But I don't believe you understand the ten thousand other things going on in this county, including the devious and muddy winding of local politics."

Somebody across the street called, "Maude—Bill Maude."

The man said, "All right—I'm coming," and lifted his hat to the girl, walking away from her.

Tom DeLong drove up to the store porch with his wagon, sulky and impatient.

"Let's be going. Twelve-mile drive ahead of us."

The groceryman came out with the girl's box of provisions, stowed them in the wagon and watched her curiously as she stepped into the vehicle and sat beside DeLong. The latter slapped his team to a brisk run, clattering on down the street. Presently they were driving along a straight road that led into the hazy southern horizon. The town dropped behind and by degrees a series of low-lying hills to right and left closed in to form the wings of a valley; bare, sunburnt hills glittering under the strong light. All the land was yellow and parched and seemingly without power to sustain life, yet cattle grazed across the flats and up into the bench. Buzzards wheeled overhead.

"Who is Ike Lang?" demanded the girl.

DeLong stirred and cast a somber look at her. "A rider of the country," he said, and seemed to convey the impression that this was the end of the topic. But the girl was in no frame of mind to be discouraged.

"And a bully."

DeLong shifted his chew. "Around here, chickens come home to roost. Never saw it fail. The less you say about other folks and the less you butt into affairs of no consequence to you whatsoever, the happier you're goin' to be."

It was a rebuke plainly delivered. The girl colored and stared ahead of her for the next three miles.

"And who is this man Bill Maude?" she asked at last.

"Owns an outfit down in NoNo," grunted DeLong. Once more the coloring of his words betrayed him; he seemed to hold a suppressed scorn of the man. The girl wished to press deeper, but remembering the previous rebuke she throttled the impulse and sat back. DeLong, meanwhile, was eyeing the figure of a rider kicking up a thin banner of dust on the left-hand rim, traveling also to the south. This occupied him for a half hour and he was diverted from it only by the noise of a body of horsemen overtaking him from town. Looking back, he suddenly muttered something to himself and pulled the wagon entirely off the road, bumping along a rocky ditch. The cavalcade went streaming by, leaving a souvenir of thick and strangling powdered earth in the wake. DeLong reined back to the road, lifting his neckpiece over his nose. The girl saw the wisdom of this and knotted a scarf around her face likewise.

"That was Lang, wasn't it?" she asked.

After a considerable silence DeLong formulated another maxim. "It don't pay to advertise what you see and who you see when you see 'em. Yuh might have to testify to information some time yuh wouldn't really care to. That clear?"

"In other words, keep your mouth shut, or die?" asked the girl. "Admirable and brave outlook, Mr. DeLong."

"I never had no dislike of bein' alive," observed DeLong sententiously. "Now, havin' seen what you saw, yore prob'ly convinced it's better to stay with sensible people than to go through with this entirely foolish idee of livin' by yourself."

"On the contrary," replied the girl. "I'm more convinced I should live my own way and not be under obligations to others."

"You'll have good cause to regret it," said DeLong sullenly. "And that's the last advice I'll throw away on a person who seems hell-bent to be stubborn."

Accordingly, he wrapped himself in a mantel of impenetrable silence and urged the team to a faster pace. The sun's shafts were striking out of the farther west and exploding on the eastern ridge with a shower of brilliant rays. To the dun of the earth was now added streaks of red wherever the road cut into the soil; the hills narrowed down upon the road and it in turn began to wind tortuously along some ancient river bed. They crossed a creek that was nothing but moist mud and for a little while were lost in the shade

124

of a narrow chasm. Coming out of this, the girl found herself staring at a three-way division of the road. It ran left up a wrinkle of the eastern ridge and seemed to pass over; it traveled straight ahead to an apparent continuation of the same valley; and it struck to the right, climbing a distinct and nearby butte. Off in a level area stood a large house with empty windows. DeLong turned, the wagon vibrated over the hard soil, swerved at the doorway and stopped.

"Home sweet home—to you," grunted DeLong. Unceremoniously, he dumped out her box of provisions and her trunk and got into the seat again. The girl climbed down, depressed at her journey's end in spite of her will. As much as she had discounted Will Slover's old homestead house, it needed more discounting still. The place was like a barn, all angles and joints. Every piece of glass, so far as she could see, was broken out. Weeds grew up between the parched porch boards and when she looked through the open doorway she saw nothing but dirt and debris. Inevitably the echo of her discouragement came to her face, but she felt DeLong's prying eyes on her and so she stiffened her lips, overlooked the fact he had not offered to carry in the trunk, and gave him a small smile.

"I'm very much obliged to you, Mr. DeLong."

"When you find what yore goin' to find," said he, "you'll be wantin' to move in a mighty big hurry. Straight ahead on this middle road four miles is the Settlement. G'bye, and good luck." Flicking the whip over the horses, he rattled away. Louisa Cherry, calculating the distance in which he would go to be out of her sight—and beyond her call—suddenly felt the need of exploring the house before she had altogether lost the possibility of help. Turning, she ran inside. The front room was a mess and through the slack inner doors she saw other rooms, equally messy. But pressing through to the kitchen she came to a startled halt. The floor was clean and in the air was the smell of recently disturbed dust from a sweeping. Fresh wood was in a box beside the stove, and in the stove was a small fire. A pail of water stood on the table.

Her instant reaction was one of fright. Dominating this, she ran back into the front room, saw a pair of stairs leading up to the second floor and took them. As fast as her feet would carry her, she explored every corner—to find nothing, Returning to the kitchen, she went out the back door, made a complete circle of the house, ran to the shed, on farther to the sagging barn and back again, quite out of breath. It was after this spell of panic that she saw a slip of paper folded and tucked under the edge of the water bucket. Lifting and opening it, she found this message for her—

Go slow on the wood. This is all, till you get more. Prime the pump with a dipper of water or it won't work. Boil it before you drink it. Well's got to be cleaned. The place is full of squeaks and funny sounds at night, but don't worry. That'll be rats and loose hinges. However, there is a gun for you to use. Look in the cupboard.

She lost no time in locating the gun, a heavy, well-oiled forty-five. A man's gun quite evidently, signifying that the person who had been here within the last twenty minutes had been a man—and one that to her was thoughtful and kind beyond any other in her own bitter experience with the breed. Encouraged, she walked to the front door. Dusk was not far off. Putting aside her coat, she began the labor of dragging in her belongings.

Late that night, she woke from a troubled and fitful slumber. She had done this a dozen times since dark and each time remembered that the uneasy sounds dominating the house were those described in the message. Yet this time her reasoning could not reduce the fear. The sound now rising to a steady murmur came apparently out of the east and would not die. Rising from the bed, she went over and crouched beside a window, looking down an angle of the roof to the ground. High overhead the stars were gleaming, but the moon was gone and no glow of light dispelled the abyssmal black that seemed to press against the house. The murmur rose to greater strength; a point of fire flashed out of the high eastern ground and then in a rush that trembled the foundations of the house, a body of horsemen came beating by on the dead gallop.

Listening, she thought they turned into the road that led south to the Settlement yet she was not sure. What she was sure of was that after the noise of the band had quite died there was another and newer sound below that froze the blood in her veins. A man's step distinctly came dragging across the porch of the house. Rising from the window she ran to the closed door and put her body against it. Afterwards she thought of the gun under her pillow and went to get it; but before she had returned the sound of a shot broke the quiet. The creeping marauder on the porch yelled and went plunging across the loose boards. When she got to the window she saw a weaving figure racing away. Another shot rocketed out of the blackness, answered by a second and more frantic shout from the prowler. Then silence.

III

BILL MAUDE'S CROSS IRON

THAT ROAD which turned to the right in front of Louisa Cherry's house and zigzagged up the butte face kept going straight to the west through a very rough and uneven country for about four miles—or until it halted directly at an enormous lodgepole gate twenty feet long with a high cross-member connecting the posts. In the center of this cross-member was burned a great brand, the Cross Iron.

One hundred yards beyond the gate stood a low-lying house with oaks all about it and a galleried porch. To either side of the house were the inevitable scattering of bunkhouses, corrals and sheds marking a ranch of considerable size; and behind the house the western ridge ran up to the hot, cloudless morning sky. Somnolence hung over the place and nowhere was the sign of life except on the porch where Bill Maude sat indolently in a chair and talked to his foreman, Jubilee Carew.

"So they came down the gulch last night?" mused Jubilee, who was a slim young fellow with a deceptively smooth face.

"Like a bat out of hell," agreed Bill Maude. "As usual. But they brought no beef this trip. Like as not they smelled smoke in Lost River valley and figured to lay off."

"I never knew them to be that bashful," opined Jubilee Carew. "More likely they got their beef and drove it to shelter some place up in the pockets. Ten miles a night is about their limit of drivin' critters."

"Maybe," said Bill Maude. "I wasn't interested in that angle. What took my attention was the fellow that dropped off from the bunch and tried to break into the girl's house. I laid a shot across his stern and he yelped like a bit dog. When I sent number two after him he was a hundred yards away and seemed in a hurry. They don't like the girl bein' there, Jubilee. They don't want anybody livin' in the neighborhood of that trail. It spoils their game. So they'll raise heaven and earth to scare her away. If scarin' won't do the work, they'll try something else. From now on, Mister Carew, one man of this outfit will have to camp on his belly near that house from sundown to dawn. That's orders from headquarters."

"Easier to put a bug in the girl's ear and have her move," suggested Carew.

Bill Maude emitted a dry chuckle. "You think so? Not that girl, Jubilee. She's dynamite. She knows what she knows and she'll do what she intends to do. Advice has been offered—and refused. I gathered that much in Buffalo Crossin'. In fact I sort of felt the lefthanded backwash of her temper."

"If she's stubborn then let her get the hell scared out of her proper," grunted Jubilee.

"No-o, I wouldn't like that," mused Bill Maude. "We'll keep a watch down there for a while."

Jubilee shrugged his shoulders and changed the subject. "Get that man you went after?"

"Ahuh. Link Whitehorn. All meat. Tough, rough and able to absorb punishment. Just the kind to add to our happy family."

"And he can keep his mouth shut?"

"Just so," said Maude. "He won't work on the ranch, though. We've got all the hands we dare carry. I told him to get supplies and just cruise around the ridge, keepin' an ear down for signs from me."

"That's seven we got staked out on demand. Plus twelve here. Which about fixes us for trouble."

"Which will develop," said Maude, eyes narrowing into the distance. "Lang made a play in town yesterday right under my nose. Think he wanted to suck me into it, but I minded my own affairs. The whole thing is plumb apparent, Jubilee. That gang's about got to the point of bein' big business and I'm in their way. We can expect grief any day."

Jubilee's careless, pleasant face stiffened. "What they start we'll finish."

"That's the ticket," agreed Maude and rose. "But it won't be any picnic, my son. There's angles to this business you don't get. Lang's the visible target. But between you and me there's a power behind the throne."

"Who?" demanded Jubilee.

"Don't know. I'm trying to find out. But just put this under your hat. When illegal beef begins to mean large and continuous profit you'll find the sober-minded gentlemen of law and commerce devisin' ways and means of sharin' same. And Cross Iron is in the way."

"It ain't Cross Iron, it's you they're scared of," amended Jubilee.

"Hell to be honest, ain't it?" murmured Maude and got on his waiting horse. The two grinned at each other. Then Maude wheeled away. "I'm bound for the Settlement."

"Careful there."

Bill Maude, sitting easy and sure in the saddle, cantered off to the southward. This August day promised to be a scorcher and even now the domes and turrets of the rugged land about him began to glitter and shimmer with refracting rays of light. He was on his own range and at odd intervals he spotted bunches of stock grazing in the more fertile pockets of the heaving terrain. At a point of elevation he paused, drew binoculars from one of the saddle bags and leveled them on Louisa Cherry's house off in the valley to the west. A wreath of smoke came from her chimney, clothes of some sort hung on a line, and he saw her moving about the yard.

"Determined and energetic little cuss," said he, "and she won't be bluffed. Imagine me tryin' to offer her fatherly warnin'."

In a general way, Maude's range was long and narrow, standing between the western ridge and the valley to the east; but after a matter of two miles the valley curved off and a thinly wooded shoulder of land rose between, to further add to the cut-up appearance of the country. Tackling this on a long tangent, Bill Maude passed into the spotted shelter, crossed a table-like top and slid down the farther side. The Settlement was below, a cluster of houses crowded at the end of a blind canyon. Cruising through the street, he put up at the store and went in. Half a dozen dark and slack appearing men loitered in the partial darkness of the place. Silence fell suggestively as he came upon them.

"Lang around here?"

They sat still, staring sullenly at him. Maude grinned. "Yeah, I know you're hard and mean. Real wicked. Big around the chests and broad in the pants."

"You talk too much," rapped out one of them.

"Maybe that's because my conscience is clear," suggested Maude, evenly. "I asked you dumb brutes a question. What's the matter—too tired from last night's ridin' to answer?"

"Damn you, hush! Lang's not here! Never will be here to you, Maude!"

"Fair enough," cried Maude, and turned out. As he started for his horse the lean, slant-jawed Tom DeLong came around the building. When he saw Maude he stopped on his heels and stared, but recovered and went to the door of the store. Maude, already in the saddle, spoke sharply. "Hold on there, DeLong. I've got a piece to recite to you."

"Yeah?" growled DeLong, swinging around. "What you doin' in the Settlement? It ain't yore stampin' ground."

Maude studied him coldly. "Maybe I'm like you and get in the wrong places now and then."

"What's that mean?"

"If I ever catch you putterin' around that girl's house after dark again, DeLong, you'll turn up missing. Make no mistake about it."

"So it was you!" snapped DeLong. Inside was a scraping of chairs. One by one the loitering men passed out to the porch and arranged themselves against Maude. DeLong swore. "There's the answer to those shots last night! Maude, yuh take in too much territory! If I'd of know who it was I'd of rammed into you plenty."

"Instead of which," observed Maude, ironically, "you broke all the known records getting away from there. Mister, you went so fast you punched holes in the atmosphere."

"You can't bluff me!" yelled DeLong.

"I don't bluff," said Maude and lifted the reins. "Mark it down—fool around that house any more after dark and you're done for." Setting the pony to a lope, he passed along the gulch and out of the Settlement. "The handwriting," he observed to himself, "is on the wall. It used to be that the gang made an attempt to be civil with me. They've got orders otherwise now, that's plain. The word's out—I'm in the way."

He galloped around a point of rock and straightened into a level reach of road that gave him view of Louisa Cherry's house. The girl was on the porch and a man

—whose thick and rounding body betrayed him even across the distance—was in the act of climbing up to the saddle. Maude stiffened the gait and came hurriedly over the ground, catching the scene with sharply observant eyes. The girl's face was flushed and one hand lay across her breast in an attitude of defense and defiance. Ike Lang's heavy cheeks were compressed with wrath. There was another emotion on them, too; an acquisitive and lustful desire that sent the blood racing through Bill Maude's veins. He wheeled his horse in front of Lang, whereat the other changed front with a brooding watchfulness.

"Good morning," said Maude to the girl, lifting his hat.

"Good morning, Mr. Maude."

"You seem in a hurry," grunted Ike Lang.

"To get here," was Maude's cool reply.

"Well, yore here," challenged Lang.

"Yeah. Sorry to see you go so soon, Ike. Bye-bye."

"Who said I was goin'?"

Maude scanned the powerful figure thoughtfully. "You have all the earmarks of a man on his way to other parts, Ike. Don't let me detain you."

"Mebbe I'll stay, and what do yuh think of that?"

Maude hooked one leg over his saddle horn. "In such case we'll have a nice time chatting about the weather, the old folks at home, and things that pass in the night. You look sleepy, Ike. Didn't get much rest last evenin', did you?"

The girl stepped back into the door. Lang's horse had fiddled away, apparently without urging, until there was a space of twenty feet between the men. As this happened Maude dropped his leg and straightened in the saddle. So the two confronted each other, Maude, casual and cool and with that sober, sleepy gaze about him she had noticed in town—while Lang's cruel mouth was pressed in a downsweeping line, and the veins on his temples stood out like dark scars. When he spoke again the girl observed his voice was even and stiffly polite.

"Yuh do a great deal of talkin', Maude."

"I was told that up at the Settlement a few minutes ago."

"Lookin' for me?" asked Lang with an increasing wariness.

"I had something to tell you," assented Maude. "But meanwhile I told it to DeLong. He'll give you details."

"It was you, huh?"

"Exactly—and next time it will be more serious. I mean that, Lang. I've kept my oars out of the dirty water flowing down this gulch so far, but there's one thing I don't propose to stand for. You know what that is."

"Grandstand stuff," snorted Lang.

"You think so?" drawled Maude, and tipped his body a little forward in the saddle. A long, uneasy quiet fell between the men. Ike Lang's black eyes were smouldering and hostile, his chest rose with an increasing of breathing.

"You figurin' to start the ball rollin'?" he demanded. "You want to take a hand?"

"I'm going to leave that entirely up to you," said Maude.

The girl thought this duel, with its increase of unspoken threat and suppressed fury, was about to break out violently. But Lang suddenly threw up his knob-like head, shifted his body and spurred off. Maude sat still, never turning to see the man depart, which in itself seemed queer to her. She broke the silence.

"Thank you for your help yesterday. I am really obliged."

It came out so stiff and formal that the man grinned. That only made matters worse. Louisa Cherry's temper rose instantly. "I suppose you came for your thanks. There it is."

"Hoop-la," said Bill Maude. "Did I put my foot in it again? Bless your heart, I never thought of bein' thanked. It's been years since anybody did that to me and I wouldn't act natural. So forget it."

"Then why did you take the trouble of cleaning the kitchen—and those things?" she wanted to know.

"Because the kitchen was in awful shape. You couldn't of fought your way through it with an axe. The pump was out of order and I thought I better get the fire goin'. The stove is temperamental."

"And the gun?"

"To open your cans with," said Maude, cheerfully.

"Who has been using this place?" demanded Louisa Cherry.

Bill Maude turned indefinite. "Oh, whoever had happened to be here at sundown."

She nodded back of her in the direction of the road that ran eastward up the ridge. "Where does that go?"

"Lost River Valley."

"Why should bands of riders come from there after dark?"

He cast a reflective glance at her and proceeded to roll a cigarette with an unconcern that was maddening. "About that—I wouldn't be too curious."

"In other words, mind my own business."

"Not a bad idea."

The storm signals rose on her cheeks. "And now I suppose you'll be advising me in that wise and fatherly way of men that I ought to be moving."

"Nope," said Maude, lighting the cigarette. "I've got better sense. And I learn from the mistakes of others. You came to this country with an idea. You intend to go through with it. You mistrust anybody that attempts to tell you different. You wouldn't move if dynamite was put under the porch. Why should I advise you, I rise to ask?"

"Then what are you doing here?" asked the girl sharply.

"Gosh, I wonder," sighed Bill Maude. "Absorbin' punishment, I guess." He took time to study her more closely. She was angry, no doubt of that. And it was apparent that she had a mind of her own and a good sturdy body to support it. Yet the clearness of her features and the rather gentle set of her lips belied the apparent storminess of her nature. She didn't look like a spitfire. She looked more like a girl who had seen bad times and now refused to believe or trust. Maude glanced around at the growling echo of a wagon coming off the bluff.

"As a matter of fact, Miss Cherry, I've got no intention of botherin' you whatsoever. You want peace from folks —and I'll promise that's what you'll get from me. No ulterior motive, no schemin' designs. My idea in cleanin' up the house a trifle was just the normal act of neighborliness. I take no credit for it. If I hadn't done it, somebody else would have. Here comes some fuel for you."

"From where?" asked Louisa Cherry, more friendly.

'School board's sendin' it, I guess. By the way, if there's any sort of trouble here, or if you need any kind of help, my place is back on top of that butte three miles. Goodday."

She started to speak again, but he was cantering across the flat. She saw him come abreast the load of wood, speak to the driver and then head toward Buffalo Crossing. For quite a while she watched his slim form retreating while the hardness and bitterness left her features. But the respite was only for a moment. When the wagon drew abreast of the house she challenged the old codger driving it. "Where is that wood from?"

"Don't know a dang thing about it," was the old fellow's too-prompt reply.

The girl bit her lip, trying again. "What is the trouble between Mr. Maude and Mr. Lang?"

"I never heard," said the man.

Louisa Cherry flung herself into the house, simmering with anger. The conspiracy of silence dominating the land was absolute, it was like a thick curtain she could not lift or penetrate; and by every evasive answer given to her she realized the isolated position she held as a newcomer in a country gripped by clan spirit. Nor did it soothe her feelings to know she had thanked Bill Maude poorly for his thoughtfulness. To be truthful he had treated her with indulgence and ridden away with a slow smile in his eyes. Despising masculine egotism as much as she did, this last item hurt her most because she had to admit she deserved such treatment.

But if Bill Maude had ridden off with a smile he did not long maintain it. A furrow of perplexed doubt crossed his forehead and from time to time he swore mildly. "She's a thoroughbred, no mistaking that. She's had a lot of grief somewhere along the line. She's runnin' away from it. She's bent on fightin' her own battles and won't ask for help. And how in thunder can a fellow get around that?"

He was so immersed in this train of thought that he neglected his habitual vigilance; and so came to Buffalo Crossing without having watched his trail. In town, he rode the length of the business street and came back to dismount in front of the stable. To an observant eye the parade meant one thing—he was advertising his presence. And there happened to be one in Buffalo Crossing who possessed just such an eye; this man, an under-cover adherent, ambled across the street in front of Maude without giving a sign of recognition. Some time later the both of them met in the covert angle of a rear corral, passed a very brief interval of talk, and parted.

All this roundabout movement was a part of the game Maude knew he had to play. Buffalo Crossing was not the frank and open town it once had been. As a free and easy puncher three years previously, he had walked the street full in the knowledge that men were what they seemed and that the expression on their faces was the actual mirror of their minds; but in the elapsed time Bill Maude had climbed to prosperity, and in that length of time also the rotting influence of intrigue and treachery had spread through what once was a fine, frank and robust country. Good men crumbled before the pressure of dishonest money, partisanship became a cold and evil and ever-present thing. In three years Ike Lang had developed from a common ruffian to a master of outlawry—with organized backing. That was it. The individual crook became a part of a machine, and the machine crushed whatever lay in its unscrupulous path. It took no son of a seventh son to see that Maude was in the way of that machine and soon was to suffer. Every act of his was watched, and weighed for meaning. And consequently on this visit he had to conceal his real reason for coming to town with other apparent reasons. He went to the store and set aside a load of groceries for future freighting, he bought himself a new pair of spurs at the saddle shop, he drew a little money from the bank. Passing out of this latter institution he was joined by a man who seemed there entirely by accident.

"Mornin', Bill."

"Same to you, Sheriff," drawled Maude.

The sheriff, Sid Lickshaw, was thin and sorrel and narrow-featured. His clothes flapped on him and he kept his face always slightly turned aside from people, as if listening rather than seeing. "Funny," said he, "I should run into you the very minute I had somethin' on my mind I wanted to see you about."

"Spread it," urged Maude.

"Let's go for shelter."

"I'm in a hurry, Sheriff. Let 'er blossom right here."

The sheriff nodded briefly and allowed himself one scant look at Maude. "I want you to help me. Take a deputy's star, Bill, and watch your end of the county."

"What for?" demanded Maude.

"I'm too busy to watch everything," complained the sheriff. "And it's a tough end down yonder. You drag a lot of water. You could keep the slate clean."

"I don't see the need," objected Maude, rolling a cigarette. "We never kill anybody in the NoNo but ourselves. Spectators never hurt."

"It ain't that and you know it as well as me," pointed out the sheriff. "It's somethin' else I want you to go after and clear up."

"Who's so anxious to have it cleared up?" inquired Maude skeptically.

"Me," said the sheriff with a ravenlike gloom. "I got sworn duties to perform, but I need good law-abidin' men to help. The finger points to you."

Maude chuckled. "Now, now, Sheriff. Do I look that green? Honest, would I be such a sucker?"

"How?" grunted the sheriff, sharp and aroused. "Don't be funny. The county likes you. If you did that job I'm hintin' at there'd be a lot of public approval—"

"Yeah? Well, Sid, I think I can bear up under the loss of public approval. You go drag your bait in front of some other simple lookin' pilgrim."

"What makes you so all-fired suspicious—"

"I never buy a horse if I can't see his teeth," opined

Maude, and walked off. Mounting his pony, he left Buffalo Crossing. "That," he murmured, "was raw. Good Judas, what a downright crude way of tryin' to hook me! Well, if they're that anxious, it won't be long now."

The sheriff, after watching Bill Maude depart, turned into the courthouse and went to his office in the rear. There was a man waiting for him, a man with a plump face and plump hands laced over a rounding belly. He was lounging in the most comfortable chair of the place, a neat, bland and soft appearing fellow completely at variance with the rawbone type of the land.

"Get him?" he inquired.

"Wouldn't fall for it," grunted the sheriff.

The other displayed no disappointment. "Didn't think he would," he observed. "But there's no harm in tryin'. Well, we'll have to find another way."

Sid Lickshaw rounded the room, struggling with his doubts. "Grannis, I don't know that you're wise. It never pays to make unnecessary enemies. Bill Maude's been mindin' his own business, even though he knows what's goin' on. You better lay off the man. If he gets pushed into this game you're goin' to hear fireworks."

"Got to be put out of the road," said the neat little Grannis.

"I don't get the necessity of it," argued the sheriff.

"For one thing," said Grannis, summing the points on his fingertips, "he knows more than he should. He's too active and too contrary to trust with that kind of knowledge. In the second place we need his ranch. It sits on the trail from Lost River valley. It's a range exactly suited to our needs. It's rough and full of odd pockets. Stuff could be hid in there forever. That isn't all. It has several good outlets from which in due time we can drive stuff without too much attention."

"Plenty of other wild country down there to use as a storehouse for the cattle we pick up."

"Not as good as the Cross Iron outfit. Not nearly as good. No, I've made up my mind to have his place. He's to be pushed aside."

"I'm warnin' yuh Bill Maude don't give in easy."

Little Grannis stared at the sheriff speculatively. "He's just one man."

"He's one hell of a hard man and he's got some hard hands to help."

"Nevertheless, he's to be put away," Grannis said imperturbably, "Trouble with you fellows is you don't understand the magnitude of the game we play. One man or one outfit, or even one valley, is only a drop in the bucket."

"You know what that means?" inquired the sheriff. "It means recourse to plenty lead. It means—"

"Yes," said Grannis softly. "Just that. Better get used to it, Lickshaw. What of it? We're making a fortune. Come on."

Side by side the inoffensive appearing little Grannis and the doubtful visaged Sid Lickshaw passed to the street, mounted and rode out of Buffalo Crossing. Once clear of town they cut off the road and ran their horses toward the eastern ridge. A dry wash took them below the horizon and they followed it a mile—or until at a sudden bend they found Ike Lang waiting.

"The order of business, Ike," Grannis said, "is to take care of Bill Maude immediately. Sid tried to pin a deputy's star on him, so we could send him out on some job—from which he wouldn't come back. But he's shy. So, it's up to you."

"Dirty work's always up to me, ain't it?" grumbled Lang.

141

"You do it well," was Grannis' purring answer. "And he's got to go."

A brightening glow came into Ike Lang's sullen eyes. "Then here's the way to do it." He came closer and spoke in curt phrases. When he had finished, Grannis nodded.

"That's good. Do it tonight."

"But, my God, it's cold-blooded!" protested Lickshaw. "DeLong—"

"—is a bungler and a weak-kneed rat," finished Lang.

The sheriff pulled himself together, licking his lips. "Judas, but this is gettin' to be a black business!"

Lang and Grannis exchanged significant glances. Then the trio split up. Grannis called over his shoulder to the departing Lang. "Tonight, for sure. I'll take care of our end."

IV

BLACK BUSINESS

At dusk a file of riders led by Ike Lang left the Settlement and disappeared in the heavy rolls of land to eastward. By full starlight they had reached the summit of the ridge. Ahead was a meadow studded with pines and beyond that the ridge fell away rather abruptly to Lost River valley. Behind them, not on the trail they had traveled but on the more public road, lay Louisa Cherry's house at a distance of four miles. Lang suddenly halted his oufit. "Be still," he said. In the ensuing silence the night wind bore up the chant of a coyote complaining from some remote part of the deep mystery surrounding them.

"Boys," said Lang, "we've got to watch sharper. I've been warned of trouble. We'll be comin' back with the beef and passin' that girl's house. Before we jam our heads into trouble I'm siftin' down there for a smell. And I believe I'll station one man there. DeLong, you come with me."

DeLong protested. "You know what Bill Maude told me."

"He's got yuh buffaloed, uh?" sneered Lang.

"He's hell on doin' what he says he'll do," said DeLong.

"So am I," retorted Lang, "and I said you'd come with me. Rest of you fellows go ahead to the same place and wait for me."

Lang and the reluctant DeLong went down the grade at a gallop, reached a comparatively level stretch and steadied to a set pace. DeLong continued to argue. "This business gets tougher and tougher. Sometimes I figger we'd ought to draw in our horns before we get busted proper."

"Cold feet," grunted Lang. "That's what you got. Always was timid."

"It's a good man who knows when it's time to quit. In the old days, Ike, we stole our beef without a lot of advertisin'. Now, by God, we go at it like an army. You mark me, there's trouble in that."

Lang said nothing until they had swung wide around a curve of the road. Ahead of them a light glowed with a crystal radiance. Without order they fell to a walk and so approached nearer Louisa Cherry's place. Lang began to murmur. "Her comin' to this district has just raised hell. When we come by with cattle we might just as well tell her to come out, tally and read brands. We've got no more privacy. Nor that ain't all. She's the honey pot to draw busy bees. DeLong, you sit down around here and listen. It'll be midnight before we're along. When you hear us in the distance, come back. I'll know everything's O. K. But if you flush any queer birds, start back before time and catch me higher up."

"I don't like it," said DeLong, very uneasy. "Maude, damn him, sees and hears too much."

"Yellow as Swiss cheese," was Lang's bitter answer. "You've had the willies for a long time now. Pretty soon you'll have all my men too nervous to be worth a damn. This is a big game, Tom, and you ain't growin' with it."

"I don't want to," snapped DeLong. 'I'm willin' to quit on my winnin's right now. I got a queer feelin in the pit o' my stomach—"

"What's that yonder?" whispered Lang.

DeLong swung around in the saddle so that his back was toward Lang. Lang's body swayed, his hand fell and rose, and a single shot blasted the soft dark like a change of dynamite, to go rolling and rocketing away up the canyon. DeLong caught his breath and fell from the saddle. He was dead when he struck the ground. Lang turned and galloped toward the summit.

It had all been deliberately planned in the cold and conscienceless mind of the outlaw leader; yet there were twists to the plan he could not have foreseen and one particular after-event he could not, in his most optimistic mood, have hoped for. Louisa Cherry was in her kitchen when the echo of the shot came beating against the house. Her first reaction was to drop a dish to the floor, her second to whip out the light. Running to the second story, she put her head through the window. The echo of hoofs was even then dying out in the distance; but somewhere in the black pall the fugitive seemed to pause and return, coming around and approaching the house by a different angle. The man came straight in, drawing up under her very window. She saw the outline of horse and rider all blended together, and then heard the man calling to her.

"Miss Cherry—are you all right?"

She recognized Bill Maude's voice instantly and it was on the very tip of her tongue to say so. But some deeper impulse stayed the announcement. Instead she answered: "Go away."

"Fair enough," drawled Bill Maude, and forthwith departed. Immediately she was sorry, for the returning silence pressed against the house like an actual threat and every minor sound inside it kept plucking at her nerves. Rather irritably she wondered why the man always insisted on taking her at her word, so after an hour's vigil she barricaded the door with her trunk and went to bed.

But not to sleep soundly. Around midnight she was wakened by the passage of a band of riders. Remembering what had happened the previous night, she slipped from bed and stood guard at the window again, vainly trying to penetrate the shadows. Nothing moved and no skulker's feet scraped the porch boards. Relieved, if not altogether convinced, she tried to sleep once more. After a long dreary interval of taut and miserable consciousness she subsided into something that was neither slumber nor wakefulness. And so early dawn came and she rose dispiritedly, to go down and make her breakfast. She had not quite finished it when she was aware of another considerable group of riders pounding along the main road from town.

By this time she was thoroughly on her guard and kept inside the house, watching from a window. Perhaps fifteen men shot into sight, came to a milling stop at the forking of the road, and seemed to debate courses. One of the outfit dismounted and climbed up the trail leading to the top of the bluff; he had no more than reached it when he raced back again and made for his horse. At command the group retreated down the road and were shut off from sight. Considerably puzzled, Louisa held her place. Not more than five minutes later she was rewarded by sight of a single rider who came over the butte and cantered across the open, directly toward her place. Bill Maude.

Two thoughts flashed through the girl's mind simultaneously. Lang and Maude hated each other, and the hidden group might be Lang's men waiting to trap Maude. So strongly did she believe this that her next move was to pull open the door and run out to the porch. Bill Maude was only a few yards off, reaching for his hat.

"I only called to see if anything had disturbed you last night—"

"Do you think," she cut in, to be herself interrupted by the sudden reappearance of the cavalcade. It swung for the house, the men of it spreading fanwise. Bill Maude turned sharply, arm dropping, and the girl saw how incredibly fast the lazy, serene humor of his face gave way to a tight and mask-like expression of watchfulness. The horses came on and a part of Maude's rigid attitude vanished, though not all; for as the flanks of the party spread around him, he slowly backed his pony as far as the porch and squared himself to command them. The party halted and one man came forward.

"Want you, Bill," said he, solemn as a sphinx. "Hand over the gun."

Maude drawled dryly: "Lickshaw, you get some of the nuttiest ideas a man ever heard of. Yesterday you wanted me to be deputy. This mornin' you want my gun. Settle down and explain."

"You know why, Bill."

"Yeah? Well, let's hear your version of it."

"For the murder of Tom DeLong right here in this clearin' last night. Shot him behind his back, too. Hand over your gun and do it damned gentle."

Louisa Cherry leaned against the house wall, struck by the terror of the word "murder." Yet even then she observed that Bill Maude's countenance, or the part of it open to her, displayed little change. Lip and nose grew thinner, the eyes narrowed, the body seemed to stiffen. But the drawl of the man's voice remained even and unshaken.

"I was wonderin' when you heavy-handed big business men were going to think of that old trick. DeLong was the goat, uh? Well, if it had to be somebody, he's less loss than anybody else around here."

The utter indifference to tragedy on his part aroused in Louisa the same flare of resentment she had felt on seeing him crawl up to the corral rim with a dead horse at his feet and a careless grin on his face. It revolted her.

"Hand over your gun and do it gentle," insisted Lickshaw.

"Who told you I killed DeLong?" demanded Bill Maude. "Let's get some details on this."

"The body was found at four o'clock this mornin' back of this house by a party from the Settlement who had found him missin'. He was brought to Buffalo Crossin' and I was notified."

The girl's brow wrinkled. At four? She had heard no travel around the house at that hour. Perhaps she had fallen into too deep a slumber after the long vigil.

"And what," was Maude's ironic question, "Was DeLong doin' here at that hour to make folks in the Settlement think him missin'? Moreover, even if he was known to be missin', how was it the searchers found him without trouble in the dark? Lickshaw, I could drive a span of mules through the holes in your yarn."

"You made the threat to DeLong's face yesterday in the Settlement, with a crowd of men to testify, that you were goin' to kill DeLong."

"You bet," agreed Maude casually, further hardening the girl's anger. "But it was under certain conditions."

"Said conditions were fulfilled," pointed out the sheriff, shrewdly. "Right there behind the house he was."

"Then," snapped Maude, "it's too bad I wasn't around, for I certainly would have done what I said I'd do."

"Go ahead, hang yourself," said the sheriff.

"Hang hell," grunted Maude. "You couldn't frame a job like this any better with blueprints. It's too perfect, Lickshaw. You know what I'm thinkin' about. It's so plain it stinks. One crook killed another crook—to hang the cross on me. It's too lousy to cause me any worry."

The girl suddenly pushed herself to the edge of the porch, trembling violently. "You lie, Mr. Maude! You were here last night! You rode up to my window right after the shot was fired and called out to ask me if I was all right. I recognized your voice! You lied—you were here!"

The ranks of the posse shifted forward. Maude whirled in the saddle, astonishment on his face. Lickshaw cried out a savage, exultant question. "You heard him, ma'm?"

"I did," said the girl, voice breaking. Maude's eyes were like drills; she had never seen a man's face turn so cold and formidable.

"Maude!" said the sheriff, "I want your gun now or I'll blast yuh to hell and gone with pleasure!"

"Fair enough," was Maude's brief reply. He passed over his gun, butt first; then ranks of the posse closed about him and moved away, disappearing into the throat of the canyon.

Somehow Louisa Cherry found herself standing with clenched fists, desperately hoping Maude would turn for a last glance. But he didn't. Going into the house, she dropped to a chair with misery riding her. "But he was here!" she wailed. "He was here! I couldn't shield a murderer, could I?"

VI

BY USE OF FORCE

IN BUFFALO CROSSING the largest—and the ugliest—building was the courthouse, and in the courthouse was centered the legal and administrative units of both town and country. Pursuant to the conventional idea of what a courthouse should be like, the walls were of solid stone and three stories high; the offices were numerous but very small, sacrificed to wide and high corridors which somehow were supposed to represent the spaciousness of law and justice. On the third floor was the jail block, guarded by a series of doors and gratings. To this habitation came Bill Maude in the middle of the morning. He was searched and locked in; and then the half dozen men who had escorted him up the stairway departed, leaving behind a whole train of blank footfalls further strengthened by the iron *clang* of metal jamming against metal and locks shooting home. A solitary jailer took seat just outside the farther grating; a dismal silence fell.

One barred window let in a beam of fractured light. Going over to it, Bill Maude found himself looking down on Buffalo Crossing's housetops and also on the main street which at this hour showed no great degree of liveliness. Far across the prairie he made out the smoke steamer of an approaching train, but when he essayed to scan the country to the south—along the road to NoNo—he found his vision shut off. So he sat down on the edge of his cot and manufactured a smoke.

He had not in the beginning of this affair taken it too seriously. It was just one of those things that varied the monotony of the day, an accident in the pattern of existence. More accurately, it was a move on the checkerboard of county politics. And when Lickshaw had rapped him, he had not considered the move to be a very dangerous one. But by degrees—and with the cold hard fact of four solid walls around him—he began to realize what might happen. The fact that they were desperate enough to kill one of their own members in order to put the charge against him was thought provoking. If they went to that length they would go to others. More specifically they would move heaven and earth to secure the kind of a jury that would hang him higher than a kite.

"For what?" he asked himself. "I'm not competin' in their crooked game, so it ain't that. What are they afraid I'm going to do? Well, maybe squeal on 'em. Still I haven't done it yet and they might know I'm not the kind to carry tales. Anyhow, who would I carry any tales to even if I was so minded? They've got the law bottled up. Nope, it ain't that, either. Then there's only one thing left—the Cross Iron outfit. It's a good outfit and might suit their purposes—"

His eyes narrowed as he developed the idea. "Ike Lang wouldn't do it that way. His style is to use the gun and take things without delay. It ain't Lickshaw's manner either, for Lickshaw's too numb-witted. So, there's a master hand back of all this, just like I've always believed."

He stood up and called the jailer's attention. "Hey, do

me a favor and tell Lew Nolan and Chauncey Grannis I'd like to see them."

The jailer went off reluctantly, leaving Maude with an increasing impatience. Nolan was the lawyer who handled all his business and one in whom he placed a great deal of confidence. Grannis, in the capacity of tradesman, owned half of the town and was indisputably the most powerful character around the county. But when the jailer appeared a good half hour later it was to bring only Grannis, who came up to the cell door with an air of soft regret.

"Too bad, Bill. Too bad. We've got to get this straightened somehow."

"Where's Lew Nolan?"

"Couldn't find him," said the jailer, throwing a queer half-glance at Grannis.

"Grannis," said Maude, "This is all a lot of heifer dust. You're old enough hand in this misbegotten, steeped-in-sin county to know that. A six-year-old kid with no sense could understand the trick pulled on me."

"It would seem so," acquiesced Grannis, with a slight hesitancy. Maude noted that, but went on.

"Well, go down there and do a little fixing. I want to get out of here. You know I'm no hand to run away. I never have yet. And there's nothing about this frame-up that's causin' me any worry. Get busy."

"No bail on a murder charge," sighed Grannis, increasingly regretful.

"Oh, hell," retorted Maude. "Since when has this country held a man in solitary for murder? You know better. It ain't the practice and never has been."

"Lickshaw's tightenin' up," said Grannis, looking at his chubby fingertips.

"Look here, you're beating around the bush, Grannis. You've stood sponsor for a young army of fellows in jail."

"But not for a thing as serious as this," protested Grannis.

"Serious?"

Grannis ventured a direct glance at Maude, and shook his head. "The girl saw you."

Maude's lips tightened. He stepped back from the door. "All right. Sorry I bothered you."

"Now," began Grannis, "you know I'd cut off my right hand to help you—"

"Yeah?" interrupted Maude. "I'm inclined to doubt that."

Grannis flushed slightly and turned without further talk. Maude watched him hurry down the hall and disappear. The cattleman rolled another cigarette. "I'm learnin' things fast," he mused. "Lickshaw would bend double if Grannis asked it. He owes his job to Grannis—" He let the lighted match burn clear to the end, frowning meanwhile at the wall. "Now I wonder if that's the answer. Grannis!"

On the street below was the *Cloppety-clop* of a passing rider. Maude went to the window again and stared down. As he did so a flash of light fell against his eyes and blinded him. Drawing back from the beam he saw it trembling on the far side of the cell wall; looking out again he caught a bright sparkle of something in a second story window directly across the street. There was a man crouched discreetly inside the window, operating the reflector. When he saw Maude's attention focused on him, he dropped the reflector and raised a hand.

It was Link Whitehorn, one of Maude's transitory riders, and Whitehorn was putting on a show. He spread the fingers of his right hand and added three of his left, to make eight. He pulled out his watch, displayed it and again tallied eight with his fingers. He pointed to the southward and swept his arm from thence into town and then jounced himself in the manner of one riding a horse. Lastly he lifted his gun, aimed it at the courthouse door and let it rise as far as Maude's cell. Following that he leaned back to wait. Maude nodded his head vigorously, whereupon Whitehorn faded from view.

Meanwhile the morning, the ten o'clock train had paused to drop a passenger in Buffalo Crossing who hoisted his burly body through the streets with a certain apparent antagonism and presently entered Lickshaw's office like one carrying a grudge. Lickshaw was in. On seeing the newcomer, he rose solemnly. "How-do, Sheriff Manary. Glad to see you."

"Sorry, but I can't say same," said Manary, who was peace officer in the Lost River country. "I've come to thresh out a mess of grain, and what I mean it's a-goin' to be threshed out this time. I'm sick and tired of all the arguin'. What's the matter, Lickshaw, ain't you able to control your district?"

"I do tolerable well, thanks," grunted Lickshaw, not pleased.

"The hell you do," replied Manary. "You do rotten, if you're tryin' to do anything at all."

"Got your nose all painted for war, huh?" growled Lickshaw. "Well, it'll do you no good. I'm runnin' this side of the ridge. You run the other."

"Yeah? Let me tell you this: My county's been dickerin' with you for the last year to do somethin' about the rustlers who jump over to our side, steal a mess of stock and hike back for the NoNo. We get no satisfaction. All we get is talk, talk, talk."

"We're gettin' a line on 'em," said Lickshaw.

"*Bah!* You've been gettin' a line on 'em since Bosco was a small pup. That's the old stall. But there's goin' to be no more of that. This is final. Next time we get a smell of night riders we aim to chase 'em through to the limit. And we won't stop at the county line, either. If you can't do your job, we'll do it for you, see?"

"Now look here," muttered Lickshaw, coming forward. "You'll keep your damned clubfeet out of my county. Don't let me ever catch you one foot inside of it on official duty. You got no right to pinch anybody in it, and if you ever let loose any lead inside of it and hit anybody, you'll cool off in my jug. Over this-away you're just folks and your star don't mean a damn."

"Oh, so you've thrown in with the night bunch?"

"Who said that?" cried Lickshaw. "I take that as an insult!"

"Nothin' else explains your attitude," declared Manary bluntly. "Maybe you buzzards over here consider Lost River a regular lunch box. Maybe you don't even consider it to be stealin' when you cross into our county. Well, it's been a fine, neat game, brother, but you'll just pocket your marbles from now on. Next time we flush a mess of prowlers we'll run 'em down, county line or not."

"Try it!" yelled Lickshaw. "Try it and see how quick I have you hooked in the circuit court for transgressin' your authority!"

"Authority? Listen, Lickshaw, when we come it won't be under any pretense of authority! We'll come as plain ordinary riders with the intent of wipin' out the nest of rattlesnakes you're harborin' here!"

"Illegal! Understand—it's illegal!"

The sheriff from Lost River leaned forward and shoved his chin into Lickshaw's face. "Moreover, if you trump up any resistance under the argument of protectin' your citizens we'll bust you too. My country is tired of bein' the sucker. We know what's goin' on. We don't propose to endure it another minute."

"You actually threatenin' to fight this county?" screeched Lickshaw.

"If you want to side in with a bunch of thievin', murderin' mugs—yes! There's one hundred punchers over my way in a temper fit to wreck your whole confounded town. They'll do it, too."

"Say—that's war!" exclaimed Lickshaw, thoroughly aghast.

But Sheriff Manary was in no temper to mince words. "You bet. That's what you've been conductin' right along —a border war. Don't think we're goin' to stand for it any more. Why, you confounded fool, you've let this rustlin' grow into a regular business! Last week three of our men were killed outright To hell with county lines! I come here to tell you that. You can take it or leave it. Next time a bunch crosses the pass, we're comin' after 'em, and we're just as apt to clean house for you while we're at it."

At this juncture the neat, soft-treading Grannis slipped into the room. Lickshaw, badly off balance, explained the situation, upon which Grannis pursed his lips and studied Manary with an owl-like shrewdness. After considerable silence he turned to Lickshaw.

"Did you tell him about Maude?"

"No, what's Maude got to do—"

Grannis checked the sheriff with a gesture and turned to Manary again, each word unctuous and soothing. "Don't blame you a bit. Aggravating situation. But I think we've got the brains behind your trouble. We took in Bill Maude this morning for murder. If signs read right he'll hang."

"Maude?" echoed Manary. "Why I always thought him a decent fellow. I've met him at stockmen's conventions."

"You don't know politics here," gently interposed Grannis. "Maude's young and pretty headstrong. Actually he's tried to make the NoNo country independent of the rest of the county. A regular rustler's hell down there, and something we've not been able to do much about until now. The killing was in line with his policy to wipe out all those men who didn't agree with him. Lickshaw, take Manary up to look at Maude. There's the man he should be cussing."

"Don't want to see him," grunted Manary. Then he changed his mind. "Yes, I do. Lead off."

Both sheriffs departed, leaving Grannis alone. The little man stood in the center of the room with his fingertips placed piously together and a suppressed and furtive gleam in his brown eyes. When the sheriffs returned he was at a window, legs pushed apart, hands behind his back—like a pale copy of Napoleon.

"Maybe, maybe not," muttered Manary. "It's your grief, not mine. If he's the fellow, you should of done this trick a long time ago. You've got a lousy county and a lousy reputation and unless you do somethin' about it we'll move over and annex you. I mean that. We're not fools. We can smell the rottenness, and we know just exactly what the whole scheme is."

"And what is it?" was Grannis' soft question. "I'd like to know."

"Would you?" countered Manary, heavily sarcastic. "Go tell that to the goats. I cut my teeth a long time ago. Goodday to both of you—and watch your step." Turning, he departed like a young cyclone, leaving Lickshaw thoroughly overwhelmed and fearful.

"What good did that particular lie do?" he wanted to know. "He'll know it wasn't Maude, because the rustlin' will keep right on after Maude's gone."

"Temporary bait," mused Grannis. "Don't lose your head."

"Well, that was hostile talk," grumbled Lickshaw. "I could smell brimstone in it."

"He's a fool to come here and shoot off his face. It lays him wide open. We know what Lost River might do. Therefore, we shall prepare for it. Lickshaw, you make it a point of swearing in half a dozen deputies. Also get your posse organization perfected. Also, spread this fellow's threat around town. It's mighty good fuel and it'll make folks pretty sore toward Lost River. See how things can be turned to our advantage? Now don't get excited."

"Things are comin' entirely too damned fast," said Lickshaw, shaking his head.

"If you're going to cry about it," observed Grannis coldly, "go out in the hall. What've you done about tonight?"

"What's tonight?"

"Great Judas! Don't you suppose Maude's outfit will be here trying to get him out of jail? Of course! Get going now and see that you've got plenty of guns posted around this town. And when they make a break against the courthouse, let 'em have it. *Let—them—have—it!*"

VI

WAR

SHORTLY after dusk had fallen that evening the lone watcher stationed two miles out of town on the NoNo road heard the hoot of an owl. Being of a suspicious nature and somewhat nervous because of his mission—which was to spy on any approaching Cross Iron party—he listened carefully for a repetition of the sound, for he was weatherwise in the ways of deceit. But no second call floated through the shadows. Instead, there emerged from behind him the tipsy song of a fellow riding from Buffalo Crossing. It was the sort of a song that had no moral or education value whatsoever, and the inebriate sang it with gusto and verve. At intervals there was a pause for interpellations and free hand embellishments; and presently the gentleman began to yodel. All the while he came closer and the watcher, sidling off the road, caught a dim view of a jaded horse plodding forward with his swaying, noisy burden. A little later his own pony let out a signaling whinny.

"Whassat?" called the inebriate.

The watcher drew farther from the road and held his peace. The inebriate, now about ten yards away, said *"Whoa,"* in a solemn voice. "Pardon the intrusion. Wouldn't inflict m'self on nobody. But is somebody sick?"

The watcher cursed under his breath, which had no effect whatever. The inebrite called out in a stentorian voice. "Somebody's sick. Is they a doctor in the house?" And his horse turned off the road in the direction of the watcher.

"For the love of Christmas," grumbled the watcher, "go on away from here. I don't want to see yuh."

The other one, animated by an overflowing love for mankind, placed his horse beside the watcher. His hand fell carelessly on the watcher's saddle horn. "You want to sing?"

"Dammit!" exploded the watcher, "you're advertisin' me a mile! Get out of here!"

"Sure," agreed the other and there was the metallic lisp of a gun's hammer cocking. Then he continued, still cheerful but sober as a judge. "Now, mister, you imitate total paralysis to the best of your ability a minute. What're you doin' out here—observin' the beautiful aspects of nature or somethin'. Now, now, you ain't actin' paralyzed enough. Want help?"

"Whitehorn!" said the watcher.

"Yeah, and how's everybody up yore alley these days?" Whitehorn extracted the watcher's gun from its holster with competence and sent a soft "hoot" into the night. There was an immediate answer down the road and the sound of a horse coming on rapidly.

"I might of guessed it," groaned the watcher.

"It's fate," opined Whitehorn. "Fold yore hands behind. I'm goin' to take a tuck in 'em."

The advancing horse slowed to a walk and a voice floated forward. "*Quien es?*"

"Jubilee—it's me, little Alice Ben Bolt," said Whitehorn. "And I have done ketched me a kindred spirit roamin' the shadders."

Jubilee Carew drew nearer. "See anybody else down the road toward town?"

"Nope, this is the only scout they got out."

Jubilee Carew emitted another hoot and in a little while the unfortunate captive, now on the ground and being thoroughly laced up with Whitehorn's rope, felt the shadows to be crowded with in-drifting men. Jubilee Carew was speaking. "Coast seems to be clear, but the town's probably lousy with Lickshaw's assassins. This whole thing is fishy. We'll go a little closer and wait. Whitehorn and me and Lonnie Duke will snake forward and see what we can see."

"What about exhibit number one?" inquired Whitehorn.

"If you trust your own knots, let him lay."

'Bye-bye, brother," said Whitehorn, climbing to the saddle and catching up the watcher's loose pony. "If I got time I'll bring you an all-night sucker."

The group of riders slid on a mile, crossed the road

and curved around to strike Buffalo Crossing from its more shadowed side. Carew ordered a halt again and dismounted. "Come on Lonnie—Whitehorn."

"We'll stay off the street," said Whitehorn as the three walked forward. "I took a *pasear* around the courthouse at dusk. The back door is locked. But I made it a point to go in to the recorder's office after everybody went home and unlock the ground floor window in rear of the joint. There's where we make a point of entry."

"Hold on!" whispered Jubilee and dropped flat to his belly. The rest obeyed. A slow moving figure cut across a beam of light shining out of the courthouse, cut across it and moved on. The three rose once more and closed upon the rearing pile of stone, to flatten themselves by the recorder's window. "I'm lightest," muttered Jubilee, "I'll climb your shoulders, Whitehorn."

"Hop," said Whitehorn and threw Jubilee's weight upward with his palms. The Cross Iron foreman caught the window ledge, braced himself on Whitehorn's shoulders and tested the window. It gave to pressure. Placing his fingers in the created aperture, Jubilee lifted it with an exceeding caution, bellied himself into the dark room and turned to offer his hands to those below. But even as he leaned out the two faded against the earth. Jubilee froze. There was another guard—or possibly it was the same one—patrolling by. He came within five yards of them, breath rising audibly; he walked on, halted and lighted a match and by the illumination revealed his identity. After the light died Jubilee heard the fellow go stolidly off on his appointed round. Whitehorn came up on Lonnie Duke's shoulders, hooked one leg over the sill and leaned far down to give Lonnie the necessary pull. So the three of them made a breach of the courthouse and crossed to the closed door leading from the recorder's office to the main hall. Jubilee drew it open a thin inch and peered out.

A single bracket-lamp gave the hall its light and created as well a series of thick shadows along the walls and in corners. From Jubilee's point of view the big street doors of the courthouse were visible, closed and apparently locked. From this vantage point, too, the stairway could be partially scanned. Looking over the scene, Jubilee closed the crack and spoke dubiously to his confederates. "Mighty quiet and gloomy out there. I wouldn't put it past those buzzards to be layin' for us. Still, no help for it. We'll all go out, huggin' the dark parts. I'll climb the first flight. You wait at the bottom till I signal."

They slid out of the recorder's office, moving swiftly around to the mouth of the stairway, conscious that the creaking of each loose board sounded with a hollow resonance throughout the structure. Jubilee wasted no time, but went up the first flight of stairs two at a time like a cat. At the second floor landing he collapsed gently, disappeared and was gone for a tediously long time. At length the other two saw his hand slide over the banister and beckon; and they followed. Jubilee led to the next flight and by brief gestures indicated the need for greater stealth. This flight he ascended more carefully. Three-quarters up he flattened and reached for his gun, and proceeded to inch his way to the floor level. The remaining partners saw him stiffen and arch his back. He rose full length, flipped the gun on an invisible target and spoke coolly.

"Be quiet, Abe. Make no disturbance."

Whitehorn and Lonnie Duke came up, to find the jailer risen and his back placed to the outer jail grating.

"Boys" said he, "yore makin' a big mistake. Remember now, I'm not personally opposin' you. This is my job and I got to do it. No hard feelin's at all, but as friend to friend, yore makin' a mistake."

"Lickshaw made the first one by trappin' Bill Maude," said Jubilee. "Lay aside that rifle and hand me the keys."

"Lickshaw's got all the machinery of law to protect him," offered the jailer. "You got nothin'. This means you'll be joinin' the wild bunch. And maybe Lickshaw would like to maneuver you into that exact status. Think it over."

Whitehorn meanwhile had gone forward, disarmed the jailer and reached for his keys. He unlocked the grating, passed inside and went through to Maude's cell. Maude came forward from his cot with a chuckle. "Just couldn't keep you fellows out, huh? I knew you'd do it."

"That reflector wasn't a bad idea was it?" asked Whitehorn. "Me, sometimes I'm half ways bright. But I flashed the thing for an hour on every confounded window up here before I got your attention." He tried a dozen keys before the cell lock gave. Maude walked out with a shake of his shoulders and passed down the hall, to find Jubilee Carew grinning.

"Wasn't it done smooth, Bill?" he wanted to know. "You'd think this was our steady work."

"It's apt to be from now on," warned the jailer gloomily. "You're outlawed, see?"

Maude rolled a cigarette. "You bet we are. And as long as Lang and Lickshaw and the rest of the bunch are in the saddle around here we'll continue to be outlawed. You know as well as me there's no chance for a square deal. Abe, who hangs around Lickshaw's office the most?"

"That's hard to say," said the jailer, not meeting Maude's glance. "Lots of folks."

"Grannis is here pretty frequent?" pressed Maude.

"I'm not answerin'," evaded the jailer.

"Grannis?" echoed Jubilee Carew.

"I think so," murmured Maude. "The master hand."

"That little pencil walloper? Aw, hell—"

Some stray sounds from below warned them all. Maude whispered. "Put Abe in a cell and tie his mouth."

The jailer protested. "I'm an old man, Maude. Don't gag me. I'll give you five minutes before shoutin'. My word."

"O. K. Stow him away, Link."

Whitehorn led the jailer to the nearest cell and locked him in. Closing the outer grating as well, the four passed down the flight, crept around and took the next one. As they reached the first floor and were in the act of swinging back for the recorder's office a high, shrill cry came beating after them, filling all the corridors and penetrating even to the street.

"That double-crossin' Abe!" ground out Carew. "Come on now, we're in for it!"

They flung themselves at the recorder's office. Carew and Duke and Whitehorn had passed through, leaving Maude as a rear guard just as the big front doors were wrenched open and half a dozen heavily armed men burst in. They saw Maude instantly and sprang aside. Maude yelled over his shoulder, "Go ahead—out of the window—I'll come in a minute!" And without waiting for trouble to come to him he began whipping shots at the legs of the guards. They flinched back and the accuracy of their intended fusillade was disturbed. Shots broke into the paneling over Maude's head and a slug cut up a splintered furrow at his feet. One of the guards went down, crying out in pain and then the rest fled through the door, leaving the field to the Cross Iron boss who stood not on his victory, but raced through the dark recorder's office and pitched out of the window. Trouble here too. As he landed on the ground a fresh spatting of gunshots woke the echoes of the shadowed earth. White-horn was beside him, plugging away at a careening horseman who had galloped inward and was trying to check the escape. The horse fell and the rider came sailing through the air, to fall beside Maude all in a heap. Maude heard Whitehorn calling to him to hustle along and, thus directed, he raced into the open and came to a waiting and impatient crew.

"Welcome home," said a dry voice, "and what kept you so long, boss?"

Maude swung up to the horse Whitehorn pushed at him, settled his feet in the stirrups and spoke with heart-felt satisfaction. "I can do without grub, water or blankets. But I simply shrivel and die without a horse to straddle. Boys, mark this well: it's better to be an outlaw than a pedestrian."

Whitehorn was laughing in the dark. "Wasn't it a nice party? I rise to ask, ain't the evenin' been a success?"

Jubilee Carew spoke more thoughtfully. "We're sure outside the pale of law now and no mistake. If that's the play the wild bunch wanted to bring about, they sure succeeded."

Maude stared at the outline of Buffalo Crossing for several moments without replying. A few nervous-fingered gentry over there were unleashing some gun-shots into the shadows. Lights began to die out but the beat of horses slashing through the streets and alleys became more pronounced. Maude turned on the silent outfit.

"This," said he, "has been on the wing for a year. I saw it coming and I've been preparing for it. You fellows may not know it, but each one of you was hired for hard riding and grief. I've been picking the cream of the fighting men around here for a long time—and now it's the showdown. Jubilee's right. We've got no legal leg to stand on. As long as Lickshaw is sheriff and the rustlers run politics we'll be in the same boat. I have minded my own business until now. Such a course ain't possible any longer. To be frank with you fellows Cross Iron has now got to fight until it runs and rules the county—or be wiped out complete. Is that clear?"

"As brook water," assented Whitehorn. "What next?"

"No sleep or rest," grunted Maude. "And right here is the proper occasion for any of you to slide out from under who don't care to stagger along with the white man's burden. Speak now or forever hold your peace."

"Why, you darn fool," grunted Whitehorn, "we like to fight."

"You'll get a belly full of it," said Maude. "Any other comments?"

There were none. Maude squared himself toward the town, speaking softly. "All right. The cryin' begins now. Let's go." He put his spurs to the horse and shot away from Buffalo Crossing's back side, curving out as far as the NoNo road and maneuvering his men across it. Thus they went forward and in a measure plugged the end of the street. This move would have been rash had the town lights extended outward, but they fell only across the middle portion of the street, illuminating a mass of men and horses, now seething around the courthouse. Confusion seemed to shake every soul, confusion and uncertainty. Lanterns swung from point to point, riders dashed pellmell through the ranks of those afoot, veered and charged back again, to be soundly cursed. Lickshaw stood on the courthouse steps, shouting up his helpers. Beside him was Grannis, each fist clasping a revolver. Seeing that, Bill Maude's last atom of faith in the man he had considered a friend died completely away. He lifted his own gun and placed one bullet toward the stars. Instantly silence gripped the whirling party by the courthouse. Into this silence Maude launched his issue of war.

"Lickshaw, your jail couldn't hold me. As for you, Grannis, your flimsy scheme ain't worth a damn. I warn no honest men to pursue me. Now and henceforth it's going to be give and take."

"Maude!" yelled Grannis, screeching violently, "you're buckin' this county!"

"From now on there ain't any county," said Maude. "I recognize no authority. More than that I am going to bust every lousy crook this side of the ridge. Don't try to get me—I'll smash whoever tries it! That goes for you Lickshaw, too. It goes for Lang and his hounds of hell. You wanted it—you're going to get it!"

"Knock him down!" cried Grannis. "Don't let him get away! Knock him down!"

Maude whirled about, his last view of the street a confused impression of men boiling in an endless circle and the small Grannis lunging madly forward, both guns blasting the shadows.

"Get to your horses—go after him!" Lickshaw was bawling. After that the pound of Maude's retreating outfit drowned out the clamor. Sitting free and reckless in the saddle, Maude ran down the road toward NoNo valley with the deep night cloaking him and the frosty stars gleaming overhead. He knew that he should be regretting the rash step taken and that he should be fearing for the future. Yet he could not suppress the fierce and exultant pleasure sweeping over him like a flame. He had been practicing a hateful neutrality all his mature years, he had been moving softly, speaking guardedly, closing his eyes and his heart to the surrounding evil. That was past now. Whatever came of the decision, he was free to follow the dictates of his conscience and the urgent promptings of a nature fashioned not to compromise but to strike out.

"If I win I'm a good citizen," he reflected grimly. "But if I lose I'll hang higher than Haman. What of it?"

The posse in Buffalo Crossing started raggedly in pursuit, found itself leaderless, and faltered in the edge of darkness. Lickshaw was in the saddle, but he moved uncertainly, keeping his eyes pinned to Grannis. Grannis had emptied his guns and now was pouring out the wrath of years' accumulation. No man had ever seen this neat and precise little man exhibiting such emotion; Lickshaw frowned, gnawed at the ends of his mustache and appealed for a final word. "Well, what'll I do?"

Grannis flung his guns to the ground. "Come back here! You've lost your chance now! You let him catch you off guard! Come into your office!"

Lickshaw followed, silent and morose. Grannis lit the sheriff's office lamp and sank into a chair. "I've got to do all the thinking," he complained. "Nobody else knows how."

"It's a mess," grumbled Lickshaw. "Maude's got a lot of popular sympathy. And we've sorta had our hand exposed. I don't know that public opinion would hang with us if we caught him again."

"The hell it won't," snapped Grannis. "We're not going to give public opinion a chance to pass judgment. We're going to find Maude—and leave him right where we find him. Never mind public opinion. When a thing's done, it's done. I've got a better idea. Tonight you'll strike out with your men. Better boil down the fellows you're uncertain of. Just take along those that we know are sure and solid. Keep to his trail. If you lose it, camp till morning and pick it up. You're certain of his going as far as the NoNo anyhow. That's the first thing. Next, get word to Ike Lang to take his whole outfit and raid

Lost River. Tell him to make a wide loop, raise hell and destruction—and to come home through the pass. Then tell him to draw back of the Settlement a few miles and watch for Maude. That puts you on this side of the valley and him on the other. Maude's got to operate between you. You've got him pinched in."

"If he stays between us," muttered Lickshaw. "But, he won't do that. He'll cover ground and lots of it. He'll hit for the pass and cross into Lost River, like as not."

Grannis almost shouted. "Fine! That's what I hope. Remember what Manary said about bein' on the watch for any more raids on his country? That's why I want Ike Lang to ride over into that country and just slash things right and left! Manary will get his posse together and start lookin'. If Maude escapes us and gets into Lost River Manary will sink him. He'll be huntin' for Maude. And he'll never let Maude out of that jam alive. See?"

"Yeah," murmured Lickshaw, rubbing his hands together.

"You and Lang make a point of pinching Maude between you. He'll strike for the pass and cross over. Manary and the Lost River men will do the rest! But even so, I don't think friend Maude will ever get away from us this time. I've got another plan of my own and I'm not telling you for fear you'd bobble things like you always do. Now get goin' and obey my orders down to the last dot."

VII

STRATEGY

LOUISA, this morning, was on an exploring trip. Two days before a man who said he was Jubilee Carew, had come to her house leading a fine black gelding saddled and ready to ride. Rather vaguely he said he worked around the district and that in obedience to the customary habit of furnishing teachers with means of locomotion he was bringing the animal in question—guaranteed sound, sensible and nowise skittish. Before Louisa could query him Jubilee Carew had departed at a high lope.

Therefore she was headed up the trail to the eastern ridge, determined to see what lay up there that so attracted night riders. As a matter of fact, the house had gotten on her nerves. All during the dark hours just past, the converging roads had emptied one party after another into the clearing. They came hurriedly and departed the same way, the reverberation of their progress shaking the flimsy foundations of the place. By now the thing had become so common that her initial fears were pretty well worn down; yet the constant play of hoof-beats throughout the night had seemed to indicate some extraordinary event and to further alarm her there had been a crackling of gun-fire up on top of the bluff to westward sometime preceding daybreak. Directly after that a cavalcade had come hasting by—and twenty minutes later another.

She knew nothing of the art of reading sign but nevertheless she could not escape finding the yellow dust of the road scuffed and pockmarked with hoofprints. On upward a mile the brush beside the highway was rather beaten down and it seemed to her a considerable group had smashed through it. As she paused to study this, she heard something move behind her. Whirling about she saw only a blank line of pine and thicket facing her with the bright sunshine streaming down on the dust-coated greenery. All around her the land was fair and bright, giving the lie to the swift thrust of fear she had felt.

"If I am to live here," she told herself impatiently, "I shall have to get over this."

Accordingly, she went on, rising with the sharper incline, passing through heavier timber. The road narrowed to a pair of double ruts above which the overhanging pine boughs formed a heavy, sunless arch. But this lasted only a half mile or so and then the girl found herself on level land and looking across an open flat, across which was the white and brilliant horizon of another valley. The flat area was only a few hundred yards wide and she started onward to find a good viewpoint from which to inspect the country yonder. As she did so a figure moved into the corner of her vision, and throwing herself around in the saddle she saw Bill Maude coming leisurely forward. His hat was in his hand and the lean, watchful face seemed to be sharper and graver than she had known it to be. Coming abreast of her, he wheeled the horse to a stand.

"Mornin'. You're draggin' your picket some distance from home."

"Why—I thought you were in—in jail!"

"All good outlaws break jail," drawled Maude.

She felt her cheeks turning crimson. "Then it was you I heard spying on me down there in the brush?"

"Where?" said he, jerking out the word. He seemed to stiffen.

She pointed, watching him closely. "Do you have to do things like that?"

But he brushed aside the question. "How far down did you hear that?"

"About half way to my house," said she, angered at his manner.

"But you didn't catch sight of anybody?"

At this point she rebelled. "Why should I let you cross-examine me, Mr. Maude?"

"Fair question," he admitted. "Why should you answer a notorious killer, a thief and a jail breaker?"

There was irony, gentle but neverthesess apparent. Somehow she found herself on the defensive. "Well, you were around my house the night that man was killed. You can't deny that?"

"Nope. Was."

"Then—then why did you lie to the sheriff?"

"Didn't," said Maude in the same level voice. "My statement was that I had nothing to do with the killing."

"How can I believe that?"

"Lord bless you, I'm not askin' you to believe it. Why should I?"

This again was a repetition of his indifference toward her. It hurt her worse than she dared to admit. "No reason, I suppose," she said, eyes falling. "But you have no right to condemn me for not shielding you. I told the truth. Perhaps law means nothing to you. It does to me."

"That's too bad," said the man. "For there is no such thing in this county right now."

"That brands you as an outlaw," snapped the girl. "There is a sheriff in the county and a court."

"You mean there is a fellow who passes for a sheriff and a place they call a court."

"When a cry baby loses his marbles," was the girl's scornful reply, "he always says the game wasn't played right."

Instead of an explosion she evoked an approving chuckle. "You hit hard and fast, don't you? That was a pretty neat statement. All right. You believe in law. Supposing I had stepped into that play the other day between Ike Lang and old man Meek. There would have been a shooting. That's against the law, yet you wanted me to interfere."

"There is such a thing as justice and fair play," said the girl.

"You bet," agreed Maude.

"I don't understand," broke out the girl, impatient both with the man and herself.

"Then I advise a little more toleration for other folks until you do understand," suggested Maude quietly.

"I have heard pious advice from men before," said Louisa Cherry, bitterness coming to her face.

"You've got no love for men, that's plain."

"Why should I have when all that I believed was destroyed—" She checked herself.

"By men?" Maude added. "Or more particularly, a man?"

She flung up her head. "That's true. I have no faith in men. And I think I have reason enough for that. They are not considerate or kind. It is always selfishness, desire, boldness—and cowardice in the end."

He was watching her, steady eyes contemplative and kind. Unwillingly she admitted he made a fine, gallant figure in the saddle and that about him was a vigor and an honesty she had never seen in another. It was hard to believe him crooked. Meanwhile, he had shifted and was studying the throat of the pass, glance striking all through the trees. A horseman came rapidly from a thicket and halted, far enough away to be unrecognizable. He lifted his arm, in response to which Maude turned to go.

"You're a great hand to do what you want to do," he told Louisa. "And I'm a great hand not to waste unwelcome advice. But I'll break the rule to suggest you really ought to visit Buffalo Crossing for a few days. The country around here isn't going to be safe for anybody. So-long." Lifting his hat with a pleasantly flamboyant flourish, he spurred off. The girl swung about and de-

172

scended the trail, no longer desirous of seeing the land off to eastward.

Maude rode over to the man, Jubilee Carew. "I got uneasy waitin'," said the latter. "I don't believe I'd pay any head to that girl, nor let her pin you to one spot very long."

"I'm trustin' her," was Maude's instant answer.

"After what she done to you?" was Jubilee's rather astonished answer.

"She was following out her convictions, which is a hell of a lot more than most of us do, Jubilee."

"Well," pointed out Jubilee, "it might be her conviction to help get us hung. Can't never tell about no woman. Let's make tracks."

"I don't think she wants us hung," mused Maude, and said no more. Louisa Cherry had not seemed particularly disappointed at finding him loose. To the contrary, there had been something like relief in her eyes at the meeting. The memory of that strange glance was with him as he cantered along the slope and reached his hidden outfit. He had recruited to full strength in the hours following jail break and there stood around him now close to twenty men, not counting four he had placed out as scouts. Those four, he discovered, were still missing.

"Watch and wait—is that it?" queried Jubilee.

"No, I think we'll move on to the Settlement," decided Maude. "The longer we delay the more sure it is that Lickshaw and Grannis will add to their hand. We've got to catch Lang's party before it joins Lickshaw and bust it up proper. I want Lang. I want him alive and squealin'. That jug-head has got to be twisted on the rack till he bawls what he knows—and when we get that dope there'll be nothing left of the crooks around here.

All right—we'll ease along without speed. Slim, you slope down this side trail and keep a hundred yards ahead of us. Sing out if you see trouble. Lee, I want you to go pick up the scouts. Let's go."

It had all the earmarks of a cavalry troop in action. As the point man forged ahead, another dropped behind to cover the rear; and at the first opportunity Maude motioned a couple men to drift off to each flank. Thus guarded, the Cross Iron outfit moved down along the sinuous and secretive trail leading to the Settlement— the same trail blazed by Ike Lang's marauders traveling to and from Lost River Valley. These rakish, debonair punchers sat loosely in the saddle as if it were just a day's work to them, but Maude casting a sharp glance along the line, saw that they were keyed up to a fighting pitch. Behind the grave mask of each face lay tell-tale signs; the hard cheek muscles, the compressed lip, the eyes flashing back and forth through the screen of brush. He had built his crew with care and he saw now how well his handiwork had been. Hard and shrewd and capable, the men expected trouble and hoped their expectations would be fulfilled. The two upon which he placed most reliance had silently posted themselves as platoon leaders might have done. Jubilee Carew was to the fore, Link Whitehorn brought up the file.

At the end of a half hour the scouts were still out. About them was the stillness of a hot hill morning. Occasionally a pheasant drummed heavily up from covert and occasionally a woodpecker's whirring bill sent out waves of harsh sound to accent the clinging silence. All this while the trail led them diagonally away from the main road and the junction by Louisa Cherry's house. A little worried over his scouts and believing it might be well to catch a view of the open country to the north, he brought his party to a standstill.

"Wait here till the boys come in. I'm going off to the right. Be gone about fifteen minutes."

"Now hold on," objected Carew. "This ain't no time to straggle."

"If you hear sounds of trouble, come on," said Maude, and rode away. Within the count of ten the curving side trail shut him from view. Going at a canter, he fell into a shaded hollow, worked out of it, turned again through the pines, and then aimed directly up a slope which he knew would bring him out on a commanding eminence. The route was devious and suggestive of trouble. More than that, his ears brought to him faint disturbing sounds that appeared to come from the general direction of Louisa Cherry's house which was now no more than a mile off. Man-made sounds, if his ears were to be trusted. More and more impatient, he elected to go straight through the brush, leaving a wake of snapping branches behind him. He climbed a last inclined surface, passed between a line of stunted pines and halted on the edge of a small cliff. Below him ran the main road between the eastern pass and the junction. Ahead of him was a long view of the open prairie leading to Buffalo Crossing; but these landmarks he swept at a single glance, for his turning eyes had fallen upon Louisa Cherry's house down to the left. From the back end of that house a thick smoke was pouring. Fire!

Even as his attention struck it, his fist was gathering the reins and his spurs dropped, to whirl the horse down a precipitous, breakneck stringer of caved-in soil. He reached the road with the loss of his hat and swept along it at full speed. The house itself was immaterial, but his first thought was that the girl, green to Western ways, had left a lamp too near her stove and had suffered an explosion. Rounding a point, he shot across a level meadow. The girl's horse stood by the barn, reins

down. Otherwise the scene was empty of life. Flashing
by the barn—and casting one rapid glance into it—he
swung from the saddle and shot ahead of the halting
pony. The back door stood open and he flung himself
through it, to be met with a gush of fire and smoke. The
girl's figure swayed through the pall. She was beyond it,
standing in the living room door and fruitlessly trying to
beat down the blaze with a blanket. Maude covered his
face and crossed the kitchen in three lunging jumps.

"Are you burnt?"

"No—but the house—"

He seized the blanket from her and started to beat
down a licking streamer of fire crackling up the papered
wall. "What did you do?"

"Do? Nothing! I only got home a minute ago! It was
burning then!"

Maude cursed and dropped the blanket. Rushing
through the living room, he took one look out across the
front yard. That was enough. Swinging back, he reached
down for the blanket and threw it over Louisa Cherry's
startled face. "Trap!" he bellowed. "They set it!" Picking
her up, he bent his head to the increasing heat and
reached the back door. There was no enclosing posse out
here, but the tumultuous drum of hard-driven ponies
surged around from the front. Maude snatched the
blanket from her, set her down and pushed her toward
the barn. "Run like the devil—ahead of me!"

One unoccupied cell of his brain registered admiration. Louisa Cherry never stopped to ask foolish questions; picking up her skirts, she ran. Afterwards even
that lone brain cell was swamped in a fury of speed and
action. Maude raced beside the girl for twenty feet,
wheeled and took up a slower retreat, gun raised. The
posse—he had recognized Lickshaw's face from the first
glance through the front door—broke against the house

like a wave, split and came around it on either side. There was some hesitation as the members of the group glanced about them to line up the situation. No single man, it was evident, wished to place himself so far forward as to be a conspicuous target; and it was this slacking off of the charge that gave Maude his opportunity.

Lickshaw was on the right. Maude placed a shot at the sheriff. He sent a second to the extreme left end. Lickshaw's horse went down and the sheriff spun through the air in the manner of a pinwheel. Those two bullets brought the pursuers to a dead halt.

Still retreating and still firing, Maude passed inside the barn and reached to close the door; but the girl was before him, waiting to do exactly that chore. Swinging her whole body against the rusted hinges, she brought the barrier home. That was one surprise, and there was to be another. Maude's attention, hitherto concentrated on the business of pushing back the posse, now collected on his horse and the girl's horse which were standing in the barn. There must have been a high astonishment on his face. She looked up to him, breathless, eyes clear and shining, and a catch of emotion in her throat.

"They were right in front of the door, so I caught them up and brought them through. I knew the posse wouldn't dare fire at you if I stood behind. Have I—have I paid back for my original mistake?"

His answer was to take her around the waist and half carry, half push her into a corner aside from the door. Louisa Cherry's head snapped back and her arms gripped him tightly. There was an astonishing strength in that pliant body pressing against him; and the deep and moving shimmer of light still rested in her eyes. No fear, no nervousness. She seemed in fact as cool as himself. He held her until she straightened. Then he let her go with an apology. "They'll plug the door full of holes. Lay down behind that pile of boards."

She obeyed submissively.

"Have I paid back?" she asked again.

"Lord bless you, yes," said Maude. "But why did you do it?"

The remote smile grew more elusive. "I have surrendered to your country. I wanted you to know I can be as good a fighter as anybody, asking no reasons and no questions. Right or wrong, I'm on your side of the fence. If I am to be sorry for it later, I don't care."

"You won't be," muttered Maude, turning about. He had been watching that front door and now decided Lickshaw had other tactics in mind. So far the posse had not fired a shot—due to the girl, Maude guessed—and there was no sound of a rush on the structure. But the back door of the barn still stood open, leaving his position pretty well exposed. Starting down to close it he was arrested by Lickshaw's voice from some position near the house.

"Maude—give up."

"Not likely," called out Maude.

"Listen—what kind of a man are you to put that girl in danger? We can't fire on account of her. But if you're goin' to be hostile about it we'll open up—and God help you in case she's hurt."

"Don't let them influence you," whispered the girl swiftly. "They won't dare fire."

Maude shook his head, a crease of worry showing. "You've still got something to learn about those people. They'd kill their own mothers to get me. Lay nearer those boards."

Lickshaw yelled again. "I'm givin' you just about

thirty seconds to answer me, Maude. Then I go into action."

The girl rose and came toward Maude, whispering rapidly. "Does it mean something terrible if they catch you again?"

Maude's answer was a slow smile and a motion of his finger across his throat. The girl laid a hand on his arm. "Then, here. I'll get on my horse, open the front door and ride toward them. You take that chance and run out the back. I'll be between you and the posse. They'll have to go around me to shoot at you. And by that time you can be half way to timber, can't you?"

"Good girl," approved Maude. "But it's no go. I'm not goin' to use you that way."

"Why not?" insisted Louisa Cherry.

"You might get hit. Nope, that's out."

He learned something new about the girl then. "I mean to help," she said, and walked toward her horse. She was in the saddle by the time he reached her. He laid a hand on the beast's bridle.

"Don't do that. I'll wiggle through this another way."

Lickshaw bellowed: "I'm comin' after yuh now, Maude, and not all the help in the world will keep you from the gallows!" At the same time riders galloped along the walls of the barn, aiming for the rear. Maude sprang toward the back door to close it. As he let go of Louisa Cherry's horse the girl dropped her spurs and aimed for the front door, crying out.

'Sheriff—I am coming through the front!" she screamed.

Maude wheeled and raced toward her, but was too late. Leaning from the saddle, she forced the door open sufficient enough to give the horse passage room and pressed through. Maude turned, flung himself to his own pony and pointed for the back exit. She had forced his hand, leaving him nothing but the necessity of breaking clear before the posse, now unhindered by her presence in the barn, closed in and smothered him. He had no illusions about their intentions. It was a kill they wanted. So thinking, he passed through the back way on the dead run, swinging his body alternately to left and right.

The first thing Maude saw was a single rider race abreast him on the left; and as he saw the man he let go a single shot. It struck fairly. But the posseman rounding the other side of the barn was thus given a free chance and before Maude could quite recover and protect himself a carefully aimed bullet pierced the body of the straining horse beneath him. His own replying shot winged the posseman. Then his pony buckled at the knees and fell. Maude's feet were already out of the stirrups. He made a wide leap, cleared his kicking mount and swung about to regain the protection of the barn.

There was no chance of it. Lickshaw's men were streaming forward and to run for the barn would be walking directly against them. Turning back, he dived for the flimsy protection of a shed directly in front of him. The door of it was closed and from the rising volley of bullets clipping all around him he knew he dared not stop to fiddle with opening it. Another leap brought him to the far side of the shed where he turned in.

Instantly the boards of the shed began to grumble and snap with the impact of slugs. A more reckless member of the posse came to view, angling out across the meadow and lying flat in the saddle as an Indian would lie. Maude tried for a hit and missed. The horseman curved and started directly in, his example rapidly bringing others in pursuit. Maude held to his position with grim patience, laying the sights of his gun on the bellwether of the posse. When he squeezed the trigger, horse and man both went down.

But there was no possible hope of staying longer behind the shed. Already some of the outfit were dismounting in plain sight, reaching for their rifles. Thus with the ponies for a shield they meant to snipe him across a distance too great for effective revolver work but exactly suited to a long-barreled gun. Looking back of him, Maude saw the corner of the homestead corral beckoning like a charitable finger. It was but three jumps and a run. He wheeled and tried for the broader if flimsier shelter. The move was timed to catch the posse members as they were adjusting their rifles, and it worked with a precision that left no margin whatever for self-congratulation. He had no more than rounded the corral's corner than a whole cloud of dust began boiling up on that strip of earth across which he had fled.

It was only a temporary respite, a utilization of cover even more exposed than the last. His situation was something like that of a man treed by a bear; the farther he climbed the higher came the bear and the weaker became the supporting branches. Beyond the corral there was no point of safety, no refuge. The open prairie extended between himself and the nearest trees of the bunch—and those trees were utterly outside of consideration. To the southward was the road leading up toward the pass and beyond that road lay tantalizing shelter, to be reached only by a stiff run and a still stiffer climb up the face of an earth slide. This too, was impossible.

Meanwhile Maude was creeping along the side of the corral toward another corner. As he did so the riflemen suddenly ceased their efforts and ran boldly parallel the corral, to cover that far side he was working for; and to make the capture inevitable, another group appeared from behind the shed, guns raised, and slowly followed him.

A trembling quiet fell over the premises. Maude, reaching the absolute end of his tether—which was the corner of the corral—wheeled and faced his more immediate pursuers. Breaking open the cylinder of his gun, he thumbed in fresh shells, let the weapon hang and waited.

Over the droning, suppressed stillness cracked the brittle bark of Sid Lickshaw's voice. "Now—all together! Get him!"

Immediately a flare of dust and a spatting rain of lead rose no more than a foot behind him—the enfilade fire of those possemen who were checking him from turning the corral corner; and with equal suddenness the group following him broke into a shambling, ragged advance, also opening up.

Through alll this echoed a scream, Louisa Cherry galloped around the shed and aimed straight across the pathway of bullets. A mounted posseman threw himself after her, came abreast and pushed her horse aside. Then, from a different direction there was a confused and staccato sound of pounding hoofs and over it a riotous, full-throated yell. Lifting his head, Bill Maude saw the Cross Iron crew come down the throat of the ridge road, spread out into the meadow and charge against the flanking possemen. The whole scene changed at the snap of a finger. A warning cry broke out from the possemen by the shed. One and all, they turned and fought for their horses by the barn. Maude plunged after them with Lickshaw's narrow back the center of his attention. Louisa Cherry galloped toward him and jumped to the ground.

"Take the horse!" she called.

She had a smudge of dust across her forehead, but it

could not conceal the flush of her cheeks and the glow of excitement in her eyes. Maude, even in the rush of this bittler, vengeful fight, caught the clearness and the strength of the girl's character. He wanted to speak then but the encounter had swept beyond the barn and beyond the house, out of his reach. So he spurred off.

Dust lay all about him, the crack of guns struck continuously against his ears and beat against the higher land like claps of thunder; and to all this fury the roar of the flaming house added its throaty, sinister note. A part of Maude's outfit swept around the house, caught up with him and carried him on the far side where posse and Cross Iron were weaving and rushing and swirling from point to point.

The posse had taken to horse again and were giving ground with a sullen obstinance. Link Whitehorn and half a dozen men drove forward like the point of a spear, oblivious of death, carried on by a wild and reckless courage. Maude, seeing Lickshaw retreating on the trot toward the NoNo road, galloped in pursuit with the rest of Cross Iron after him. That was the last stand of the posse. Before the consolidated smash it weakened, broke and fled—pouring through the gulch mouth in the direction of Buffalo Crossing. Charging directly at that mouth, Bill Maude heard his name cried out imperiously and he swung to see Jubilee Carew, the forehanded and ever-cautious Jubilee, wigwagging him with an arm from near the house. It spelled urgency and Maude galloped back, to follow Jubilee's pointed hand.

Out of the ridge road poured a heavy cavalcade of men, all riding low and fast.

"Great guns," muttered the surprised Maude, "must be thirty or forty of 'em!"

"Who?" grunted Jubilee.

"Don't know," was Maude's terse reply. "But we can't

afford to stand and find out now. We've got to run for it."

"Which way?"

"Home this time," called Maude, racing past the barn. The girl still stood by the corral. Leaning down he swept her up to the saddle, turned and went back to Jubilee who had hurriedly assembled the outfit. Without more ado these still fuming fighters paired off behind Maude, who led them up the western butte and toward the great front gate of his own ranch. Looking back at the top of the butte, he saw the band of newcomers spreading into the clearing; more than that he saw the remnant of Lickshaw's posse riding back to meet them.

VIII

THE POT BOILS OVER

THREE hundred yards beyond the edge of the butte, Maude suddenly called his party to a halt, dismounted and helped the girl to the ground. "Jubilee, she'll ride with you. Take the boys to the ranch and spread 'em out for a scrap around the house. I'm staying behind a minute. Link, Louis and Happy, stick with me. Bust into it, boys."

Louisa Cherry obeyed without comment, swinging up in front of Jubilee. Jubilee, embattled as he was at the moment, showed the frozen countenance of one considerably shaken. To actually hold a woman in his arms was worse for him, than to slap a cougar on the whiskers. He cast a stunned glance toward Maude and received no sympathy at all. Maude grinned briefly and motioned his foreman to be off. So the crew broke into a dead gallop and departed. Maude wheeled and led his three partners to within a hundred yards of the rim, or as far as he dared go without exposing his presence of those below. Dismounting and taking his binoculars from a saddle bag, he crawled forward on his stomach. There was, along the rim, a ridge of caked and buckled-up clay and this he used for shelter, commanding a full view of what went on below.

His glasses were not necessary. Immediately he recognized the members of that second outfit which had swept down from the Lost River trail—recognized them to be more men of the county who by personal grievance or political allegiance were against him. Lickshaw, meanwhile, had rallied his followers and was motioning them to collect. At the same time the sheriff rode over to a small, round figure who sat like a sack of meal in the saddle. It was Grannis.

"There you are," grunted Maude to Link Whitehorn, who had crawled beside him. "Chauncey Grannis threw away his mask and now he's on my trail like a wolf. He brought that second bunch of hammerheads on top of us."

"Dirty little pup," growled Link. "Lemme go back and get my rifle outa the boot. I can reach him sweet from here."

"Not now," countered Maude. "I want to see what he figures to do next. He thought he had a swell plan. Lickshaw was to bust into us from the front and Grannis was to crush us from behind. Almost worked, too."

"They ain't collectin' any prize money on 'almost,' Bill. But why ain't they on our trail right now? That's what worries me."

"Probably afraid to storm this cliff. Grannis maybe figures we could lay along here and drop a lot of his crowd while he was comin' up. He'll tear the landscape upside down to get me, but he's far too slick to let himself into a wholesale slaughter. I tell you, Link, he's more dangerous than Lang and Lickshaw put together. He uses his bean."

"And supposin' Lang's swingin' around to catch us off guard at the ranch?" worried Link. "Daggonit, they've got too many young armies floatin' around here."

"There's your answer," grunted Maude, nodding his head to the scene below. Grannis beckoned a man to come near, talked earnestly with him and presently motioned semicircularly toward the west—toward Cross Iron. The designated rider hurried off down the road in the direction of the Settlement.

"Ahuh," said Link. "You think he's sending that jasper out to notify Lang about somethin'?"

"Exactly. Lang's around the Settlement. Now we've got to move. Louis, I want you to stay on your belly right here and observe what happens. If they decide to storm this bluff, you've got time to get away and reach the ranch. If any part of the gang splits off and goes some other direction you hotfoot it back to me anyhow."

He crawled to the horses with Link and Happy beside him. Mounting, they swung toward the ranch. "This beats me," growled Link. "Which way we goin' to turn first?"

"Lang," said Maude. "He's the fellow I want. And I want him alive to squeal on Grannis and Lickshaw. I want him to spill the whole dirty scheme. I'm morally sure he's still at the Settlement. Probably Grannis told him to stay there to keep us from retreating through the hills in that direction. Ike's only got about twelve men and we can handle 'em nicely."

"Yeah," observed Link, "but even if we take 'em, that don't make much of a dent in the goshawful crowd Grannis and Lickshaw have collected yonder. I'm dubious to the point of doubt."

186

"It's a long day," mused Maude, "and we can run as fast as they can. If it isn't possible to bust the crowd as a whole then we can try to split it in pieces and catch each piece on the bounce. Main thing right now is to nail Lang's jugheads before they move away from the Settlement. Happy, you turn off to the north here and hide yourself in some hollow about four miles yonder. In case Grannis considers rounding the ranch on a flank move you'll see him coming and backtrack to give us a signal. Link, you go straight on to the ranch and bring all the bunch, except one man to stay with the girl, to that big moss rock which lies beside the trail over to the Settlement. I'm splitting off here to do a little scoutin'. I'll meet you at the rock."

"You got no business—" began Link. But Maude had already spurred away into the south. Over his shoulder he threw a phrase:

"Work fast. No time to lose."

Roughly speaking, the Cross Iron range extended from this general point on southward to a rising, broken country. It was directly into this strip of country that Maude pressed, aiming for a ridge whose darkly timbered slopes made a kind of barrier between the range and the lawless Settlement. It was then about four o'clock and the long rays of the sun were burning across the sky like actual shafts of fire. Knowing that Grannis probably had spies situated on commanding points, Maude drove straight for an area broken by gravel domes and by deep arroyos, and when he reached one such arroyo he immediately dipped into it. His whole life had been spent in the NoNo country and so, below the horizon, he curved from one depression to another with an unerring judgment as to where the next protective runway could be found. Indeed, when he finally rose up from the maze of gullies it was to pass directly into the trees of the ridge and halt by a great, square-faced rock all overgrown with moss. Pausing and turning for a brief moment, he looked back to the haze ridden outline of his ranch quarters in the distance. A dark line and a train of thick dust appeared over there—his men already coming.

From this rock it was not more than two miles over the hump to the Settlement. Judging he had considerable time to make a preliminary scout, Maude cantered up the trail. All about him stood close-ranked second growth pines. Sunlight streamed over the tree tops but very little of its penetrated the thick branch layers and such vagrant shafts of light as did press through, only accented the stillness and the shade and the stifling heat of the hillside.

For perhaps a quarter mile Maude kept to the trail. Presently he began to see fresh hoofmarks in the soft earth. On impulse he dodged from one small glade to another and brought up before a kind of green wall of underbrush. An exceedingly narrow aperture showed where other travelers, probably animal, had passed through.

It was an invitation to Maude but, standing there with the profuse sweat rolling down his cheeks, he caught the sound of some moving thing ahead. Directly afterwards there came a flutter of wings and the booming drum of a pheasant flushed from shelter. Through the small interstices of the timber he caught sight of the bird's bronze and golden body flashing by. The heavy waves of echo faded reluctantly down the avenues of the ridge and silence came again; Maude pushed his horse through the aperture.

Instantly two things registered on his mind. He had reached the summit of the ridge and now stood in the middle of a roadway. And he stood thirty feet, no more, from another horseman whose blackened features and bullet-like head, registered enormous shock at this meeting. It was Ike Lang, alone and probably on the same sort of scout work. As with Lang, the abrupt turn of events caught Maude in a slack moment. He had mistaken the sound of the pheasant as being also the source of the other faint disturbance he previously had heard. Now, one hand on the reins and the other lifted to rub his sweaty cheeks, he froze. Lang's reckless head turned slightly and the round, staring eyes began to gleam.

"Damn yuh!" bit out Lang, the report of the words flat and sustained in the dull air. "If I had known— Now what's it to be, Maude?"

Maude's mind ran rapidly ahead to cover the situation. Lang's followers might be nearby. Hiw own crew was approaching. Gunplay at the moment would bring the outlaws to the scene and set them on guard against the Cross Iron riders. He wanted no gunplay now. With a strong effort at seeming casual, Maude let his lifted hand drop to the saddle horn, "I want to talk with you, Ike. Let's get to the ground."

He swung down, pulling the pony slightly around to protect himself as he did so. Lang matched the move, and thus they stood with still thirty feet between them and each still staring at the other to weigh every twist of muscle and every fleeting passage of emotion. Suddenly sweat stopped crawling on Maude's face. Some remote nerve power made him cool. Realizing he gambled heavily on the passing moments, he broke the taut silence. "Where's your men, Ike?"

"You'd like to know," grunted the outlaw, black lips twisting apart. "Go on—speak out. I know yore playin' with a joker up yore sleeve."

"You heard the firing over at the fork of the roads?"

"What of it?"

"Why ain't you there?" drawled Maude. "That's where the kill was to be, wasn't it?"

"You think so?" parried Lang. There was a wild, straining net of creases spreading along his face; and color seemed to turn still deeper. Not by the breadth of a hair had he moved since dismounting, but his head was slipping forward now and Maude knew the meaning of it. Lang was balancing himself for a play. At the thought a savage recklessness swept through the Cross Iron boss.

"Listen—I won't beat around the bush," he said. "You're stalkin' me and I'm stalkin' you. I think I could beat you to the draw, Ike. I've slung lead as long as you have and I've been practisin' against the day when we'd bump."

"Hot air!" jerked out Lang. "You can rip to it any time you want!"

"I don't want you dead," said Maude. "I want to beat that miserable hide of yours to a pulp and I want to wring the dirty secrets of your gang out of you with my two hands. How about it—we'll drop the guns and try fists and the winner can do what he damned pleases afterwards."

There was a long, packed silence. Lang's glance never ceased its sullen, burning watchfulness, but some of the strain went off his face. He was the bigger man, infinitely the more solid of bone. No fist had ever taken him off his feet. The advantage, after being even through the nerve-tightening vigil, swung to him. "All right," said he, croaking the words. "But I'll kill yuh just the same—with my fists! Expect no mercy from me!"

Maude's fingers dropped to his belt buckle, unfastened it, halted there. Lang followed suit. And when

Maude let one end of the belt drop, the outlaw did likewise. Maude stooped down and let the belt lie on the ground, fingers brushing the leather and remaining so until he saw Lang stoop. Thus far each gesture had been guarded, stealthy. But there was no longer the chance of that trembling, split-second move of treachery and it was Lang who first stood up, unarmed. And as Maude straightened, a crooked, infinitely evil smile broke the malevolent cast of Lang's face.

'Yuh fool!" he yelled. "Yuh'll wish for a bullet in the brain before I'm through breakin' yore bones! Come on!"

Maude stepped a pace forward of his grounded belt. Seeing that, the outlaw's head dropped like a ram and he came charging across the earth, the enormous arms breaking into piston-like blows and the muscles of his shoulders swelling beneath his coat. To the crouching Maude he was like a force of nature rolling forward, destruction personified. But after that thought there was no time for another. The outlaw had thrown caution to the winds in his blind charge, as if believing no punch or succession of punches however terrific, could throw him back. The dome-like head bent farther down and Maude made a target out of the slanting, brutal eyes. Putting all his body into his arm, he hooked a solid smash up into the downcast face. It brought Lang to a staggering halt and lifted his chin. Maude exploded another blow underneath the chin and stepped aside from the crushing arms that came out to trap him.

Lang whirled about. There was a trickle of blood running from his mouth, but he laughed and charged again. Maude, feeling the swift agony of some wrenched bone in one fist, backed off a few steps then he sidestepped, wheeled and beat Lang on the temple with a smother of punches. He landed fair and hard and Lang swayed away defensively. And before the outlaw had quite receded from range, Maude leaped in with a down-driving fore-arm blow across the nape of the man's neck. He was savagely seeking to dull the fellow's wits and in a measure he succeeded for Lang launched a wild punch that went completely to one side of the Cross Iron boss. Seeing this, Maude jumped forward and lashed away at Lang's kidney. But Lang's arm swept out again in that sinister grope and Maude sprang aside.

The outlaw turned once more, like an enraged monster slavering at the lips. There was a film over his eyes and his drooping head swayed from side to side, peering at Maude first from one angle of vision and then another. A sardonic cry heaved out of his chest. "Come on—gimme some more of that! See how I take it! You damn string bean! I'm goin' to strangle yuh when I get my grip on yore body!" And he plunged at Maude madly.

Maude veered. Lang, shaking his head clear, matched the shift of directions and railed the Cross Iron boss with one lone blow on the chest. Literally it lifted Maude from the ground and sent him backward, to land on the soft earth, plunged in a kind of roaring darkness. His heart seemed to go wild and wrench at its ligaments. Long shafts of pain went through and through him and his breath was agonizingly gone. Through a film he saw Lang's face approaching and bending, all distorted, all black. The man meant to leap on him and grind his stomach out. That threat brought Maude's feet up—catching Lang full in the mouth. The sharp-pointed boot heels did the rest. Lang whirled back with a half-screamed roar. Maude rolled over and stood erect.

Strength came back to him in a rush of breathing. Throwing the last of his wariness aside and pressing for the kill, he leaped against the outlaw's relaxed body and sledged blow after blow at the stomach pit. Lang reeled. His arms rose and started to encircle Maude. The latter wrenched himself back, fighting now against the certainty of being broken in twain, but Lang clung doggedly, ever tightening his grip and the flooding pressure of his muscles. The blood of his face dripped on Maude and the hot torrent of his words came spilling out vengefully.

Maude, feeling his ribs being slowly pushed into his vitals, tore one arm free and beat it up against the jutting chin. Again and again. Lang's head rolled aside, but he clung on like a bulldog, certain as death of his power and his purpose. Something seemed to crack. There was the least surcease of pressure; Maude fought for his other arm, at the same time caving from the terrific pressure applied to his spine. There was but one thing left to do—desperately he shot his thumbs into Lang's bloodshot eyes.

Lang dropped his arms and bellowed. His hands rose. Stepping back, Maude measured the distance with as much care as was left in him and spent the last of his energy on one hooking smash under the chin. Lang fell over, struggled on the ground a moment and then lay still.

Maude, utterly exhausted, staggered to his horse and leaned against it, every fiber in his body caught up in a palsy he could not for the moment control. He was sick at the stomach and there seemed to be actual cavities opened up on his body where Lang had hit him. He thought he was going under and he cursed himself for the weakness. But what broke the swirling night in his brain and steadied him was the sound of shots farther along the ridge. It seemed to him they had been sounding for some time but that he was only now becoming aware of them.

Pushing himself clear of the horse Maude looked about. A little to the south the brush crashed. A man shouted, and more shots poured on top of the words. Warned, Maude retrieved his gun and kicked the senseless outlaw's weapon into the thicket. He started back for his horse and was on the point of mounting when the gunfire stopped, another yell skimmed over the tree tops, and a rider pounded into view—Link Whitehorn. A gun swung restlessly in his fist and a broadening alarm on his face. When he saw Maude he drew up with an oath of relief. "Good Judas, where you been? I thought—Hell, what's happened—"

"Yonder is the relic," said Maude, testing his muscles gingerly.

Whitehorn sprang from the saddle and went to Lang. He prodded the outlaw with a boot toe and turned to Maude. "With yore fists alone?"

"Finish fight," grunted Maude. "I wanted him alive, and I got him alive. He'll live just long enough to turn state's evidence on the whole crowd, Link. Then he'll hang. What's going on yonder?"

Link swore. "I'd give all my pay for the next thirty years to've seen that scrap. You look kinda gray all over. Hurt bad?"

"I'm comin' out of it. We've still got a lot of work to do. What's up?"

Before Whitehorn could answer a group of riders filed into the clearing and halted. Maude saw his own men making a ring around half a dozen of Lang's outlaws. Jubilee came on. "Christmas, what's happened here? Don't tell me that's Lang in the dust?"

"Consider it thoughtfully," said Whitehorn. "He did it —our boss—Mister William Maude. Don't it stagger you that anybody could bust a human battleship into small fragments thataway." Then he thought of Maude's question. "Why we come to the moss rock and din't find you. So we barged right along and directly busted into Lang's hellions. There they are, mighty humble now and—"

A single rider shouted through the trees and came on at a dead, run, bringing up in front of Maude. "I sauntered up to the high point and what you suppose I saw? Lickshaw and his bunch. Evident, they been to the Settlement because right now they're headed back around the base of this ridge, like they either intended to climb it or strike for Cross Iron."

"See anything of Grannis?" snapped Maude, brightening.

"No. From there I couldn't ketch much of the country yonder. But it did sorter look like they was a dust cloud off towards home."

"Towards home?" grunted Maude, and rose to his saddle. He pointed at the captives. "Climb to the ground. Lou Lord, you'll have to stick here and handle this Settlement crowd. Shoot the first man that bats an eyelid. That includes Lang when he wakes up, though I doubt if he'll give you much argument. Think you can do it?"

"Why not?" retorted the designated puncher.

Maude nodded and turned north down the roadway with his outfit hard on his heels. "They've heard the firing here and I suppose they figure to come up the back side. I know a place—if we can reach it first—that will make a fine trap. We licked that outfit once and I think about one good round of shots will settle the question. But Grannis bothers me bad—Turn here."

They flashed through deeper timber and heavier brush. Presently the ridge became a long, descending grade and brighter daylight glowed between the pine tops. Once, down a narrow lane, Maude caught sight of the prairie. Seeing no risen dust he swung somewhat to the west and spurred rapidly toward the edge of trees. Near it he raised a warning hand and brought the calvalcade to a halt; immediately the not far removed rumble of approaching horses came strongly along the hillslope.

Soundlessly Maude gestured for the Cross Iron outfit to deploy. To the right he saw the flash of a rider passing around the foot of the ridge, followed by a long line of other riders. Maude motioned and flung himself onward. The trees ran past, dwindled to seedlings and died out altogether. Lifting himself in his stirrups Maude yelled, and at that moment Cross Iron hit the unsuspecting sheriff's posse hard on the flank.

There was one concerted volley and then the posse broke to pieces. A few shots whined back and after that the yellow dust of the open country rose as beneath a whirlwind behind the posse members in full flight.

Maude's eyes, however, were rivetted on one man who suddenly lagged and flung himself about. It was Lickshaw, and Lickshaw carefully raised his gun and began to fire on the advancing Maude. Maude saw the kickback of the gun at each hammerstrike. Once he felt the touch of lead near his cheek. Lickshaw's face was a gaunt mask of fear and anger blended. As Maude took aim, he wondered what terrific change had come over the hireling sheriff to make him stand and fight back. His gun roared and Lickshaw, crying brokenly, slipped out of the saddle.

Maude turned and lifted a high yell at his scattered men. "Never mind—come back here! Come back here!" Off across the prairie he had caught sight of Grannis' party at this moment verging on the Cross Iron ranch quarters. Jubilee and Whitehorn, hearing the summons, dashed away to round up the members of the crew who were now in full cry on the fading heels of Lickshaw's vanishing posse. Lickshaw rose on an elbow and yelled.

"Yore damned nest is goin' to be burnt clean down, Maude!" the sheriff shouted. "Grannis'll settle with you, make no doubt about it! And I'll live to see yuh on the hangin' rope!"

Headed by Jubilee, the crew pounded back. "The buzzards of that posse are split twenty-one ways from the deuce," called Jubilee. "You'll never get 'em with a trout net."

"Pick up Lickshaw and come on!" roared Maude. Never waiting, he thrust in his spurs and raced away. It was three miles to the Cross Iron front gate and the horse beneath him was tired by its long efforts. Maude closed his mind to the ruin of a good animal as his eyes went to the horizon. Grannis was yonder, no doubt about it. The long line of horsemen verged toward the ranch buildings, dust behind them. Then it seemed to Maude that there was a sudden recoiling from the house. Distinctly he made out a split in Grannis' faction. Riders broke off and went whirling around the place, Indian fashion. He checked his pace slightly to let Jubilee run abreast. "Who did you leave there with the girl?"

"Oley," said Jubilee.

"Well," ripped Maude, "you left a good man He's holdin' them back. Jubilee, if they so much as touch that girl—"

"Say," broke in Jubilee, "they're a-comin' this way, ain't they?"

Maude studied the blurring, shifting outline. In a little while it narrowed to a single black point; dust rose higher.

"You bet they're a-comin'," added Jubilee. "Now listen. They's about forty in that bunch. We're out-weighed."

Maude forged on, still watching. The spearpoint of that outfit drove steadily toward him; and before many minutes had passed he came to recognize a slighter, smaller figure in the foreground. At that, Maude looked around to the left and his attention dropped on an irregular, roughened strip of earth. "With Grannis along they might turn the trick," he muttered. "He's got his back to the wall. He's got to get me or be ruined. He knows it. That's why he's comin' from shelter and exposin' his own part in this business. Jubilee, he's a bad one."

"Look out, look out," warned Jubilee, voice rising. "We're damned near on top of 'em!"

Maude pressed his mouth together and held his peace. Over the narrowing interval he heard the shrill cry of Grannis himself. "Now—spread out and smash 'em!"

Catching the signal, Maude pulled his horse to the left and raced for the rough area of the prairie. He turned in the saddle to yell: "Arroyo—pile into it!"

The two outfits had been racing head-on. Maude's rapid shift of direction was in effect a parrry. The men under Grannis, already spreading in a skirmish formation, were lost in sudden confusion as they shifted and rammed each other. Maude veered again slightly and the mouth of an arroyo yawned in his face. His horse took the jump, stumbled and raced on. Maude pounded across the gravel fifty yards and suddenly reined to a halt, jamming his party behind him. He cleared the saddle, bawling out: "Make a stand for it!" And leaning against the natural parapet, he faced the attacking party.

In column formation and with half a minute's more

time Grannis' men could have swept around the flank of
that arroyo, enfiladed the defenders and left them
dead. But the maneuver had been calculated by Maude
to produce the present situation, and it had worked.
Pulled into an irregular line that faced the full length of
the depression, the attacking outfit hurled themselves
onward, too near to withdraw without loss or to shift the
emphasis of their assault.

Grannis alone seemed to have kept his head, for as
the whole group came bearing thunderously down
upon the arroyo he swung and raced for that far end
where Maude was stationed. He was yelling at the top
of his treble voice, his hat was off and all his neat
clothes were stained and streaked; but as dishevelled as
they were, they could not compare with the sweaty,
swollen face of this man who had lived so well and so
aloofly calm all his life. His eyes were hard set on
Maude and the latter saw the small lips moving in some
sort of speech entirely lost in the clamor. He gripped the
reins of his horse cruelly and set the animal on its
haunches within twenty feet of the arroyo, he lifted
his gun with a grinning effort of lips and laid the sights
of it on Maude with a careful, astonishingly cool deliber-
ation. And it was thus that Maude last pictured him
alive—one who had gambled and gone out with the
inflexible purpose of making his gamble stick. In the
concerted roar of sudden firing Maude never heard the
beat of his own weapon. But the muzzle kicked up and
the acrid smoke curled back. And Chauncey Grannis
went sprawling from the saddle. The horse bucked clear
and for a moment the man was lost in the dust. When it
rose, Maude saw him lying face down, quite still.

Elsewhere was yelling, more gunfire, and the com-
mingled confusion of the attackers rearing back from a
hot, blasting wall of resistance. The charge had failed.

Horses were down and men as well, crying and cursing. The fact of Grannis' death swept through the ranks of his followers like a devastating force. Leaderless, all coherence and purpose seemed to dissipate in the air. Three or four of the more dogged ones wheeled to rip the edge of the depression with a last volley and then fled. But the main body slowly recoiled beyond range and huddled together in some dispirited conference. Silence came uneasily into a sky filling with twilight. High up, a last reluctant ray of sun blazed against the heavens and expired. A few more of the attacking party left the scene at a dead gallop.

"No more firing." Maude said briefly. "Into the saddles. Guns on 'em. Up we go!"

With a heave, the Cross Iron outfit came from the arroyo and confronted the remnant of the Grannis party who gave ground sullenly. Maude's voice twanged curtly over the space. "Drop your artillery to the ground —and do it now!"

"No more shootin' from you?" came a troubled voice.

"No more," promised Maude. "I'm tellin' you something—Grannis is dead, Lang and his outfit are caught tight, and Lickshaw is right here. We've busted the back of this crooked ring. Now drop those guns or I'll open up!"

One man flung his revolver far from him; and as if that were a signal the rest of the attacking party followed suit. Maude motioned to his crew and the members of it closed quietly around the aggressors. "You're through," said Maude.

"Fair play," muttered a spokesman for the other outfit. "We know it's all over. The big fellow's dead—and we ain't goin' to play a dead man's cards. Fair play."

"You'll get it," said Maude, and suddenly felt a desire to bring the long fight to a definite close. There was a harder edge to his words. "From now on and for a long time to come I'm going to run this county. Every crooked mug in Christendom has tried a hand, and it's time for an honest man. You fellows pick up Grannis and the rest of those poor devils lyin' yonder and take 'em to town. That's item one. Item two—get out and stay out. Don't let the sun shine on you in this country tomorrow."

"By God, that's hard," protested somebody of the opposing faction.

"Sure," interrupted Maude. "Hard, after you had your minds set to wipe me off the earth and plunder the county. You heard my terms. And if I ever find any of you tarryin' I'll come after you personally." He lifted his eyes and saw, across the prairie, a figure standing in the Cross Iron gateway, waiting. At that, a long suppressed impatience took hold of him and he turned to Jubilee. "You take care of this. Send a couple boys back to help Lou Lord with Ike Lang's crowd. They're going to jail. So is Lickshaw. And that winds the whole bloody story to a finish. I'm on my way."

Trotting past the group, he aimed for the ranch. The darkness gave way across his eyes, gave way to a sparkle of light. He raised his arm in a kind of reassuring signal; and from Louisa Cherry at the gate came a similar reply. As Maude neared the place, the girl ran forward to meet him.

THE FIGHTING CALL

I

THE HILLS BECKON

TWENTY-SEVEN days after commencement the Skillet beef round-up ended in one last blistering stretch of dust and sweat. Late of an evening the crew staggered into the home bunkhouse and fell to sullen slumber, dogtired, red-eyed, sand-bitten and saddle-galled. Next morning young Len Gann, foreman, stepped forth to curl a smoke under the crisp sunshine; and as he did so there came to him from the dim distance a far call of the red gods. As sudden and preemptory as that. One moment routine was in his soul, the next he was keening the wind while the cigarette remained unfinished in his fingers. All six feet of his willowy frame stiffened, the ash-blond head turned westerly like the point of a compass and out of the normally sharp and humorous eyes flickered a kind of narrow, mongol glance. Thad Burchevain, Skillet owner, was at that moment crossing the compound and when he saw his foreman standing thus, he knew what it meant even before Len Gann's soft drawl broke the spell.

"Make 'er out," said Len. "I'm long gone right now."

"I catch on," replied Burchevain. "A lot of funny bugs ketch holt of a man when he's whipped low from roundup. Tomorrow you'll feel better. But today—"

"I'm makin' dust," reiterated Len, "and a lot of it."

"Many fiddle-footed fools I've seen in my time," grunted Burchevain, "and all of 'em died lonely and busted. You been workin' three years for me. Don't toss off your advantage. Don't drift. Only pluggers inherit the earth."

"Message for me yonder," said Len Gann, the blue glance breaking into a hundred dancing points.

"God hates a quitter, Len."

"Maybe," agreed Len, and went thoughtfully on. "But look at me. I'm twenty-eight. Hell, I'm pretty soon an old man. What've I got out of the shuffle so far? Sand in my craw, a lot of hard labor under my belt. Slep' so long in the same bunk it's creased exact to my frame. I'm tired of lookin' at the same mugs all day long, tired of the simple-faced heifers. No, somethin's over the hill I got to see."

"Wait," urged Burchevain. "Wait till you can go like a lord, on a milk-white horse and your own brand scattered like tumbleweed around the landscape. Wait till you've earned your fortune. Don't sacrifice your prospects now."

"Which are what?"

Thad Burchevian faced his foreman squarely. "Never made you a promise yet I didn't keep, Len. After me, you're next. All my range and all that's on it. I'm no longer young and my son-in-law gets the spread. You're a better man than any."

Len Gann's reckless, high-boned cheeks broke from the horizon for the first time and veered toward the flutter of a woman's bright dress over on the house porch. The mongol glance softened, but immediately thereafter grew sharper. "That's the biggest compliment anybody ever paid me, Thad, but I'd be old then and there wouldn't be any call from the hills. You see?"

"I know," admitted Burchevain reluctantly. "Felt the same way when I was young. Made me sweat at night to think of all the green country I hadn't left my pony tracks in. But I stuck. Never get anywhere travelin' down the trail."

"Well, you've got your milk-white horse now. . . . and what of it?" said Len Gann. "You ain't ridin' with the breeze. Why? Because the hills quit callin' you long ago."

"Then go, damn you!" cried Burchevain, and turned away.

Fifteen minutes later Len Gann swung to his seat, geared for travel. A rifle stood butt up in its boot, saddle bags and blanket roll rested behind the cantle, a canteen depended from the horn. All his possessions were with him, all but one—and that something he could neither take nor entirely leave behind. As he drew beside the house the brightly burning fire in his eyes suffered a sudden dimming and he stared at the girl on the porch with a sober, half-puzzled straightness. This act of his was in a way cruel, but beyond his helping. And to make matters worse, he had no words to explain. But if he was proud, Louisa Burchevain was no less so. Slim and straight and with a quiet courage that was like a shining light, she confronted him. And she was the first to speak.

"Going, Len?"

"Going," said the man, lifting his hat. "And I don't know why."

"I haven't asked why, have I?"

"No. And bless you for that, Louisa."

"So long, then. And be a good partner to yourself, wherever you go."

"So long," said Len Gann. And lifting his arm in one

gay sweep, he cantered away. Into the west he ran, with the fresh brilliance of the morning sun following his supple, swaying form; and at last he became but a seemingly stationary figure against the dark strip of hills running along the horizon. Skillet's best man had gone, leaving behind a colorful memory. Louisa Burchevain turned and found her father watching.

"There was an understanding between you two," said Thad Burchevain. "And if you'd lifted your voice, he'd have stayed."

"Yes," said the girl with a calmness that only accented her inner havoc. "But he would have hated me the rest of our lives for fighting what's in his heart. He's a full man, Dad, and I'll never want him tied to me with his longing elsewhere."

"He'll come back, you think?"

"I hope so," said the girl. And under her breath she repeated it with a hungry softness. "I hope so!"

Thus Len Gann traveled, a lengthening wake of dust to the rear, rising and falling with the heave of the prairie and the char marks of his successive fires making a die-straight line onward. It was strangeness he was after and as long as he remained in familiar country he avoided ranch houses. His coffee can grew black from many flames, and the long-suppressed carefree instincts swelled and left him a little giddy with the pure delight of living. The brilliant black heavens lay over him at night and the lonely chant of the coyotes evoked in him a sense of wildness and mystery. He left the flat terrain behind, rose with the bench lands, plunged into a rugged country where broken ridges swept like vast waves against the sky and tangle glens beckoned him to deeper isolation. Never caring, never reckoning, Len Gann drifted. And on the seventh day he rounded the sharp bend of a canyon wall to find the message he had been seeking of the hill gods. The muzzle of a gun was leveled, bleak and black, against him.

Behind the gun was a man who half leaned and half crouched against the wall, hat gone and face stretched in a series of haggard, downsweeping lines. He was young and not bad looking; but at present the two eyes traveling steadily along the gun barrel were like rubies blazing against the sunlight. A lathered horse stood a little to the rear.

"Sorry," rapped out the man. "Climb off. We trade. You take my brute, I take yours."

Len Gann's cheeks relaxed. He got down, chuckling softly to himself. The transfixing threat of the gun made him a little careful of his gestures as he paced backward, but the cadence of his voice was undisturbed. "Seems to be what I'm lookin' for," said he. "What's the trouble here?"

"I'd have to go back thirty years to tell the story," said the man, running for the fresh horse, "and I ain't got time. I'm runnin', mister, because I never learned to crawl. Sorry about the horse."

"It don't grieve me too much," drawled Len Gann. "Is this a private war or open to all comers?"

The man was in Len Gann's saddle, swaying a little, and his glance constantly flickered toward the canyon's ahead. "I done you one bad turn already," was his answer, "and I'll not increase it by urgin' you to meddle in the sudden death and disaster of these hills. But, look here, you can do me the favor of lyin' to whoever comes clatterin' this way durin' the next five minutes. Say I've doubled up the rim."

"Done," said Len Gann. "I'll go you one better and fort up right here to cover your retreat."

"Oh, my God, no!" exclaimed the man. "Don't attempt it! You're proud but they'd bust you like a strawstem."

He bit off his words and strained forward. Somewhere on higher ground was the faintly increasing echo of a cavalcade in progress. And when the man caught it his harried expression grew more pronounced. Back went his head in an unconscious defiance. The ruddy color of his face died utterly away as he stared at Len Gann. "Do me another favor, will you? I'm Pete Strawn. Go find the Strawns. Tell 'em I did the chore. Tell 'em I'm wiped out, but that I'm not sorry. Tell 'em good-bye and good luck!"

"Hold on—hold on," interjected Len Gann. "You ain't that bad off yet. . . ."

The fugitive Pete Strawn was in motion. Turning briefly in the saddle, he sent back a last call. "You don't know what I'm up against, brother! And mebbe I've done wrong gettin' you into it. Adios!" With that he ran recklessly around the bend and was shut from sight. The murmur of his pony's hoofbeats struck sharp and crisp against the canyon walls and gradually died.

Len Gann stood in his tracks and curled a cigarette. "Here am I with another man's steamin' horse and mebbe it's stolen. I can't prove a blamed thing about myself. If these jaspers are tough. . . ." His lips curled back on a widening grin and blue glance brightened with a reckless, anticipatory gleam. A line of riders ran violently out of the upper trees and came headlong into the canyon. Len Gann was instantly seen. A single shot burst thunderously between the rock walls and over it rang a brazen, deep-chested yell.

"Watch him sharp!"

Len Gann knew better than to make the mistake of precipitate movement. He remained quite still, cigarette drooping from his lips, almost indolent. The line of riders swung into a semicircle and guns veered against him. His roving glance counted an even dozen men, all of whom had a slantwise, sullenly hostile look. Somehow they seemed like members of a single tribe, but he had little time to consider. The advancing party halted out of the ranks rode a slender, whiplike man; he had cat eyes, green and cold as the heart of an ice chunk and when the full weight of his scrutiny fell on Len Gann it had a dead, unrevealing flatness that was at once merciless and unwavering.

"You're no Strawn," said he in a still, sing-song voice. "How'd you get mixed up in this—right in our path with Pete's Strawn's pony?"

"A forced swap," drawled Len Gann. "He seemed in a hurry and I was of no mind to halt him."

"Which way did he go?"

Len Gann turned a little and indicated a narrow fissure leading off the canyon floor to a higher area. "Yonder."

The man raised one hand in half a gesture. Instantly four of the group sprang to action, galloped for the fissure and started upward. The leader gestured again and another trio raced straight down the canyon. But before either party had quite got away, there sounded from the lower depths of the hills a sudden rising of gunfire. The echoes came rolling back, settled and died into a complete silence. Immediately the dispatched men wheeled and started to return. The leader of the cavalcade watched Len Gann with an unchanging face. "You're a pretty bald liar. Don't suppose I'd be tarryin' here if I didn't have other scouts circlin' to catch Pete Strawn, do you?"

Len Gann shook his head, the pleasantry leaving his features. Pete Strawn had forecast his own fate pretty accurately. The boy was dead now. "Hell on gettin' what you start after, ain't yuh?" he countered.

"If you knew anything about this country you'd never

have meddled between a Strawn and a LeStang. You're in trouble.

"For helpin' a man?" asked Len Gann.

"Nope. For buckin' the LeStangs."

"I'll make up my own mind about that," retorted Gann.

"Hate to disappoint you," was the leader's emotionless answer. "But we'll make it up for you."

Gann was on the point of speaking again when three other men came up the canyon at a steady rack. Approaching, one of them called out, "That chore's done, Nick."

The leader nodded briefly and pointed a finger at Gann. "Mount and ride with us. And I'll have your gun."

"Never question a better hand than mine," muttered Len Gann and lifted his revolver butt first to the now identified Nick LeStang.

"Wouldn't pay you to," said the latter.

"But," added Len Gann, "I always count on the next deal."

"Too bad. In this game the cards are all stacked."

"Ain't it hell?" drawled Gann and got aboard his horse. Silently the cavalcade enveloped him and moved back up the canyon, entering a dim trail between the densely pines. There was no talk among the men and this very muteness began to oppress Len Gann. They rode with a grim certainty of their power, as unmoved by the recent kill as if it were but a casual chore. With a leisure at hand he studied his captors more closely and liked them the less. All the faces around him were shad-sided, swarthy, without the ruddiness he expected of a well-living man. Lips were thin and for the most part bloodless; and between hair line and eyebrow was a uniformly narrow forehead. It was a coldhearted clan, moving with a kind of machinelike unimagination. And

Nick LeStang, he judged, was the ruler.

In silence they passed through the pines, down a circling road and abruptly into a town whose two buildings rows were backed up against the sides of a deep ravine. A small, slanting bar of sun struck vagrantly across the house tops, but otherwise the crowding slopes and massed timber made this low-lying habitation darkly dismal. Street dust rose in dense balls as they passed along, and a few idle citizens retreated indoors. Then Nick LeStang brought up in front of a house and said briefly: "Down and inside." Len Gann obeyed, passing through a door. A giant of a man appeared from some other recess of the place and stood passively surveying his visitors. Nick LeStang spoke again. "Lock him up, Jud. And keep him locked till I tell you otherwise."

"What's the nature of the crime?" interrupted Len Gann.

"Anything or nothing," replied Nick LeStang. "But mostly because it's my pleasure to have you put away. If I read you right, brother, you're a trouble maker. I'm going to cut your claws. Take him away, Jud."

The giant Jud pointed at a stairway. Len Gann, two sharp creases running the full length of his brow, climbed up, entered a cell and heard the iron door slam behind him. That metal echo spun him around in his tracks, to confront not only the jailer but Nick LeStang, who had followed and now lounged outside the bars. LeStang's cold, calm face was more alert than usual; he seemed to be probing Gann, weighing the inner merit of this stranger. "I told you," he murmured, "the cards were stacked."

"Yeah?" grunted Len Gann. "Well, I've been known to play in crooked games with some success."

"Maybe you're just the average rider battin' through the country," reflected Nick LeStang, "and maybe you're somethin' more. Others have tried to spy this scope of territory with no due success. None of them ever got away. I don't know your business yet, but I will."

"I'll clarify one item for you," said Len Gann. "I'm no friend of yours."

LeStang's cat-green eyes expanded and for one slight moment a flicker of inner feeling came through the dead flat windows. "I guessed right. You're a hell hound for action. Doubtless you're proud of your vinegar. But it's no go now, mister. You never bucked this kind of a deal before. I've about decided to sink you. Come on, Jud."

Len Gann rested against the barred door and watched them vanish down the stairs.

II

KATHERINE LeSTANG

"WELL," said he to the empty hall, "I got my wish. I found what was over the hill."

He turned and began to tramp the floor. It eased him, furnished an outlet for the rapidly accumulating temper. If Len Gann hated anything more profoundly than false imprisonment it was the still greater outrage of a cold killing; and both of these things had occurred within the space of the last hour. What lay behind the death of Pete Strawn he didn't, of course, know. But the mode of the man's death was plain enough. Moreover, the utter, conscienceless calm of Nick LeStang's purpose increasingly oppressed Len Gann. That green-eyed individual had no nerves. "Cool as a cucumber," reflected Len Gann. "Never gives a man a break if he can help it. He'd think no more of puttin' me out of the way, if it fitted his purpose, than he'd think of kickin' a dog in the ribs."

His reflections were interrupted by the reverberation of a fast-running horse in the street below. Going to a front window opening directly from the cell to the street —the hallway was on the back side of the floor—Gann looked through the bars and into the heart of the town. His first observation was of the number of times that Le Stang name appeared painted on the various stores within view. There was a "LeStang Gen'l Store," a Mountain Tavern, A. LeStang, Prop." and "Jim LeStang's Livery and Feed Barn." More citizens were venturing abroad than when the cavalcade had brought him into town, and in front of the Mountain Tavern a considerable number of horses were racked. LeStangs, judged Len Gann, were strong for patronizing their relations. At this precise moment a woman dressed in a buckskin riding skirt and boots swung off by the Tavern and paused a moment. Her head turned and Len Gann briefly saw dark, alert features beneath the sweeping brim of a Stetson. She lifted an arm, beckoning; and in response to the summons, a hump-shouldered creature with a chest like a barrel crossed the dust and stood patiently opposite her. She said something to the man and he walked at a livelier pace into the Mountain Tavern, reappearing a little later with Nick LeStang. Len Gann's idling eyes focused. LeStang and the girl talked, head to head, and there was a considerable display of force on her part which the man met stolidly. In the end, both of them left the tavern porch and crossed the street; and Len Gann had turned to face the hallway when they came up the stairs and down to the cell, followed by the giant, Jud.

"Open it up, Jud," said the woman, crisp and arbitrary.

She was no more than twenty-five, with the faint mark of kinship to Nick LeStang apparent. But whereas the man was coldly unmoving, this girl seemed tremendously alive, impatient. Jet hair curled beneath the edges of the Stetson and her eyes were a clear, restless gray. Even in the man-like attire she was fully woman, with a supple swell to shoulder and breast and a tint of fresh color in her dark cheeks. Only in her glance, which clung to Len Gann steadily, did she display a certain family pride.

"I'm Katherine LeStang," said she. "Who are you?"

"Len Gamm, from the Big Cloud country, just ridin' along."

"My people," said she, "suspect you."

"From my short observation," drawled Len, "I'd say they was a suspectin' race."

"And set in their ways?" urged the girl, the full red lips curving at the corners.

"Well, I'm here—and that's your answer."

She came to a decision, lifted her head suddenly. "Let him out, Jud."

But Nick LeStang broke in with a cold protest. "Let's get together on this, Kathy. I do one thing and you change it. Let me run this affair."

"Open up, Jud," repeated the girl. "Look here, Nick, we've got no right to manhandle folks like this. Here's a rider comin' along, and you haze him. I've told you to be more civilized."

The door was unlocked and opened by the giant Jud. Len Gann walked through, a faint smile covering fast-moving thoughts. He was no hand to believe in Santa Claus and this situation had a funny look about it. But at the girl's silent command, he moved down the stairs and halted in a jail office half full of those same riders who had escorted him through the canyon. All were silent, standing against the walls of the room. Nick Le Stang asked the girl a sharper question. "Well, what now?"

"He's free as the air," said the girl. "Let him alone, you hear me?"

"Not so sure," replied Nick LeStang, slow and cautious.

The girl turned on him, color staining her temples. "I have something to say in this family, Nick. There's been enough things done behind my back, but this is not going to be one of them. Don't let your ambition crowd you too far."

"Maybe he's an average rider—maybe he's somethin' else," retorted LeStang.

"Never mind. He's free to do what he pleases."

She was holding Nick LeStang's glance and fighting it, chin lifted. Nothing was said for a long interval. The men along the walls kept perfectly still. Len Gann, reading the affair through detached eyes, thought the girl was making a lone play, not only against LeStang but all the others. And it surprised him when LeStang gave in with an abrupt nod. "You're the doctor—this time. Gann, you can ride. But it had better be out of here."

"I'll appreciate my gun," said Len Gann.

LeStang walked to a corner desk and picked up Len Gann's belt, passing it over without in the least showing his feelings. Gann buckled the belt about him, and through long established habit, lifted the gun and threw open the cylinder. It had always been his practice to carry five cartridges in the weapon, hammer resting on an empty space. But there were six cartridges instead of five in the gun now—and the sixth had been fired. Looking up, he found LeStang's eyes narrowed to an infinitely cold watchfulness.

214

"Who's been monkeyin' with my hardware?" demanded Gann.

"That empty shell," snapped LeStang, "contained the slug that killed Pete Strawn. You shot him, Gann. Any remarks?"

"So I'm framed, huh?" muttered Len Gann. "I might have figured something like this."

"Framed?" echoed Nick LeStang, a faint note of malevolence in his words. "Now I wouldn't say that. Ten men witnessed the fact of that fired shell in your gun when we inspected it."

"Never overlook a bet, do you?" countered Len Gann, blood turning hot in his veins. "But if you've got this country tied up in a sack, why bother to shift a cold killin' on somebody else."

"To keep you humble, mister," droned Nick LeStang, "We've got the goods on you. That's for you to consider when you ride free. Be humble—or a LeStang jury will hang you higher's a kite."

"Would you take time to go through that unnecessary formality?" grunted Len Gann, forcing back the imminent explosion. It would not pay, he knew, to show his fighting disposition now. Katherine LeStang had gone to bat for him, made an issue of her authority, and he couldn't jeopardize her slim victory. She had taken a backward step, dividing a deeply puzzled glance between himself and LeStang. Holstering his gun, he turned out of the jail office and saw his horse—the dead Pete Strawn's horse—being led into a stable at the end of town. That way he turned.

"The play is strictly up to me," he muttered. "I can deliver my message to the Strawns and put this country a long ways behind, or I can take the stack of chips this LeStang gave me and play 'em out." But even as he stated the proposition he knew what the answer was. By no stretch of the imagination could he see himself running off with a murder darkening his name. That was impossible. Not much less impossible, perhaps, than electing to buck the solid ranks of the LeStang clan, but nevertheless beyond an instant's consideration. What he had to do now was to find where the Strawns holed up. So thinking, he walked into the stable and into another unexpected situation. His horse was standing there, held by the hump-shouldered, grotesquely enormous-bodied man he had seen answering Katherine LeStang's beck; obviously, he was waiting for Gann.

"Yore horse?" said the fellow, and winked a heavy lid.

"Mine," replied Gann, closely watching. The man was a little shy of reasoning powers. A clouded brain showed through small eyes. Lumpish, physically powerful, there lay over him a kind of dumb sadness as if he realized, in a dark intuitive way, his own lack. A fetch-and-carry creature, good only to obey exact instructions. He made a mysterious business of scowling about the empty stable and came nearer Gann.

"Ride out the south end of town. . . . take the first trail to yore right."

"Whose orders?" demanded Gann.

The creature's face became wreathed in a deep network of lines. Clearly he struggled to meet an unforeseen question, and presently gave up. His pendulous lips closed on a pout. "I wasn't told to tell."

"Was it Nick LeStang?" pressed Len Gann.

"I take no orders from Nick," said the creature, suddenly glowering.

Len Gann made up his mind on the turn of a thought, mounted and rode from the stable. The shopkeepers had again retreated to the depths of the buildings, but as he passed between the jail and the tavern, a row of silent, staring figures stood to either side and watched him with an unblinking taciturnity. The girl was gone. Nick LeStang remained by the jail door, wrapped in an aloof calm that held a more potent threat than any number of words. Here was an unyielding deadliness that Gann knew he had to guard against. Going by, he came to the southern edge of town and turned into the first righthand trail leading up into the hills. The dust of a recent traveler lay over it, and much higher on the grade he turned to see some evidence that he was to be tracked. Pressing forward into the reaching pines, Gann considered these signals.

"I'd be dumb to consider that they'll let me alone. Better get into deeper shelter and start huntin' for the Strawns."

There was somebody preceding him, as evidenced by the fresh-risen dust. The slope grew steeper, leveled off to a parklike area. Right here the dust died and the trail forked. Alert and wary, Len Gann halted to consider the margin of the encircling pines. A woodpecker sent out its sharp drumroll; and Katherine LeStang moved into view from the left. She cantered across the meadow, sure and easy in the saddle. She held her hat in one hand and even under the shady light the jet hair shone against the white surface of her temples. Reining in, she measured Len Gann coolly.

"You're a cagy animal," was her final decision. "You knew somebody was near."

"That was a-b-c," replied Len. "You sent the message for me to ride this way?"

"I did. Want to talk to you. Come on. You're probably being trailed."

Without answer he accepted her lead. She crossed the meadow but swerved away from the beaten pathway and went along a dimmer, lesser-used route. For a long time they rode single file, the girl to the fore. Laconically she threw a question over her sturdy shoulders. "Not in with the Strawns, are you?"

"Wasn't, but my ticket seems to read that way now."

"Keep an open mind on the subject for a little while longer," urged the girl. "Who killed Pete Strawn?"

"I didn't."

"I know it," was her rather impatient answer. "Give me credit for some sense. But who did? Which one of my crowd?"

"It happened outside of my sight. But I heard it."

"Where was Nick?"

"Talkin' to me at the time. Wasn't his shot."

A small silence followed. The trail bent, dipped, struggled up to another of the frequent clear spaces. Katherine LeStang halted and let Len Gann draw abreast of her. She folded her hands on the horn. "No, but it was his order. I know him."

"I don't get this," said Len Gann, eyes narrowing. "Considerin' you and him are of the same family, you're spillin' a lot to a stranger."

"I battled Nick and got you out of jail, didn't I?"

"My thanks for that."

"Well, then," said Katherine LeStang, a deeper color on her cheeks, "use your head. You've got one or I'd never risked the showdown with Nick."

"You're playin' your own hand and you want help?"

"That's right," said she. "But, look here. It wasn't altogether because I needed help. The LeStangs have pulled enough crooked deals and I couldn't see this happen—to you."

"Make up your mind about a man mighty quick, don't you?" murmured Len Gann.

The girl raised her chin. It was, he discovered, her

manner of coming to the point. "I made up my mind about you mighty quick, Len."

He reached for his cigarette papers, built a smoke, lit it, blew a wreath to the branch-laced ceiling of this glade. "Odd," he reflected. "Here's a country just lousy with LeStangs and yet you pick on me. Well, what's up?"

She pointed to the north. "That way five miles is the Strawn country. Go tell those people I had no part in the killing of Pete. Knew nothing about it and would never have agreed to it."

"I'm to be the bearer of friendly offerin's?"

He saw temper rise in her. It put a live glow in her eyes, set her lips stubbornly, and made her the more striking. "Friendship with the Strawns? Never! That family and mine have fought each other for two generations. But I believe in fighting fair. There's no blood on my hands and I want them to know it. I don't ask for friendship. I do ask for peace. This has gone on long enough."

"Yeah, and what would brother Nick say to that?"

He observed a let-down of her spirit. It was as though cold water had been poured over her body. "You know the answer to that as well as I do," said she, slowly. "That's why I sided in with you at the jail. Well?"

"I'll deliver the message," said Len Gann.

"Then what?"

A quiet grin came to his face, creating crowfoot wrinkles about the steady eyes. "Better do one chore before figurin on another. Probably won't run, though, even if I ought to."

"I didn't think you'd run," said she, in a tone that was suddenly hopeful. "Keep to the small trails and never, under any circumstances, let a LeStang catch you off guard. You can trust none of my people except Modoc

Hutchins—the one who delivered my message to you."

Having said that she lifted the reins of her horse and moved on. Len Gann caught her with another question. "You're gamblin' on me?"

She turned her head, the darkly alert features fixed enigmatically. "Yes—a gamble. And the last left me." Then the trees absorbed her.

Len Gann wheeled into the brush. A few rods onward he swung to scan his back trail—and saw the lowering form of the dumb Modoc Hutchins slipping quietly across the glade on foot, dogtrotting after Katherine LeStang. What Gann did not see as he pushed ahead and entered a slight alleyway was the prone figure of still another lurking man sheltered behind a deadfall adjacent the glade. After Gann had quite disappeared, this one rose and retreated to a hidden horse; mounting, he followed Gann by a parallel trail; and from time to time he maneuvered himself into certain vistas down which he checked Gann's progress.

Meanwhile Len Gann slipped from one fissure between the trees to another, always avoiding any common, traveled opening. By degrees he rose with the incline of the ridge and fell down the other side. He crossed a creek, went circuitously around a darkling glen in which the sound of charging waters rose tempestuously, and reached a well-worn corduroy road. This led definitely somewhere. Wood smoke lay in the slight wind and he knew that he was approaching the Strawn stronghold.

"Damned dangerous business—me ridin' on an armed camp with a horse they'll recognize instant. I'm not makin' up my mind very fast as to what next."

But if he meant to battle the whole situation to a conclusion, he was to be delayed. He had kept edging along the flank of the corduroy road. Now, without much warning, the trees quit him and he faced a rambling log house squatting at the throat of a canyon. Outhouses and corrals—all weather beaten and stoutly built—circled the main quarters. A lone man sat on a stump nearby with a rifle beside him. A brindle dog rose from the dust, poked its snout into the vagrant wind and began to growl. Instantly the man reached for his gun, rising to gaunt height. Len Gann rode calmly into view, closed the distance.

As he anticipated, the fellow's reaction was one of instant and hearty suspicion. "Stand there!" he called out. "Where'd you git that hawss?"

"You a Strawn?"

"I am—and I don't know you. It's the hawss I'm askin' about."

"The man that rode it asked me to bring a message back."

"Where's he?"

"Dead."

The questioner's face showed no surprise, but it began to settle and grow barren of feeling. His head dropped in a half nod as if the news were not unexpected; and without moving he sent out a long call that rang through the still afternoon air with a reverberating clarity. It was a summons instantly obeyed. Men ran out of the house and from the sheds; they galloped from the wings of the surrounding pines. Hands folded on his saddle horn, Len Gann watched them assemble around him. All were solid, rugged people, heavy of bone, straight-glanced and stamped with plain honesty. Without stopping to question his impulses, Len Gann decided that he liked the Strawns. Presently the rough circle opened to let through one who somehow seemed representative of the tribe to the last degree. This one, quite tall and symmetrical, was hardly thirty, but he possessed a pair of penetrating eyes that dug into Len Gann sharply and without malice. The guard made a brief explanation.

"Phil, this fellow says Pete's dead."

Len Gann noticed the general tightening of lips and the instant darkening of eyes. But again it seemed that the news was half prepared for. The man called Phil, apparently the mouthpiece for his people, spoke to Gann with a crisp directness. "Say what you come to say."

"I rammed into the kid's gun when I came around the bend of a canyon," explained Len Gann. "We swapped horses. He was pretty badly tuckered. LeStangs were on top of him. He considered he was done for and he asked me to find you people and say this: that he had done the chore he set out to do and was not sorry to die. He pulled out in a hurry. The LeStangs caught him somewhere outside my sight about five minutes later. I heard the shot and I heard the LeStangs later say they'd dropped him. That's all."

"It's enough, by God," said one of the Strawns, hard and bitter. Silence gripped the party and lasted a long interval that was at last broken by Phil Strawn.

"Go on, mister. There's more. How'd you get away from the LeStangs? I know they took you because it'd be the way they do things."

"For a fact," agreed Len Gann. "Nick LeStang threw me in jail. Katherine LeStang used her influence to get me out. Ridin' up the hill trail she met me, told me to come here. So I'm bearin' another message. It's her desire that while she has no friendship toward you, she wants it understood that it was none of her planning that killed Pete Strawn. She knew nothing about it and she wants peace. There's the story, gentlemen."

At mention of the girl's name it was noticeable that

Phil Strawn's attention became more fully centered. After Gann finished, another pervading quiet held the group and there was a general turning of eyes toward the Strawn leader. Finally he broke the silence. "What's your name and where from?"

"Len Gann, out of White Cloud country and no business in particular."

"Well, Len," said Phil Strawn, "I'm takin' you at your word. That goes for the rest of us. Come over to the house—"

He broke off and faced the trees. Deep down the corduroy road rose the surging rush of hoofs. Strawn ripped out a savage order. "Back to shelter! Make a run for it!" And in response those on foot wheeled and flung themselves toward the house. The four or five mounted Strawns, who had come riding from the trees a little before, started to shift as well, but Len Gann, on the alert, challenged them bluntly.

"Stick fast, you! We'll cover the boys till they get settled! Spread a little—back away a little—rake the mouth of that road!"

The mounted Strawns caught the idea and swung to obey. Len Gann lifted his revolver, poised it and waited. Venturing a fugitive look behind, he saw the dismounted men halfway to cover, and then the fresher, higher gush of sound from the road claimed his grim attention. There was, a few rods beyond the mouth of the road, an obscuring bend. Of a sudden the threatening thunder of pony feet turned into a two-abreast cavalcade streaming around the bend. There were a dozen men, all riding low and fast; and as Gann plugged a checking shot down the roadway he recognized the slim, black and infinitely cold cheeks of Nick LeStang staring at him. Immediately all the other guns abreast of Gann blazed out, erupting volcanically

223

into the close, still air. The man beside Nick LeStang flung up his arms protectively as his horse stumbled and fell, end over end, pitching the rider far out. Nick LeStang yelled a throaty command and swerved, leading the attacking line off the road and into the brush. Gann wheeled instantly and spurred toward the house, mounted Strawns filing after him. Then the LeStang party cleared the brush, also aiming for the house.

Thus, for a brief, flashing space of time the two riding factions strained, parallel to each other and probably sixty yards apart. Gann, whipping his lead headlong at the chief LeStang, saw the whole line open up on him and felt a touch of blasted air at his cheeks. Gun reports rolled and rocketed furiously across the open, smashed into the canyon wall and came booming back. Eddies of powder smoke lifted, bomblike, above the moving lines. Nick LeStang yelled again and the column swerved away from the house, to cut a circle about it. Abruptly here was a concerted crash of rifle firing from the Strawn's who had gained shelter. Another LeStang horse went down, ripping up a long lane of dust. Gann saw the rider strike on his back, bounce and rise on the run. But the man had gone no more than ten feet when he seemed to be plucked on the arm by a restraining hand. He came around, faltered, staggered and fell motionless in the dust.

Meanwhile, Gann led his own little detachment behind the Strawn quarters to avoid masking the fire of those stationed at the sheds. When he reached the far side of all this, the LeStang faction, never faltering, had swept away up the canyon. A few desultory shots came back; Strawn rifles banged out a final volley and the end man of the disappearing group slid to the earth, horse pounding away from him. Then the attackers turned a shoulder of the canyon and were gone. The fight was over. Gann cantered back to the Strawn yard, sudden sweat creeping below his hat brim.

III

A RESCUE AND A TRAP

HE MET Phil Strawn walking back from a shed, a thin streak of smoke eddying out of the rifle on his arm. There was a deep anger in the man and a still roused battle spirit. But all he said was: "They're gone."

"A damn fool play," grunted Len Gann. "The caper of a wild man. All he's got for his little raid is three dead horses and two dead men."

"There's more to it than that," said Phil Strawn. "It's his way of declarin' open war. He'd done damage to us, too, if you hadn't been quick enough to stage a play of your own. I'll thank you for that, Gann. You've got a head."

"That outfit stronger than you numerically?"

The Strawn chief nodded. "If all the LeStangs in the country collected and busted us, we wouldn't last a week. But they ain't all actively hostile. Its only about a dozen or fifteen of the wild bloods under Nick that want to see us go. Even so, we're some outnumbered. Our bunch musters only about ten hands. We were more, but it's been a bloody thirty years—and the Strawns have lost the most."

"What's the beginning of this?" questioned Gann.

"Same old story," said Phil Strawn. "My grandfather and Nick LeStang's grandfather collided over land.

225

The feud's kept on since then. Last two years I have sort of held a tight rein on my crowd and there's been a degree of peace. Pete ruined all that. He was the hothead of our family. Always broodin'. So he went out and dry-gulched the LeStang that had killed his dad sime time back. Now Pete's gone and the war's alive once more. Damn such a situation. There'll be no more serious work done in these hills until a lot of blood is spilled."

"Strawn blood mostly," put in another of the group now surrounding Gann. It seemed to mirror a general feeling of depression, for a weary quiet came to the yard. Gann, sizing up the circle, could see that this outfit had been so long on the defensive that there had arisen a common attitude of almost grim hopelessness. These men expected to be wiped out, even though they were too stubborn to retreat. It was a bad state of mind.

"Two sides can play at this Indian stuff, gentlemen," said he. "If you want to win this war you can. Maybe it sounds like the advice of a fool, but I've had my look around here and I've also witnessed my share of scraps."

"Move out against 'em?" countered Phil Strawn.

"Surround their place and bust 'em to flinders."

"No," said Phil Strawn so emphatically that even his own men looked oddly at him; and one undertook to explain the meaning of that force to Gann.

"We're no hands to skulk, stranger. But even if we was, there's a woman yonder that Phil wouldn't never care to aim his gun towards." Then the man added a doubtful phrase. "Sometimes, I think we're too squeamish."

Phil Strawn seemed to consider his authority challenged. "As long as I ride herd over you fellows, I'll never do it. I've done my part to let this feud die. So has Katherine LeStang. Thunderation, she and me went to the same little school over there. That was durin' one of the peaceful spells. I like her. If she had her way there would never be any more trouble. But it's that confounded cousin of hers. He's moved in on the ranch her dad passed to her. He's runnin' it. He's got the hotheads all corralled there. She can't do a thing. Can't change the sentiment except among the more sober folks of that clan, and they're afraid to back her up. Nick's the black devil of the lot."

Len Gann rolled a cigarette deliberately, turning the explanation over in his mind. He lit his smoke, blew a studious wreath to the sky and asked: "Well, you intend to stand and take it?"

"I don't see my way clear," grumbled Phil Strawn.

Gann smiled faintly. "Is it peace that holds you back the most—or the girl?"

That struck home. A slight flush invaded Phil Strawn's cheeks and he turned a steel-straight glance at Gann. "I'm thankin' you for your help, but you're pryin' pretty deep for a stranger."

"Well," put in another Strawn, "ain't it a fair question, Phil? We're all in this jackpot, not you alone."

"I'll send a bullet against her house. . . ."

A guard posted beyond a shed called back. "Come over here. Something funny."

That roused the group to alertness again. Len Gann and Phil led the way around the shed. The guard pointed toward the tree line. "Fellow yonder behind a stump tryin' to attract our attention."

Gann, closely watching, saw a hat bob up and down back of the stump. A little later a red bandanna waved vigorously; and following that signal a man rose to plain view with his hands elevated. "Modoc Hutchins," grunted Gann. "And he must want somethin' pretty bad to venture here."

"Pay no heed to the crazy loon," said the Strawn guard. "Bats in his belfry. If he don't vamoose in a minute I'll spray some dust in his face."

"Now hold on," adjured Len Gann, eyes narrowing at the grotesque body of the LeStang henchman. The latter waved both arms, beckoned, made a circling gesture that ended southward in the direction of the LeStang range. Gann said: "He ain't crazy enough not to know what he wants. I'm goin' over there." And he stepped forward.

"Be careful, this may be a swell trap," said the guard.

"Keep me covered," replied Gann and went on. Half across the clearing he saw Modoc Hutchins draw back into the trees. This caused Gann to scrutinize the timber line more watchfully. But seeing nothing, and all the while recalling that the daft fellow was Katherine LeStang's bound servant, he pressed on and entered the trees. Modoc Hutchins faced him with a dull registering of alarm in his small eyes.

"You got to come," said he, without preliminary explanation.

"What's up?"

"She's bein' held in the house by Nick," moaned Modoc Hutchins. "They won't lemme go near her. Nick told me to git. You got to come."

"When did this happen?" asked Len Gann.

"Minute she got home from seein' you. Nick was a-waitin' for her. Forcibly threw her in the house. She's all the same as tied up, I'm tellin' you! They took my gun away from me and kicked me out! I'd like to kill somebody! You got to come!"

"Why me?" countered Gann, trying to read behind the agitated countenance.

"She likes you," said Hutchins, as if that answered everything.

"Stand fast," directed Gann and returned to the Strawn crowd. "A new move. This Nick's got the girl prisoner for some reason of his own."

"What difference does it make if one LeStang hurts another?" grunted the Strawn guard. "Don't go believin' Modoc Hutchins."

But Phil Strawn cut in, angrily. "Modoc wouldn't lie about that girl. He'd cut off his arm for her. By God, I've a notion to crawl up there alone tonight! This business is gettin' past my endurance!"

"If you're runnin' this spread," was the half-surly reply of the dissenting Strawn, "you better stick to it and not go helpin' LeStangs."

"Correct," added Gann, and watched how Phil Strawn's face settled. The man was caught up in a struggle between warring emotions. As before, Gann felt the existence of some deeper feelings in the man for Katherine LeStang, some old emotion that the feud could not kill. Whether or not the feeling was shared by her, Gann had no means of knowing. The fact that she had sent him to tell the Strawns of her regret over the killing might indeed indicate such a reaction; but at the best it was a blind guess in a blind game. However, Gann was swayed by a sudden sympathy for these two characters who so futilely tried to rise above the blood lust of their clans, and he made a decision. "You're head of this young army and you've got to stick. Me, I'm a lone rider. I think I'll make a pasear with Hutchins. It'll be dark pretty soon and I might be able to learn a little something."

There was an instant flare of gratitude visible in Phil Strawn's glance. "You're all there, Gann. I'll back you up any manner you say."

"Stand tight and listen for my yell," drawled Len. "Can't do nothin' around that bunch of cagey lead-throwers," said one of the other Strawns. "They'll trap you and pull your fingernails one by each. It's a fool idea."

"Paradise is full of fellows who had fool ideas," countered Len Gann, and went for his horse. Mounting, he rode back through the group. "I'll need a rifle." When that was handed him, he added, "And the solemn prayers of all. So long till you see me." Spurring across the meadow, he joined the waiting Hutchins who had swung to the saddle. The latter led silently away into the deeper green of the forest. The sun was beyond the western hills when they left the Strawn meadow; half an hour later it was a gray, dreaming dusk with every faint snap of underbrush echoing through the utterly still air. Modoc Hutchins' dim mind comprehended little enough, but his craftiness was like that of a followed animal. Never for an instant did he follow a straight trail. He slid from thicket to thicket, wound circuitously from glen to glen, doubled back, halted, moved on again. His eyes were forever restless and he kept sidling his ears against the vagrant breeze. Only once did Len Gann break the spell, and that was to satisfy a rising curiosity. "This Nick ain't the girl's brother?"

"A kinda half cousin," grunted Modoc. "She's got no close kin among them black brutes. They're a-crowdin' her out o' her own ranch. Hush now. Echoes carry a long ways down these canyons."

Night fell, deeply black and without a moon. Wind straightened, washing through the trees. And it must have been a full three hours after they had left the Strawn place when the wary half-wit paused in a break of the timber and pointed. There was a sweeping, downward roll of land. At the foot of this open stretch sat the vague bulk of a house from which many lanes of crystal light emerged. Sitting forward in the saddle, Len Gann watched. Occasionally a figure moved across these lights and after a full quarter-hour he detected some kind of periodic patrol of the premises. Horses stood by the front porch. Hutchins murmured a warning and moved back into the timber, beginning an interminable roundabout course that ended much later on an opposite ridge. From here Len Gann observed the back side of the ranch. Hutchins touched his sleeve and whispered. "Second-story window. Her room." Then the pressure of the half-wit's arm increased. "Right below—couple hundred yards—near the shadder of those twin pines—look sharp."

The man's eyesight was uncanny. It was a long interval before Len Gann dissected the general shadows about the two tree trunks and discovered the crouching body of a man there. Night guard. The half-wit whispered again. "Wait. More of 'em. I'll find out where they stand." And the man dismounted and slid soundlessly away.

Time dragged, the pressure of the dark increased. Night chill cut through Len Gann's coat and congealed his prairie blood. Once the sentry below stirred and turned about the trees. Much later a door of the house opened and a figure came out, but soon retreated. The inaction began to play on Len Gann's nerves. Keeping a steady observation on the yard, he at last saw the door open again and four men pass through. They separated. One of them advanced toward the twin trees and he presently heard a muffled conversation down there. Then one of the pair went back to the house. Guards being changed. Only by the faintest crush of leaf mold underfoot did he know of Modoc Hutchins' return.

"Got 'em placed," whispered the half-wit. "Four-five boys out nighthawkin'. Nick's hell for protection after dark. The boy yonder is the only one between us and the house. We can slide around."

"No," said Len Gann. "It leaves him between us and the horses. We'll get him. That's our first chore. I'll try it."

But the half-wit's arm restrained him. "If you want him, I'll do it. I'll make no noise."

"Go ahead," approved Len. "Here's my gun. Use the butt of it."

Accepting the gun, Modoc Hutchins disappeared again. In the ensuing minutes, and they passed with a leaden slowness, some of the house lights died to leave at last only a single beacon shining from the lower floor and the one still glimmering out of the girl's room. A sense of impending trouble oppressed Len Gann and with it arrived a feeling of tremendous impatience. The sentry by the twin trees made a turning move and halted. He called out crisply, "Who's that?" It was his only challenge. The shapeless bulk of Modoc Hutchins rose from the dark. A dull impact echoed up and then the shadow of the guard and that of the half-wit sank away. Ripping his riata from its thong, Gann ran forward.

Modoc rose, breathing hard. "Got him. What next?"

Lenn Gann took his gun from the half-wit's fist, at the same time passing over the lariat. "Tie the brute. Get his hardware. Sit tight and wait for me."

"I'd ought to go yonder with yuh," whispered Modoc. "I know the way best."

"Stay and watch," insisted Gann.

"You ain't got long," the half-wit warned. "Nick makes his rounds between ten and eleven."

Len Gann went down from the pines. The last

232

fringes of brush gave way to the clearing and this he ventured upon for about fifty yards, or about half the distance to the house. At this point he halted and studied the possibilities. He faced one end of the house. To the right was the rear side of it and a back porch whose roof led to the window of the girl's room. To the left was the larger main porch, across which ran the only beam of light leaving the lower part of the place. There were more windows facing him but all were dark; or rather the shades were drawn, for he saw the thin slits of yellow glow seeping around the corners. A few horses still stood in front of the house; and a click of the door latch caused Gann to drop full to his belly. A man sauntered out, left the porch and came around the yard. He had a cigarette in his mouth and as he passed, Len Gann caught a dim outline of the sharp LeStang features from the cigarette's sudden livid glow. A little later he was lost in the farther darkness.

Len Gann considered this thoughtfully. "Quick or not at all. These hounds are restless. As long as the girl's light burns I can't climb without making a target of myself. After it does go out I can do the climbin' stunt, but supposin' one of the menfolk has decided to use it for his room?"

But time ran fast. So, swiftly deciding between a careful game and a risky one, he rose, ran against the house wall and crept along it as far as the porch. Here he crawled to the boards and went softly in the direction of the door. Beside that door was a window, shade drawn but sash up. And inside was the murmur of idle talk. He understood it, but after a few taut moments heard nothing of importance. Going on, he dropped off the other end of the porch and passed to the rear. Immediately he discovered the girl's light to be out. And this decided his next maneuver.

A post of the back porch was right beside him. Moving to it, he paused again for an intent study of the surrounding shadows. Somewhere about him men lay in covert watch, and somewhere as well the exploring LeStang was on the loose. All this was part of the risk, and waiting wouldn't diminish it. Reaching high, he wrapped his arms about the post, hauled himself as far as the porch eaves, hooked his elbows over and by main strength gained the shingled top. Necessarily he had made some noise, but nothing happened and he advanced. Two windows broke the upper wall. Passing by the first, he laid himself underneath the sill of the second. A warm odor of coal oil fumes came faintly out and he heard the still fainter breathing of somebody within. At this point he realized how swiftly the turn of a word might plunge him deep into disaster; but even as he thought about this he lifted himself to the opening and tapped on the sill.

The breathing seemed to stop. There was the move of a body. Katherine LeStang's voice returned through the absolute black of the room, softly questioning. "Modoc?"

"Up on the ridge with the horses," whispered Len Gann. "Come on. We'll run for it."

She came to the window, a slim outline. "You never should have dared it!"

"No time to argue that now. Come on."

"Wait a minute. I'll—"

A door squeaked directly beneath the porch roof. Boots scraped across the boards and Nick LeStang's dead voice said: "Well, it's mighty funny. Somebody came across the front of this house no more than two minutes ago."

"Wasn't me, I'm tellin' yuh."

"All right. But somebody did. Now you stay right here and watch sharp. I wouldn't put it past Katherine to try to crawl through the window. I'm going to find out who's snoopin' around."

Lying flat and still, Len Gann heard the door close. One man went back and one remained. This latter fiddled around the porch and finally struck a match, the glow of it shuttering into the night for a brief second. After that, he moved off the boards and halted at some immediate point near the building corner. Len Gann knew then he would never be able to make his departure by the porch post; lifting himself with infinite caution, he slid into the girl's room.

She had heard the transaction below. Standing beside him, she whispered a swift warning. "If they find you, Len, you are dead!"

Gann's senses were all on the race. "Got to get out of here before your cousin makes his tour and finds one of his sentries conked. What's your door open on?"

"Hallway. It leads down the stairs to the front room where the men are."

"No way of turning off before we hit the main room? Where's the kitchen?"

"Yes," said Katherine LeStang. "You could do that. But you'd still have to cross a corner of the main room to reach the kitchen."

"Can you go down to the men without excitin' suspicion?"

"Yes. Why?"

"Do it, then. Go in front of me. Talk to the gang a minute while I get the hang of things. Count twenty-five to yourself—slow. Upset the lamp, and run for the kitchen door. I'll be there then."

"It isn't possible!"

"Got to be. Don't argue."

She still paused. But Gann heard Nick LeStang in the yard again. "Hank—did you come around to the front of the house a minute ago?"

An answer came from the hillside. "No."

"Bill—did you?".

No reply; Gann knew then that Bill was probably the one Modoc Hutchins had knocked out. It would only be a matter of moments before Nick LeStang would go look. Gann pushed the girl gently to the door and opened it for her. They passed through, slipped down a dark hall as far as the stairway. Light came out of the lower room along with the mutter of voices. As near as Len could judge from the sound of talk, there were three or four below. At the same time he located the kitchen door slightly to one side of the stairway's foot. This much determined, he motioned Katherine LeStang on. Her hand touched him and she took the steps slowly. As she reached the bottom one of the outfit beyond Gann's view, someone challenged her bluntly.

"Thought we told you to go to bed?"

She moved on, answering casually. "If you'd make less noise around here perhaps I could sleep."

"Better get back before Nick comes in."

Len Gann had counted ten methodically. Turning, he went into the girl's room and to the window. Out of the yard boomed an insistent call. "Bill, why in thunder don't you answer me?" Len Gann pushed his gun through the window and along the wall of the building to keep the roar of it from flooding back through the house. He had reached the count of seventeen when he fired; the encircled meadow erupted with the rocketing explosion and bedlam cut loose. A wild yelling ran from guard to guard along the hillside. Tiptoeing out of the room, Gann came to the stairs and went halfway

down. All those inside seemed to have rushed for the
yard. He heard them calling and the thump of their
boots on the boards. Then the light went out and he
threw himself to the foot of the stairs with great leaps.

Katherine LeStang collided with him at the kitchen
door, breathing hard. She started to speak, but he
kicked open the portal and shoved her ahead, keeping
a hand to her shoulder as she led around the tables
and chairs of this infinitely black cubicle and arrived
at another exit. It gave before her. Both passed into
the yard, to immediately flatten against the wall as a
man tore around from the back and went lunging away.
The confusion seemed most general out back; accordingly, Gann turned the opposite direction with the girl's
hand gripped in his own free fist. At the front porch
it seemed that the coast was comparatively clear. The
galloping LeStang's shadow was just then disappearing
behind the far side of the house.

"Keep up your nerve," cautioned Gann. "Everybody's
on the lope and we won't be spotted if we do the same.
I've lost those confounded twin pines. Head right for
'em. Let's go!"

There was no lack of courage in her. She threw herself beside him and as they cleared the house she
pulled him more nearly across the diameter of the
yard. This brought them closer to the turbulent eddy
of the LeStangs, all of whom seemed concentrating on
that area directly adjoining the rear of the porch. Nick's
maddened voice poured furiously over the heads of
his henchmen, one curse whipping into another.

"Back—one of you—back into the house!"

"Light's out!"

"By damn, I'll kill somebody for this trick! Some of
you to the house! Rest spread out! There's Strawn
smell around here!"

"Who's that crossin' the yard!"

The girl let out a half-choked murmur. "They see us!"

"Steady—we're almost out of this!"

She faltered and nearly fell. Gann's arm closed about her waist as they approached the brush and the now apparent outline of the twin pines. Suddenly Nick LeStang's raging command overtook them. "Stop in your tracks!" Gann thrust the girl in front of him as a volley of lead drove into the brush, smashed against the twin pines, ripped along the rising earth. The girl was badly spent. Reaching the solid face of the pines she sagged behind the protection of them while Gann paused to pick up Modoc Hutchins. He called softly and had no answer. Looking a little farther along the earth he saw the bound LeStang guard still silent, but of the half-wit there was no sign. Waiting was impossible, for Nick LeStang had scented his quarry and now came forward with all his men, guns smashing away the night's peace. Judging that Modoc had returned to the horses, Gann picked up the girl and fought his way over the stiffly rising slope. It was only a matter of fifty yards, but when he reached the trail he was winded. There was, moreover, another surprise in store for him. Only one horse remained.

"Modoc!"

The echo was lost in the strengthening fire. All the shots were low, yet gradually rising as Nick LeStang's crowd reached the brush and began beating through it. Gann called the half-wit's name again and swore to himself.

"We can't go without him!" said the girl.

"Got to," muttered Gann and pushed her to the saddle. Mounting behind, he dropped his spurs into the flesh of the pony and wheeled upgrade into the farther darkness. Behind him there seemed to be a sudden resistance. A rifle began spitting back at the thicker crash of the small arms. Gann, feeling more secure, halted to listen to that rifle. But as he did so it ceased answering; and within a few moments he caught the stumbling advance of a man on foot. Swinging his gun on the dark strip of the trail, he challenged abruptly: "Who's that?"

"Me—me!" panted Modoc Hutchins. "Was goin' to cover yuh! But they got my horse and I had to run! Go on—I can trot thisaway all night!"

"You know the country," said Gann. "Lead off. Not back to the Strawns—Nick will expect that. Lose us somewhere higher up."

Modoc slipped ahead. Gann, holding the girl, followed at a slow pace. Much later and on some high point of the world, he called a halt. The horse beneath him was tiring, the girl silent with strain, and Modoc Hutchins lagging perceptibly. As for himself, he wanted daylight to fight in. There were other reasons, too, but these were sufficient. Throwing off the trail, he unsaddled and picketed the horse, made a bed of his blanket and slicker for the girl, and settled himself down for a catnapping vigil. Modoc had mysteriously vanished in the yonder dark again. A gunshot exploded somewhere below and behind.

IV

SURROUNDED

AT DAWN, when the fog tendrils rolled thickly along the lower slopes, Len Gann ventured a small fire over which he cooked coffee and bacon. The girl roused herself and Modoc Hutchins returned from his long absence. Around the cheerful heat of the blaze the three of them ate while Gann broached the problem in his mind.

"I don't like movin' through strange country after dark. That's one reason why I stopped. Also, if we'd aimed for the Strawns it's possible we'd either have run into Nick or drawn Strawn fire. Can't tell where they are now. But the question becomes, miss, do you want to go to the Strawns?"

"They'd never shelter a LeStang," said the girl, "even if the LeStang was willing."

"Mistaken," contradicted Len Gann. "They're a pretty civilized bunch. And this fellow Phil Strawn likes you."

The girl lifted an inquiring face. "How do you know?"

"Said he wouldn't strike your ranch because you were on it. What more proof do you want?"

"Phil," said the girl, quietly, "was always a kind man. But I'm not going there—after all the hurt we've done them. It's asking too much. I've got some pride, Len."

"We can't stay here. Where's another way out?"

From the high point on which they stood the world ran away descendingly to east and west. The fog was gradually rising, and when the girl turned and pointed eastward it was to indicate a long, flat prairie horizon in the distance. "There's another country and I have friends in it. Nick never would dare go that far for me."

"Then that's the ticket," said Len Gann and began saddling the horse. But the girl suddenly swung about and faced the heart of the hills, all her features dark with anger. "I've given up everything!" she cried. "My father and mother pioneered it. I love every acre and every tree! Now Nick's got it all! Oh, if I were only a man, I'd fight back!"

"You hate to run, huh?" grunted Len Gann, watching her closely.

"Can't you see it? It's my country. And after I go it will be Nick's black and bloody ground."

"Maybe—maybe not," said Gann. "First thing is to get you away. Then I'll talk with Phil Strawn. Fact is, I'm sort of interested."

"I wasn't wrong about you," said Katherine LeStang.

"Climb up," said Gann. "Got to make tracks before all of this fog goes. Modoc, you find a good hidden trail down to the prairie. I'll trot behind."

Modoc rose and set off immediately, the girl following in the saddle and Gann bringing up the rear. They passed the crest of the ridge and sidled downgrade into timber. The timber led along the sides of a gulch into which the trio gradually descended. A kind of rock shoulder stood in front of them and they dropped lower to pass it, Modoc crouching like some Indian trailer. Gann, meanwhile, saw a flutter of movement behind him and he paused to study the flashing green edges of the timber, thus letting the other two pass around the shoulder and out of sight. Satisfied that no LeStang was following, he ran down the gulch at a faster pass —and abruptly halted in his tracks. The girl came galloping back with Modoc in hot pursuit. . . .

"They've found us!" she cried. And directly on the heels of her statement came a double burst of shots from beyond the shoulder.

"Four of 'em!" muttered the half-wit. "Comin' fast!"

Gann turned back. But that previous sign of something moving at the head of the gulch now became significant; and so he pointed to the steep, densely wooded northern wall. "Up there! Get goin'! Modoc, give me the rifle!"

Modoc passed it over and then clawed at the heavy brush. The girl, now aroused and fighting, called for him to stand aside and put the pony forward to take up the shock of the tangled growth. Watching until both she and the half-wit were buried in the timber, Gann posted himself at the foot of the climb and raised his rifle on the quartet of LeStangs galloping around the bend. He took a straight, sure aim and fired; the leading man screamed and pitched from the horse, and before Gann could jam a fresh shell the others swung and fled behind the protection of rock. Gann turned and followed the sound of the two fugitives up the slope. They had made good time and when Gann overtook them they were on the spine of the ridge. Behind was the gulch they had been forced away from. Below was another, untried and uncertain. Modoc dropped to his haunches and the girl watched Gann with a dark stare.

"I brought you into this, Len, and I'll always be sorry. Better let me go back and face Nick. He'll never do to me what he'll do to you."

"I'm gettin' my fun out of this," drawled Len. "Now, we could follow this canyon down to the prairie, but I'm afraid they'd have it blocked, too. Looks like Nick figured we'd hit for the open. Therefore, we'll go back to higher ground. I'll lead off."

Modoc suddenly grunted. "Look away up."

Gann turned, eyes running to the divide they had started from. A file of riders was at that minute crossing an open patch and turning downward so as to strike the head of either gulch. Apparently this outfit hadn't yet spotted its quarry, for the rate of progress was rather leisurely. But sooner or later, both gulches and the intervening ridge would be explored. The sound of the shots had drawn them. Gann turned to Modoc and the girl.

"They think we're pinned in here. Modoc, you get aboard that horse behind the lady, dive into that gulch

242

and go up the yonder side. Keep right on travelin' till you hit the Strawns. No other way out."

"I won't go," protested the girl.

"This is no time to hate the Strawns," Gann reminded her.

"It isn't that," she answered swiftly. "But I won't leave you here to be killed! I got you into this quarrel!"

"I die hard." Len Gann grinned. "Didn't I say I was gettin' my fun?"

"I won't go!"

Gann looked at Modoc, and the half-wit understood. The girl was his life, all that he cared about, all that his simple mind could fasten itself to. And so, before she was quite aware, he had sprung up behind her, taken the reins and lashed the horse downgrade. Katherine LeStang made one futile effort to check the run; then the pony reached the bottom and started up the farther grade. Gann swung to observe the men of the descending party; and from their still methodical progress, he judged that they had not seen the escape.

"So much to the good," he grunted. "Now I guess I'll get some of this fun I been braggin' about."

He paused a moment, debating the situation coolly. The oncoming party from above had split to follow both gulches and also to cover the separating ridge. Meanwhile the three men to the rear were probably on the skulk. It left him but one avenue of retreat, which was down the second gulch. But inasmuch as he made his stand at this point to cover the flight of the girl and the half-wit, he couldn't run. Pinched front and rear, the only thing to do was fort up and spend lead.

"Phil Strawn will come," he mused. "But that's about two hours off. Well, a lot of things can happen in two hours and the best defense is a right sizable offense. Better get at it."

He was worried about the three back of him. They had been silent too long. Stepping into the deeper brush, he returned to the edge of the first gulch and had a long look. Beyond the rock shoulder stood the three horses; higher up in the timber—and nearer—was the sudden flash of metal against the rising sun. Crouched, Len Gann raised his gun and waited. A body slid between trees and vanished. Following with his sights, Gann figured the next aperture and took up the slack of the trigger. It was a long interval before the man appeared there, and then it was on a diving run. But Gann had fixed his target and his bullet crashed into the deep quiet and caught the fellow dead center, to send him rolling back down the slope. That left two to his rear—both well hidden.

He retreated, hearing an exchange of what seemed to be signal shots from the higher ground. Once more stationed on the edge of the second gulch, he saw a party of LeStangs openly rushing the slope, coming toward him. This had to be discouraged, and he brought back the gunbolt and threw it home again, only to hear a barren click. Opening the breech he found the piece empty. The half-wit had expended the rest of the shells during the night.

"This scrap ain't goin' to last any two hours," grunted Len Gann. "Can't hold 'em off at a respectable distance."

He threw down the gun and reached for his revolver. By now those on the slope had caught sight of him standing above and at once they flattened and began an aimless fire. Dirt rose in the middle ground and one slug carried past him to spat against a tree. Not bothering to waste a return shot, he retreated to the brush, mind working with an electric rapidity. A long brazen call ran from gulch to gulch. "Come up—and close in!"

It was Nick LeStang's voice, the man speaking from some point on the ridge top. It became clear to Gann then. Nick had elected to advance on the high ground while his henchmen beat the lower reaches; and knowing that, Gann ran forward. "Fight this out now before they gang me. Damn his black heart, here's a showdown between us!"

For a matter of yards he ran, heedless of the noise he made, smashing the brush savagely, circling the trees. Sweat began to trickle down from his hat brim and a prickly heat to jab his body. But inside of him was an utter, detached coolness. His nerves became hard fibers along which impulse after impulse ran free and stormy; and his mind was crystal clear. To him came the various sounds of the approaching LeStangs. They advanced rapidly and with an evident carelessness, more especially those on either side of the ridge, and from their repeated and increasingly violent calls he could gauge his narrowing chances. Behind him was no rumor at all; the two surviving members of the first party had learned their lesson well.

All at once he changed tactics. In front of him was an absolute silence where previously had been the rattle of undergrowth. And in answer to that, he stepped away from his path, ducked around a clump of pines and began a crouching, feather-footed advance. Through the darkly narrow vistas of the ridge top he saw a deadfall running athwart his advance like a bulwark; and by instinct he guessed danger laying there in wait for him. He went to his knees and turned parallel to the deadfall. And when he had reached a point beyond which he could not go without actually placing himself in full sight of the men clambering up from the first gulch, he swerved again and crawled, belly-flat, for the uprooted end of the deadfall. The call of the pack was clearer and nearer. The closest of the LeStang flankers were evidently no more than fifty yards off, though their pace was slowing down as the line constricted. When Gann reached the pit made by the torn-up roots of the tree, he sank into it and paused to consider. . . . This was a showdown—the last hand. It seemed to matter little enough which way he turned, but the fighting instincts in him, now risen high and reckless, told him to go around the log. So, pushing his body forward, he passed beneath the twisted roots and raised his head. Immediately afterwards he sprang out of the pit and stood beside the log, gun hanging in his fist. There was only one man behind the log—Nick LeStang, whose narrow and un-smiling cheeks were fixed over the top of the barrier.

Gann's muscles became ice; he called softly. "Wrong direction, Nick."

The LeStang chief whirled around, the force of his reaction carrying him almost back against the log again. His arm had shot toward the holstered gun, but when he went off-balance he checked the move and recovered like a man locked in paralysis. It was the first time that Gann had ever seen the black clan leader shaken out of his fixed calm and the sight was weird, nerve-chilling. From the infinitely black eyes poured all the concentrated fury of a blood-lusting nature and all the half-crazed desires; from brow to chin were lines like the slashes of a knife, and the thin lips had withdrawn above the white teeth as some mad dog would bare his fangs. So he stood, and Gann knew he was watching for the one precious second of opportunity. The closer sound of the pack seemed to fall off.

"Had you hipped, you dog," grunted Gann. "But I'll live with a clear conscience or die with one!"

Nick LeStang's free arm rose and pointed. "Behind you—"

"I cut my teeth on that trick," jeered Gann. "Try a better one."

LeStang opened his mouth as if to speak. Gann leaned forward a trifle and this gesture seemed to be the break LeStang waited for. His suspended gun arm streaked down and up, his body whirled away from the log. Gann never moved out of his tracks, but his own arm gesture matched the lawless man's. A double explosion shuddered through the air and a stream of slivered bark arose at Gann's very elbow. Nick LeStang's body trembled as if struck by a hard-driving fist, and he never stopped whirling. His gun fell and he himself after it in a loose, buckling manner. His free fingers closed and relaxed.

All the rush and fury of the general attack returned to Gann's released senses. Breasting the log, he saw them fighting through the brush, a long deployed line verging on the barrier. This was close-hand fighting, and Gann, maddened by the slim chance of survival he thought he saw, opened up pointblank. That bullet stopped a LeStang who had almost gained the shelter of the log. The rest of the line went flat, but over near the up-ended roots Gann saw one of the attackers leap for the pit. He caught that one somewhere in the lower body and heard the yell of pain. He heard, too, another racket back of this immediate area that seemed like a second party coming in on the run. And there was a curious shifting of the LeStangs in sight. All at once the brush began smashing as they hitched away. A detonating fire boomed and exploded through the vistas, and then a gray wave of horsemen ran out of the pines.

It was the Strawn faction. Tall and stolid, these men sat above the cornered LeStangs and ripped at the wicked answering fire. But it lasted only a moment, for over the high, spitting fury of the crushing lead came a shrilling cry. "Lay down—we surrender! Lay down!"

Phil Strawn was on the extreme end of his group. Gun poised, he yelled: "All you hounds drop your pieces! Drop 'em sudden!"

Trapped, beaten, threatened with a bloody extinction, the remnant of Nick LeStang's riding group obeyed as if by a common impulse. Phil Strawn shouted again. "Make a circle around this bunch." And in a moment the net had drawn tight. Len Gann crawled over the log.

"I knew you'd come, Phil, but where'd you find the wings?"

Phil Strawn's face shifted from harshness to instant pleasure. "Dammit, man, I figgered I was too late!"

"I die hard," muttered Gann.

Strawn was scanning the captured crowd. "Where's Nick?"

"Over the log, dead."

"Then this war is finished and I'll have my way!" cried Phil Strawn. "You LeStangs—hear this! I give you two hours to get shut of this country forever. Your prod's gone now and there ain't another responsible LeStang to back you up any more. The girl's goin' back to her ranch—to run it. She's asked my help. She'll get it, if I got to riddle the bunch of you." He turned to his nearest men. "Round 'em up. March 'em down to the prairie and see that they travel—due west."

"Where's the girl?" asked Len Gann.

"Up on the summit—waitin'," said Phil Strawn, and for a moment he studied Gann with a glance that was severe and half sulky. But his next gesture was to dismount and point to his horse. Half gruffly he said: "Go on and see her."

Len Gann nodded and mounted. He cut about the end of the log and passed along a dim trail to the open area. He saw her waiting, higher up, silhouetted against the fresh morning's light. And as he came to the summit and reined in, he saw also the deep glowing light of her dark eyes. Unexpectedly she broke the silence.

"They had heard the shots and were on the way. They met us just beyond the gulch, Len. I—I said a prayer, and that means I'm more than just glad to see you sitting here."

He nodded slightly. Off to the east the prairie lay shining like a silver field. In the dim distance lay his own country and the Skillet outfit. And the slim, serene Louisa who had let him go without a protest. Some queer current passed through him at the thought. "Yeah," he muttered. "All over. What's next?"

She was frowning at him, puzzled and wistful. "I wish I knew myself better—as well as I think I know you." Then, turning, she saw the Strawns filing up from the trees. Her face lightened a little. "That's the end of all the trouble, Len. We'll ride to my ranch and tonight the factions will meet and make a lasting peace. I promise that. So does Phil. But there is something due you, Len. Whatever you want, anything you want. You came drifting in and if you choose to stay you can be king of the mountains. That's the trust we'd have in you."

He was looking off to the east again, trying to recall the melody in Louisa Burchevain's voice. "King of the mountains or a rider of the plains on a milk-white horse," said he.

"I don't understand, Len."

"Well, I came to find a message in the hills—and I reckon I found it. Listen, girl, do you know the answer to this feud business?"

"I've told you."

"Not all," said he and pointed to the oncoming Phil Strawn. "You and him. Then there'll never be any more feud."

The color brightened on her face. "Is that your answer, Len?"

He looked at her only once and turned away, hands tightening on the reins. Seven days' journey was the Skillet, straight as he was pointed now. "Tell Phil good luck. I've had my pasear and found the answer wasn't on the trail or over the hump. As for you, good-bye and Lord bless you, Katherine. Adios."

She never answered and he didn't know what was on her face. But, five minutes later and on the edge of the trees, he turned to see her still sitting in the saddle and watching him depart. Her hand lifted and he answered it. Then Phil Strawn appeared on the skyline and stood beside her—a fine strong couple against the light. He, too, lifted his hand. And with that farewell to remember through the years, Len Gann rode into the pines, arrow-straight for the Skillet and Louisa Burchevain, eagerness in his heart. Trail dust rose behind him. The prairie called.

LOUIS L'AMOUR

122812 **Crossfire Trail**   75c

437913 **Kilkenny**   75c

761916 **Showdown at Yellow Butte**   75c

849018 **Utah Blaine**   75c

Nelson Nye

111609 **The Clifton Contract**   60c

304006 **Gringo**   60c

327254 **Hellbound for Ballarat**   60c

489187 **Long Run**   60c

801005 **The Texas Gun**   60c

896001 **Wolftrap**   50c

Available wherever paperbacks are sold or use this coupon.

Ace Westsellers

019851	Ambush at Coffin Canyon Lomax	60¢
025619	Appache Canyon Garfield	60¢
111609	The Clifton Contract Nye	60¢
142711	Desperate Deputy of Cougar Hill Trimble	60¢
609412	Odds Against Circle L. Patten	60¢
703900	Raiders From Whiskey Smith Allen	60¢
723205	Ride the Hot Wind Patten	60¢
758508	Steel Jacket Constiner	60¢
761759	Showdown at Texas Flat Hogan	60¢
824011	Trigger Trio Haycox	60¢
880419	Whenatchee Bend Cheshire	60¢
885608	White Man's Road Capps	95¢
907014	The Wolver Hogan	60¢

Available wherever paperbacks are sold or use this coupon.

— — — — — — — — — — — — — — — —

ace books, (Dept. MM) Box 576, Times Square Station
New York, N.Y. 10036

Please send me titles checked above.

I enclose $.................Add 15¢ handling fee per copy.

Name ....

Address ....

City................... State.............. Zip........
Please allow 4 weeks for delivery.   12-72-9C

Two Action-Packed Western Novels

Back to Back in One Book—at 75c

186015 **Echo of a Texas Rifle** Hollingshead
Standoff At Massacre Butte Trimble

272765 **Gallow's Gulch** West
Man at Rope's End West

307017 **Gun Feud at Tiedown** Nye
Rogue's Rendezvous Nye

317396 **Hardesty** Booth
The Stranger Lutz

419101 **Justice at Spanish Flat** Garfield
Gun from Nowhere West

488510 **Lone Star Roundup** Owen
Write His Name in Gunsmoke West

722603 **Rio Desperado** Shireffs
Quick Trigger Shireffs

Ace Tall Twin Western

Just 95c Each

060012 **Big Country, Big Men** Brian Wynne
Brand of the Gun Brian Wynne

111815 **Cliff Rider** Lin Searles
Stampede At Hour Glass Lin Searles

308700 **Guntrap At Brightwater** D. J. Stevens
The Franklin Raid Kyle Hollingshead

761478 **Short Trigger Man** Merle Constiner
Outrage At Bearskin Fork Merle Constiner

824755 **The Troublemaker** Edwin Booth
Shoot Him On Sight Wm. Colt McDonald

Available wherever paperbacks are sold or use this coupon.

ace books, (Dept. MM) Box 576, Times Square Station
New York, N.Y. 10036

Please send me titles checked above.

I enclose $.....................Add 15¢ handling fee per copy.

Name ....

Address ....

City..................... State.............. Zip........
Please allow 4 weeks for delivery.   11A

Nelson Nye

Just 60c each

019901	Ambush at Juma's Chimney
111609	The Clifton Contract
141945	Death Valley Slim
304006	Gringo
308163	Gunslick Mountain
308411	Guns of Horse Prairie
327254	Hellbound for Ballarat
373415	Iron Hand
489187	Long Run
583757	The No-Gun Fighter
629550	The One Shot Kid
722991	Rider On A Roan
759696	The Seven Six Gunners
767616	Single Action
804005	The Texas Gun
804351	The Texas Tornado
817700	Tornado on Horse Back
821215	Trail of Lost Skulls
822551	Treasure Trail from Tucson
824300	Trouble at Quinn's Crossing